HEARTBEAT BRAVES

CROOKED ROCK URBAN INDIAN CENTER BOOK 1

PAMELA SANDERSON

Cover design by Holly Heisey (www.hollyheiseydesign.com)

Editor: Lorelei Logsdon, (www.loreleilogsdon.com)

Visit the author's website at www.pamelasanderson.com.

❀ Created with Vellum

---

*R*ayanne stared at the message on her computer screen:

Sorry R. A deadline is a deadline. The retreat lodge has been rebooked for another group. They already paid. There's nothing I can do. The policy is no refunds on deposits. I'll ask the boss but I think you're out of luck.

Rayanne tapped her head against the screen. She'd been so certain she could fix this.

The executive director stuck her head out of her office. She had the bright smile you would expect from a nonprofit employee but her eyes said she was a person accustomed to getting less than she'd hoped for. "Tell me you have good news."

"Working on it," Rayanne fibbed. She typed out the beginning of a reply, but to say what?

Please reconsider your reconsideration.

Help, we're desperate.

You have to give us another chance even if it's too late, because jobs are on the line.

She let out a heavy sigh and met Linda in her office. "Sorry."

Linda closed her eyes. "Don't say it. Please don't say it. I can't stand one more piece of bad news."

"I'll say it by not saying it."

"Did you convey how deeply important this is? Did you plead? Did you look for someone to bribe? I can't walk into that meeting and tell our brand new board of directors, who were appointed specifically because of rumors that we're incompetent, that we have screwed up yet again."

"They already rebooked the space."

Linda closed her eyes, her shoulders drawing tight. Even before Margie's illness and resignation, they had struggled with everything from funding to a contract dispute. The process of buying the new building with its never-ending reports and forms had stretched them to exhaustion. They were all worn down, but Linda bore the worst of it.

"The task is to hold a retreat," Rayanne said. "Why not have it here?"

"This place is a disaster," Linda said, indicating the chaos that was the current state of her office. Their move into the new building had been delayed twice already. They were half in and half out of boxes. Stacks of extra chairs lined the wall, and computer monitors sat on the floor.

"So? We can use the front room. We push everything into a corner. Bring in some comfortable furniture and a nice rug."

"A nice rug?" Linda said.

"Make it homey. Think of all the money we'll save. Besides, what is the point of a retreat anyway? Do we need to be surrounded by mountains and trees?"

"The point of a retreat is to get work done without distractions," Linda said.

"How are hiking trails and horseback riding less distracting than the dull brown walls of this place?"

"I don't know. That's what retreaters expect," Linda said. She took a deep breath. "Can't put this off forever. Can you make a fresh pot of coffee?"

"Got it," Rayanne said. "Again, sorry."

"Not your fault," Linda said. "This one is all me. We need to organize me better."

Linda's office was a mess without the trials of moving. She liked to hang on to things, so there were files and booklets, and binders from conferences from years ago. In addition, they received oddball donations like a bag of kid-sized sneakers and boxes of insulated coffee cups from a tribal casino. She had several pieces of framed art leaning against the wall ready for bubble wrap.

Linda moved stacks of mail and newspapers around until she found a bundle of file folders. She flipped through the files searching for her meeting notes. Linda's strategy was to keep everything on her desk. She resisted all of Rayanne's attempts to put things away or at least put things in logically linked piles. For every hour they spent organizing Linda's office, they spent two hours running around because she was panicked about not knowing where everything was.

"I'll tell them you're on the way," Rayanne said.

She found her coworker Ester blocking the door.

"Did you know there is a super-hot guy sitting on your desk?" Ester said.

"Not right now," Rayanne said.

"Yeah, right now. He's has a kinda Prince Charming vibe, if Prince Charming were Ind'n. I'd hop on him."

"Very funny." Rayanne pushed around her. Ester was the person to lighten your mood no matter what happened, but they were in crisis mode. On the organizational chart, Ester was the manager of health programs but she also ended up doing everything related to computers.

Rayanne had to walk by her desk to get to the meeting room. Ester wasn't joking. There was a super-hot guy with his actual butt parked on her desk.

"Hey," she said. He looked up and her heart bounced to her toes and back. Her thoughts jumbled together in the glow of his gorgeousness. She broke into a huge smile. Dark hair, dark eyes, tall, and definitely native. "You here for the meeting?"

He smiled back. "No. I don't do meetings."

"Lucky." She pointed at the meeting room, "I gotta—"

"Don't let me stop you," he said.

"I'll be right back."

"I'll be right here."

He had an amazing smile. Pretty teeth. A surge of euphoria blotted out the frustration of the botched retreat. Maybe this guy was a good sign. Maybe her luck was changing. An actual Indian man her age at the center.

Please don't be a jerk, please don't be a jerk, she sang to herself.

She set up the coffeemaker, smiling to herself at the sudden jangle of nerves. She hated when she got like this when she met cute guys. Already she was inventing something in her head, and she didn't even know who he was. Maybe he was here to inspect something or impose a fine for some other paperwork they'd bungled.

She filled a pitcher of water, and took a couple of sodas from the fridge. She put a sleeve of coffee cups under her arm, and hurried into the meeting room.

Arnie's loud voice rang across the room. Their new board chairman said something about funding resources. He sat next to another new board member, Bernard, who was from the same tribe. Arnie mentioned a government website that any idiot who'd been working for an Indian nonprofit for more than thirty seconds would know about. She didn't know why she was predisposed to dislike him. He was nice enough. Linda had been friends with him since college, and they'd graduated over ten years ago so she must see something in him. But Rayanne caught a whiff of arrogance around him. He talked more than he listened.

He stopped talking when she entered the room.

"Linda's on her way," Rayanne said. A few of the board members remained from the previous term. She passed out sodas to the ones that she knew didn't drink coffee. She set coffee cups and a handful of sugar and creamer packets out for everyone else.

"There's a fresh pot of coffee on the way. Anything else?"

They shook their heads. Linda came in and walked to her spot at the table. She set down a legal pad and a folder stuffed with a jumble of papers. She made a tiny gesture, and Rayanne went over and poured her a cup of water.

"You introduce yourself?" Linda asked.

"I'm Rayanne," she said. "I'm Karuk. Northern California."

"Ah, another fish-eating Indian," Arnie said. "You have more diversity on the staff than I expected." He smiled like he'd made a joke, but Rayanne didn't get it.

"We're going to get started," Linda said. Her tone suggested she'd rather be doing anything else. "We'll call you if we need anything."

Rayanne backed out of the room. She tried to give Linda an encouraging smile, but Linda kept her eyes glued to her notes.

Cute guy no longer sat on her desk. Instead, he stood in front of a map that showed all the tribes in the area.

He smiled again when he saw her, and her heart thumped against her breastbone all over again.

"I forget how many tribes are around here," he said.

"We serve all tribal citizens no matter where they're from," Rayanne said.

"What do you serve them?" There was a hint of trouble in his eyes.

Rayanne laughed. "Depending on how this meeting goes, maybe not much. I'm Rayanne, by the way."

"Rayanne," he repeated. She loved the way it sounded coming from him. She stared at his perfect lips, waiting for him to say something else.

"Is that your Indian name?"

Rayanne met his eyes. "It is. My father was Raymond, my grandmother was Maryanne. My mother's idea. You?"

"Henry." He offered to shake hands. His hands were warm, his gaze confident. Here was a man with his act together. He held on to her a moment longer than necessary but she didn't pull her hand back. He smelled like the citrus hand soap Rayanne had put in the restroom.

"Is that your Indian name?"

"My dad is Henry. My grandpa is Henry. I'm Henry the third. I sound like a Shakespeare play."

"Would you be a comedy or a tragedy?" She wanted another excuse to touch him.

Henry gave a weary shake of his head. "In present circumstances,

I'm both." He pointed to a stack of boxes behind Rayanne's desk. "What's going on? Did you guys just move?"

Rayanne took in the scene from his eyes. This iteration of the Crooked Rock Urban Indian Center was located in a strip mall on a busy street with a cramped parking lot. Rayanne's desk, with all the boxes stacked behind it, sat across from the front door. On one side, there were half a dozen tiny offices. On the other side was the space they jokingly referred to as the big room. A true big room could hold a community gathering. Theirs could fit twenty people if you pushed the chairs close together. Part of the suite had mismatched floor tiles. The rest was well-worn carpet. The walls needed paint.

Rayanne scratched her head. "I guess you could say we're in transition. We're in the process of buying a building from the city but it's been delayed. We have a new move-in date so fingers crossed. Meanwhile, kind of hard to get any work done like this."

Henry nodded. "The story of our people. Roaming with all their stuff packed up and no place to go."

Rayanne waited for him to tell her what he was there for. He acted like he was waiting for her to say something. Rayanne's eyes stopped on her desk and the giant pile of work she had to do. "What can I help you with?"

"What *can* you help me with?" He smiled again, like they were sharing a secret. Except she didn't know what the secret was, and charming as this man was, she had things to do.

"Why are you here?" Rayanne said, impatience creeping into her voice.

"Oh," Henry said. He'd been leaning toward her and now he stood up straight. "My uncle is on the board. He drove out from Warm Springs rez. I live here in town. He asked me to meet him for lunch. Arnie?"

"Arnie is your uncle? Isn't he kind of young?" Arnie's nephew? Her estimation of Henry slid a bit.

"He's only, like, ten years older than me. My mom's the oldest. Arnie came along later. You know how it goes."

"You plan to get involved with the center?"

"No," Henry said, as if the suggestion were absurd.

There went that fantasy.

Her coworker Tommy came in the front door. "Rayanne, can I get a check?"

He gave Henry a curious once-over. "Am I interrupting something?"

Henry did that chummy guy thing like he was everyone's best friend. "No way, I'm Henry."

"Tommy." They did one of those handshakes consisting of numerous steps and ending with slapping each other on the shoulder. Tommy was almost a head shorter than Henry and winced before they let go.

"What do you need a check for?" Rayanne asked.

"I found a bus at an auction. It's in my budget."

"We can afford it? What's wrong with it?"

"It doesn't run. But it will." Tommy took a step back and dipped his head, as if modest about accepting applause.

"If Linda approves it and that goes well." She nodded back to the meeting room.

"What kind of bus?" Henry asked. The two of them began conversing in the foreign language of bus operations: make, model, engine.

Got it. Bus, good. Services to urban Indians, snore.

"I need to serve coffee and then do some real work," Rayanne said, to dismiss them. But they were already headed to Tommy's office, probably to ogle the auction listings.

Rayanne brought coffee into the meeting. She couldn't get a clear read on what was going on, but there was a distinct pall over the room, like everyone wished they were elsewhere. Not a good sign.

When she returned, Henry was outside the front doors, talking on his phone. She hated to admit it, but he made for a nice view walking back and forth. She wouldn't mind if he stuck around a little longer.

By the time Henry came back inside, the meeting had wrapped up. Linda had the same hollow-eyed look of distress that she'd had when she'd gone in. She flashed Rayanne an apologetic smile.

"Henry!" Arnie strode out and gave him a big hug. To Rayanne he said, "I see you've already met my nephew. You two are going to be working together."

Henry's smile disappeared. Rayanne wasn't sure what to think.

"What are we going to be working on?" she asked.

"Henry's being hired as the new project manager."

Rayanne's mouth dropped open. Linda wouldn't meet her eyes. "What?"

2

Henry didn't miss his gorgeous new friend's troubled frown as Arnie hustled him out the front door. He had half-hoped they would all have lunch together so he could spend more time with her. Rayanne with the beautiful brown eyes and curtain of dark hair that she flipped over her shoulder every few minutes. Plus they needed to talk about this crack plan that Arnie tossed at him like it was something they'd discussed beforehand. Since when was he a project manager, whatever that was?

No sooner had Arnie made this announcement, than Rayanne and the other lady had retreated to an office. His last glimpse was her cute ass disappearing behind a closed door.

"You going to drive?" Arnie asked.

"I guess," Henry said, heading for his van. It had been awhile since Henry had seen Arnie, and it felt weird to have him sitting in the passenger seat, just the two of them. They saw each other at family get-togethers, or at his mom's, but not like this.

"So, what do you think?" Arnie asked.

"What is a project manager?"

"The center does a lot of things. You help keep them going."

"I wouldn't know where to start," Henry said.

"Look, I know about your deal with your mom. You need a job. This could be a great opportunity."

"Opportunity for what?"

"You've got a college degree. How long have you been out? Two years? You're not doing anything."

"I'm figuring things out." Henry's hands gripped the steering wheel more tightly. "Is that why you asked me to lunch? So you can hassle me about *my career?*" He bit down on the word career. "Everyone isn't like you and figures it all out by the time they can stand up and walk."

Arnie had come home from college and gone straight to work in the Tribe's economic development office. He'd worked his way up through different jobs and departments until he was elected to Council. He already had a busy travel schedule, and now he joined the board of directors at the urban Indian center. It was hard to reconcile this model of responsibility with the uncle who'd gotten in trouble for stealing from Grandpa's beer fridge so many summers ago.

Arnie chuckled in a condescending way. "I always wanted to work for the Tribe. I came home. I took the first job they would give me and went from there."

"And now I suppose you are endlessly happy and fulfilled, from all the gratifying work you do."

"That's a stretch," Arnie said. "I love what I do, but it's a lot of travel. A lot of meetings."

"I hate meetings," Henry said.

"You're going to hate camping out under a bridge too." Arnie pointed, indicating Henry should turn. "There's a decent burger place down by the city center."

It took Henry a minute to figure out what place he was referring to. "That businessman overpriced chain restaurant? That's for people with a per diem who are too frightened to venture away from their hotel. I have a better idea."

"I admit I am one of those people although I wouldn't say I was frightened. I'm not in the mood for anything weird," Arnie said.

"What's weird?"

"I don't know. I'm not in the mood for Asian food that's sweet and covered with peanuts."

"So no Thai?"

"Not today. I want a burger."

The best way to keep Arnie happy was to feed him something good. Henry headed for one of his favorite spots.

"Where is this place?" Arnie asked, as Henry drove down a busy street lined with shops and restaurants.

"You gotta get away from the business district once in a while. This is a happening neighborhood with a lot going on. Parking is tight but I will introduce you to a burger that is the perfect balance of meat, condiment, and bun."

"You've been living in the city too long," Arnie said, shaking his head.

"You'll see." Henry slipped down a side street to park and led Arnie past a jammed bike rack to a dented screen door. Inside, there were a couple of narrow tables and bar seating along the walls. Every seat was jammed.

"Where are we going to sit?" Arnie asked.

"Trust me," Henry said. They placed their order at the counter, and took a number to put on their table. They grabbed icy glasses of soda and went through a narrow hallway that led to a warehouse-like space lined with long tables and benches. There was an additional upper seating area that overlooked the main floor.

"How did you find out about this place?" Arnie asked, once they'd sat down.

"That is my thing right now," Henry said. "I find out about places. They can take out the tables on that end and put in a small stage." Henry pointed to the ceiling. "Lighting. Sound system. They have DJs or bands. I heard they were doing an open mic thing, and I'm trying to get a feel for the place."

"And what would you do here?"

"I got a native rock band thing I'm trying to make happen."

"You're joking," Arnie said. "You want to be a musician?"

11

"More like a manager. They're my friends. I'm helping them. I don't know what Mom tells you but I have some ambition."

"Ambition is wonderful, but getting a rock band thing to happen doesn't sound like it will pay the bills. She wants you to have a job. She would love to see you working with Indian people."

"Doing what? I have zero qualifications for that kind of thing. Thanks for thinking of me."

"You don't even know what they do. We'll find a project that you're suited for. Give it a try. That gal you were talking to, she can help you out. Wouldn't you like to work with her?"

"Rayanne?" The woman with the beautiful hair that he wanted to tangle his hands in? Yes, he wanted to hang out her again but for fun.

"Yeah, Rayanne." Arnie raised an eyebrow.

Henry avoided his gaze and wished they had their food.

"Linda said she's smart, a fast learner, and super competent."

"Then why do you need me?"

"They're in over their heads there," Arnie said. "Have you asked yourself why I would get involved with the center?"

Henry shook his head.

"The bulk of their funding comes from a group of local tribes including ours. But their successes are marginal and several of the tribes want to put that money elsewhere. The board of directors is considering closing the center. Linda is an old friend, and that place means a lot to her. I'm trying to preserve her opportunity, but she needs help. You're smarter than you think. You can help too."

Henry had to admit, he liked the idea of spending time with Rayanne. A server brought over a tray and set down two massive bacon cheeseburgers and a pile of fries. Arnie lifted the bun and studied the meat patty covered with thick strips of bacon.

"House-made applewood smoked bacon," Henry said.

"You know the name of the pig and its last meal, too?"

"I guess you don't want to hear about the bakery that does the buns."

Arnie shook his head. He put the sandwich back together and took a bite. When he was finished chewing he said, "You're going to want to make a note of this because this is the closest you will ever come to hearing me say, you were right."

Henry had to finish his own mouthful. "I never doubted."

"What else is going on with you? Seeing anyone?" Arnie asked.

"Not at the moment. You?"

"I've got lots of friends," Arnie said with a cartoony eyebrow waggle.

When he was younger, Henry had overheard his mom and grandma talk about Arnie's dating habits. They said he was good at finding girlfriends that were totally wrong for him but luckily he never stayed with them for long.

"Some out here, some on the rez?"

"We were talking about you," Arnie said.

"I don't meet a lot of women. You go to college, you move back. It's hard to rebuild your social life. At least it has been for me." He'd almost added that he was broke but that was what started the conversation.

Arnie tried to find a grip that would hold the burger together. "I'm worried about you, with your balanced buns and applesmoke. You sound like a big city boy."

"I am a big city boy," Henry said. "A man. And I'm handling my life fine on my own."

"If you're working at the center you might meet an Indian woman. Your mom would love that. They aren't like regular women. They're like—"

"An Indian woman raised me," Henry said. "I know what they're like. They're scary when they're mad. And getting back to business, I am not your man for this job. For real, I am working on my own thing."

"How about this? I could use an eye on the inside, and you could use some money." Arnie stuffed the last bites into his mouth and wiped his hands with what was left of his napkins. "That was good but I feel like I need a shower." He grabbed some of Henry's napkins. "You don't have to do it forever. Try it for a couple weeks."

"Now I get to be a spy, too," Henry said. Already he could see how this was going to go. No matter what happened, someone was going to be unhappy with him.

"These opportunities don't come up often. It will be good for you."

"Sounds like it would be good for you," Henry said. "How much am I going to get paid?"

"As it turns out, the secret of Indian riches is in nonprofits." Arnie chuckled at his own joke. "It's not. Kidding aside, it's more than you're making now. If you do it, I can avoid your mom's wrath for failing to get you a job. Talk about scary when she's mad."

Arnie confirmed what he'd expected, his mom put him up to it.

"I'm not agreeing but I will show up and see what I think," Henry said.

"Close enough," Arnie said. "You can help them plan their retreat. That's screwed up too."

"What kind of retreat?"

"Everyone gets together to do planning for the center for the next year."

"Sounds super boring," Henry said, thinking at least he could see Rayanne again.

3

---

*R*ayanne glared until Linda said, "I'm not happy about it either."

"You're letting *that guy* be a project manager?" Rayanne said, her voice cracking. This could not be happening. There had to be something she was missing.

"*That guy* is Mr. Ear-twirler's nephew," Linda said. Ear-twirler was the nickname they gave Arnie after they met him. During the interview he couldn't stop playing with his ear.

"I know. I helped keep him occupied for the last hour," Rayanne said, like it had been a terrible burden. "But I've been busting my ass around here for almost a year. Why not promote me and make him the assistant?"

"Not my idea. Arnie was talking fast and making intimidating statements about the tribes giving up on us. No money, no center. The people with the funding have no confidence in us right now. Maybe the nephew is a well-connected organizational genius."

"I talked to him," Rayanne said. "I feel confident when I say, he is not."

"Deal with it," Linda said. "He's Arnie's family and he needs a job.

That's how Indian Country works. Arnie is trying to rescue us. He's on our side but, unfortunately, we're at the point where talking is not enough. We need some results. Do what he wants. Don't complain."

Wasn't this the story of her life? For every penny she put in, someone else got to take three pennies out. She came up with the idea, or wrote the grant, or did the presentation. Someone else got the credit or the project.

"So this is settled. Henry works here. I turn everything over to him and help him. Does he get to run the arts festival, too?"

Linda sagged into her desk chair. "Nothing is settled. I don't see why we can't keep that as your project. When we do the retreat we can nudge you out front. Show all the work you've done."

"Good. Because everything is pretty much planned. Can I finalize everything based on the current move-in date? I'm getting vendors and performers to commit but I'm worried about what we're going to do if the deal is pushed back again."

Linda stared off into the distance, like she wished to be somewhere, anywhere, else than here. She turned her attention back to Rayanne. "I worry about that too. I'm counting on it. Keep doing what you're doing. It's your project. We'll get Henry into transportation and finding funding. His uncle thinks he's so great. Give him a chance to show us what he can do. If everything goes in the toilet and we have no UIC at all, at least we have another person to blame."

Rayanne tried to picture her life without the center. There were other tribal-related jobs in town but she wanted this one. She had so many plans to see through.

"Couldn't we talk to Margie?"

Margie was the board chairperson before Arnie. She was a wonderful friend and ally. She was also eighty-two and after an illness, ordered to step down.

"Do not bother Margie," Linda said. "She's frail and she will not be able to resist getting worked up if you talk to her. I'll talk to Arnie and make sure he knows what you contribute. He doesn't want to have the retreat here, so we need to magically come up with something. Any ideas?"

"If I had ideas, this wouldn't be a problem. I think that pizza place that looks like a castle has a meeting room."

Linda pretended to laugh. "Keep trying."

RAYANNE HAD the same overwhelmed feeling she sometimes got in college when she was overbooked, and behind on studies, and then had to put in a work shift. It manifested as an electric knot twisting between her shoulder blades. She went through the stack on her desk, and set things into piles. Grants that needed to be completed were clipped together and put on the calendar. She grouped together contacts that she was hoping to develop. She had research to do, and data reporting that went on forever. Nothing could be accomplished in Indian Country without reporting on it. Sometimes she wanted to tally the time they spent hunched over paperwork against the time they were actively working on services.

She came across Linda's retreat sample agenda. Linda had tasked her with taking the first cut at coming up with the program for this year.

Number one: Talk about all the hard work Rayanne does.

That went on the implied list.

The real list included all the money talk, and a time slot for each staff member. She also made notes about meal plans and what sort of written materials they would need. She wrote Margie's name in the margin, willing the elder to be healthy enough to participate.

Technically Margie was Linda's mentor and Linda was Rayanne's mentor, but Linda was overbooked and not a great role model at the moment. Rayanne had faith in Linda but until she got a grip on the situation at the center, Rayanne was helping her more than Linda was helping Rayanne.

She was in the middle of a research project when Arnie and Henry returned to the center. Henry's blustery confidence had been replaced with a phony humble manner. He gave her an apologetic half-smile. If he thought she was going to be a friendly face, he was mistaken.

"You two could have a planning meeting right now," Arnie said. There was a little something in his voice. Rayanne wasn't sure if he was being practical, or being a jerk. She gave him a smile that showed teeth.

"We're running a center here. I can't drop everything. We provide essential services." She emphasized *essential services* but Arnie didn't get the hint.

"Tell her the good news," Arnie said. He clapped Henry on the back like he'd made the winning touchdown.

Good news from Arnie. That could only mean more work for her. What would it be now?

"I'm going to help plan the retreat," Henry said. The way he said it made it clear, it wasn't his idea and he wasn't pleased about it.

Rayanne wasn't pleased about it either. "I've got it under control, but thanks."

"Come now. Didn't you miss a deadline? Maybe you should accept some help." Arnie's tone was good-natured but the remark stung. Linda was the one who missed the deadline. Rayanne had put the documents on her desk, ready to go. All Linda needed to do was sign, attach the payment, and put it in the mail. But she'd buried it under other paperwork and forgotten about it. She was the one who deserved scolding.

But Rayanne couldn't say that to Arnie.

"Great," Rayanne said with a fake smile. "Let's meet."

"Good luck, you two," Arnie said, like he was sending them off on vacation.

"Didn't you have some place to go?" Henry said, urging Arnie out.

Arnie laughed and waved over his shoulder as he headed out the door.

"That man is going to murder me by embarrassment," Henry said. He offered a dazzling smile.

Rayanne was having none of it. "I don't have a lot of time. It's a regular ol' all-day retreat. These events are supposedly more productive if you have them offsite. Otherwise everyone is sneaking off to their office to check email. As Uncle Arnie so wonderfully pointed out, we screwed up and do not have a place. Are you connected on meeting spaces?"

"How many people are we going to have?

"Not many. Twelve to fifteen?"

"Can you give me an idea what sort of site you need?"

"Seriously? You have ideas of where we can meet?" Maybe he was some sort of secret organizational whiz.

"Maybe. I have my own history of blundering everything up so let's not get excited yet."

"Ideally, not a plain old meeting room. If we had a wealthy bene-factor we would meet in their home. I booked the smaller meeting lodge at Warm Springs because they have a nice room plus the outdoor stuff. Hiking trails and outside spaces we could use for meeting."

"I have an idea," Henry said.

"This retreat is coming up in a week. I doubt there's a place that will be available at such short notice. No one expects you to come up with something."

"Give me one second." He took a piece of paper and a pen and found a seat. It took more than a second, so Rayanne went back to work.

Tommy came out waving his signed check from Linda. "How long is your friend going to be here?" he asked, referring to Henry.

"That's not my friend. That's Henry. Arnie is his uncle. He works with us now."

Tommy nodded. "Cool. Is it okay if I take him with me to check out the bus?"

"Be my guest," Rayanne said. "I'm not his boss."

Henry finished his call. "I have a place that will give us a tour tomorrow afternoon. We can be there and back in a couple of hours."

"I can't run off and leave my desk for a couple of hours," Rayanne said.

"We can do planning in the car. Don't worry, I'll clear it with

Linda." He flashed a smile that would no doubt clear it with Linda. To Tommy he said, "You going for that bus?"

"You coming?"

They headed out the door like they were best buddies forever.

4

The next day, all Henry had to do was mention he had a retreat site, and Linda waved them out the door.

"Must be nice to so easily bend people to your will," Rayanne said, as they headed to the parking lot.

"Doesn't happen that often," Henry said.

Rayanne climbed in the van and fastened her seatbelt. "How many people you fit in this thing?"

"You're the second person who's asked me that in two days."

"Tommy?" She gifted him with a small smile. "His actual title is youth program coordinator but since he's always trying to haul a bunch of kids off to play basketball or something, his second job has become transportation. I suppose he explained all that."

"No. He came across as a guy with a healthy interest in passenger vans." As Henry pulled out, he was suddenly self-conscious about his driving. He drove like he was taking a driver's test. "To answer your original question, legally seats twelve. The most I've ever had is six. I keep the last seat out so we have room for equipment."

"Who are *we* and what sort of equipment?"

"My friends have a band."

"Oh," Rayanne said. He waited for her to ask about it but instead she said, "My car looks like it lost a fight with a dump truck. Inside and out."

"You a bad driver?" He meant to be funny but it didn't come out that way.

"Do you think anyone thinks they're a bad driver? Like some people drive crazy-aggressive and they think they're good drivers, but maybe they're part of the problem. Then there are people who don't mind holding up traffic to make an awkward left turn when they could go around the block. Do they think they're bad drivers?"

"No one thinks they're a bad driver," Henry said.

"The car belonged to my cousin. He decided he was too good for it and left it at my aunt's. He bought one of those small pickups from his friend. Of course it won't start half the time, but that's not my problem. I got his car. It's not pretty and nothing works. If you crank up the heat, it's like a puppy breathing on your ankle. If you need air, you roll down the window. The engine works. The thing runs."

"You don't have to worry about it getting stolen," Henry said.

"Exactly."

When they'd set out, she twisted her long hair into a knot and stuck a beaded hair stick into it. As they rode, it unwound bit by bit, until most of it fell back to her shoulders. She pulled the hair stick out and twirled it between her fingers. He liked her smile better than the bitter expression she offered him now. "Do you even want to work at the center?"

"I don't know enough about it to be sure, but I'm guessing it's not my thing."

"Then why are you here?"

"My mom hassled Arnie to find me a job. The nicest way to put it is that she thinks I'm a deadbeat." It stung saying it out loud.

"That's the nicest way?"

Henry shrugged. "Arnie thinks this would be good for me. He said it could be temporary."

"What do you normally do?"

"This and that," Henry said. "Sometimes I clean up at construction sites. Help people move. Power wash."

"You pay your bills, but you're not on a career path. That's her beef?"

"I guess. Family history. We don't have to get into all that right now." His chances of winning this woman over were dwindling to none and into the negatives.

"Why do you think your uncle thinks you're good for the center?"

"I went to college. I had a decent job for a while. I worked for a firm that distributes trucking parts. Got laid off. Not that trucking parts was a dream job or anything. But I can do a job."

"So you expect to come in, put in your time, and do a job."

"I'm only twenty-four. I've been out of college for two years. Should I apologize for not having it all figured out yet? When did you finish college?"

"January. I did extra classes so I could get out early and work for Linda."

"January of the year we're in now?" He had assumed she was older than him. She came across like a person who knew what she was doing.

"Yeah, that January. I'll be twenty-two in November. You don't have to have it all figured out. What is your dream job?"

"I have no idea. You?"

"I thought I was doing it until Uncle Arnie came along." She gave him a sour smile. "Listen, I wasn't kidding. I don't have a couple of hours to goof off. Can you get us there and back any quicker?"

"Sure," Henry said, pushing down the accelerator until the van coughed. "I'm not going to stick with the job, so you don't have to worry."

"Uncle Arnie comes across as a man who is used to getting his way," Rayanne said.

"You got that right. Will you tell me about what you guys do? Are all the employees native?"

"You don't have to be but we only have four—now five—people, so yes. All of us do everything we can to keep the few services we manage to offer right now."

"I don't understand why people can't get these services on their home rez if they need them."

"Everyone doesn't live on their home rez," Rayanne said. "Some people can't even get there. We want to have something for them here. If nothing else, it's a place to hang out with other Indians. Some people miss that. Don't you ever wish you could be home?"

"I am home. I grew up here," Henry said. "I love going out to the rez and seeing the family but I've always lived in the city. There's nothing to miss."

"You're lucky then," Rayanne said. "We can develop more programs when we get into the bigger place. It's kinda hard. You want more money and people so you can show that you can do the programs, but you need the people and programs to prove to the sources you can use the money." Rayanne stopped talking long enough to notice they were getting off the freeway.

"Where are we going, anyway?" she asked.

"Milk Creek Farm," Henry said.

"Milk Creek? Are there cows?"

"Maybe. A friend of a friend opened the business. According to the website they can host big outdoor events or smaller gatherings like family reunions. There's a main building, trails, and a pond."

"A pond?"

"Might be nice to swim on a hot day."

"No one is going to go swimming at the retreat," Rayanne said.

"They said they could accommodate us if we liked the space."

"You've been out here before?"

"No. I've been wanting to." Saying it out loud to Uncle Arnie had been cringe-inducing enough but how would it sound to Rayanne? "That band I mentioned? I'm interested in putting together a concert with them and some other bands."

"Is that a thing to make money?" There was hint of disdain in her voice.

"Promoting concerts? Could be. Arnie and my mom share your enthusiasm."

"Won't get any experience doing that with us."

"Wasn't asking for it. None of this is my idea. I was minding my own business when my uncle threw this at me. He doesn't have a lot of confidence in you guys."

"We need you to rescue us?"

"You told me you needed a place for your retreat. I found a place to show you."

That finished the conversation. Henry couldn't help checking her out as he drove. She couldn't keep still, first fiddling with her hands in her lap, then adjusting the seatbelt.

The farther they got from downtown, the more the landscape changed. At first there were housing developments broken up by the occasional farm. Then houses grew sparse and larger farms took over. Everything was green with stands of tall trees. Henry let his window down, anxious to get this over with. According to the directions from the owners, he would cross the creek, and it was the second driveway on the left. They told him there was a hand-painted sign marking the turn. They should be there, but they still hadn't reached the creek.

It was always like that driving to a new place. It was easy to think you'd overshot, but then you'd turn back too early and get mixed up. He kept his eye on the miles. They should have found it at least five miles ago. He couldn't imagine the scorn Rayanne would dish out if he couldn't find the farm.

"It is pretty out here," Rayanne said, "but how far out is it?"

"Is there a limit on how far out the staff will go?"

"We were going to go to Warm Springs. They won't mind coming out here."

They approached a crossroads. Henry considered an experimental left turn. Wasn't there some rule about going left if you were lost or uncertain? He turned on his blinker, then turned it off again.

Rayanne did a long slow exhale. "You don't know where we're going, do you?"

"I know exactly where we're going," Henry said.

"Rephrase: you don't know where we are."

"I'm not going to lie."

"Why didn't you put it in your phone?" Rayanne said, her voice rising in pitch.

"Put it in your phone," Henry repeated. "Why didn't I think of that? Oh, I did. Except, Polly and Pepe said that GPS was messed up out here and it would be more confusing if we used it."

"Polly and Pepe? Did they work in a circus?"

"Pepe is the college friend. They were nice enough to see us at the last minute, maybe you shouldn't make fun of their names."

"No problem. Let's go back to making fun of you," Rayanne said. "Did you write anything down? Or what was your plan for finding it?"

Henry nodded and tapped a finger against his temple. "Right here. It's all right here. Road 16 until you cross the creek. There's a sign at the turn."

"We passed the creek at least ten minutes ago," Rayanne said.

"Why didn't you say anything?"

"I wasn't in charge of finding it," Rayanne said. "An Indian man with no sense of direction. I've heard about you but this is my first time meeting one."

"The pleasure is all mine," Henry said.

He turned the van around and found that he was speeding, as if that would make up for being lost.

"You hear Milk Creek and you expect the water to be pale white," Rayanne said. "I saw a regular muddy creek. Maybe bigger than a creek. More like a small river. How do they decide whether something is a river or a creek?"

"Good question," Henry said, pleased that they were no longer discussing his shortcomings. "What about a stream? Or a brook? A brook is something, isn't it?"

"A brook sounds like something you would find next to an English cottage," Rayanne said. "There it is. Turn."

The hand-painted sign attached to the fence said 'Mill Creek Farm' in childish script.

"You sure about this place?" Rayanne said. The way she said it made it clear she was not impressed.

"We can't judge by the sign," Henry said. A gravel road ran along a grassy field and dipped down into a grove of trees. A woven wire fence surrounded the property. The road forked at an old wooden shed that was missing most of its roof.

"Where should I go?" Henry said.

"I thought you were in charge of this mission," Rayanne said.

"You took charge. I thought you knew what you were doing." He smiled when he said it, and was pleased that she smiled back.

"Go left," she said. "Isn't that the rule? If you don't know, go left."

"That's what I heard," Henry said.

She was right. The road ended at a small gravel parking lot with an old farmhouse. A young couple came out the door to greet them.

5

*R*ayanne followed Henry as they headed down the narrow trail toward the meeting lodge. Pepe and Polly led the way. She couldn't help being annoyed by how nice Henry looked from behind. Wide shoulders, narrow waist, no butt. Big surprise.

The sun was high in the sky, but the trail was shaded, and birds chirped in the trees. The pond was visible between the foliage, and a faint verdant scent floated off the water. She wished she could enjoy the peace and quiet. It was a lovely spot. But in the back of her mind all she could think of was a huge pile of work, the accumulating emails, and Linda checking her desk every fifteen minutes to see if she was back.

She quickened her step to catch up.

Polly and Pepe turned out to be a younger couple who burned out on their big city careers, and were giving country living a try. They brought them to a huge open meadow that sloped down toward the water. Picnic tables were grouped together under clusters of shade trees that ringed the meadow. The meeting space was in a rustic cabin at the top of the incline.

"You've done concerts before?" Pepe asked Henry.

"Why are you talking about concerts?" Rayanne asked.

Henry held up a finger. "Not really."

"You got sponsors or another source of seed money?" Pepe asked.

"What do you mean sponsors?" Henry asked.

"It's easy to think that you're going to bring a few bands out and charge admission," Pepe said. "A thousand people will show up and their admission will cover your costs. It doesn't work like that. You need money before you start."

"But you've met Sam," Henry said. "These are friends—"

Rayanne shook her head. "Sorry, I don't have time for this. I need to get back to the office."

"We're here for your retreat," Henry said. "It doesn't hurt if I ask other questions while I'm here."

"I need to look at the meeting space, and we need to go."

Polly caught that there was something going on. "I'll take you up there." As they walked up the hill, Polly leaned close to Rayanne. "Pepe's not trying to be a jerk. We've had this before. Someone comes up with a great idea to get their friends to play. They'll put it on social media and assume it will draw a big crowd. Everyone profits. They never get as many people as they expect. Meanwhile, we need to put up a stage, we need power, we need portable toilets, we need insurance, we need security. How many people are you expecting?"

"Me?" Rayanne said. "His band is none of my concern. I need to put on a retreat for a non-profit."

"That's easier," Polly said. She had a sweet smile and down-to-earth manner. She unlocked the meeting lodge and it took no time before Rayanne knew it was perfect. There was a large open room with couches and comfy chairs. Huge glass doors faced the pond. Polly showed her how the doors slid open to allow fresh air in and access to the deck. There was a kitchen, two small bedrooms, and two bathrooms.

"Used to be a two-bedroom home. We can reconfigure it in different ways. If there's a wedding the bridal party can get ready here. If it's a family reunion some folks can stay here. People can camp out and we have an outdoor restroom and shower. It's not fancy but it works for the right kind of group."

By this time Henry and Pepe had arrived.

"What do you think?" Henry asked.

Rayanne ignored him. To Polly she said, "It's perfect. If you can email me the agreement and electronic deposit information I can have it signed and reserved by the end of the day."

"Great," Polly said. "You've done this before."

Rayanne gave Henry a pointed look. "I have."

RAYANNE WAS GIDDY WITH RELIEF. One giant problem solved. Linda would be thrilled. Too bad it was thanks to Henry.

They hadn't spoken since they got back in the van. Henry fiddled with the radio before giving up and turning it off.

"No luck booking your band?" Rayanne said.

"Nothing you need to worry about," Henry said. "How do you do the meals for the retreat?"

"I'll make a menu. Easy meals like muffins and fruit when they arrive. Deli sandwiches at noon and then something hot for dinner. Linda and I can make a vat of spaghetti or something like that."

"Arnie can get us plenty of salmon," Henry said.

"That's a nice idea but it's got to be simple since we can't cook and run a meeting at the same time."

"I can do the cooking," Henry said. "I don't need to listen to all the funding and planning, do I?"

"You can do cooking?" Rayanne wondered what passed for cooking for Henry.

"I can hear the doubt in your voice," Henry said. "I learned not out of choice, but out of necessity."

"You were wandering lost in the woods and couldn't find a hot dog stand?"

"When I was in high school my mom broke her arm right before Thanksgiving. She was in charge of a big family dinner and she got all worked up. I suggested that we ask someone else to be in charge of dinner. Wrong response. She told me I had to get off my lazy ass and how important this was because I would be eating my entire life. I couldn't always count on someone to make my food for me."

"I want to meet this woman," Rayanne said. "I could learn something from her."

"You know how sometimes when people doubt you, it makes you more determined to show them what you can do?"

"That's the theme song of my entire life," Rayanne said.

"I told Mom I could do it all. I read a bunch of planning articles online. I watched cooking clips. I made menus, shopping lists, and timelines."

"What happened?"

"She didn't let me do it unsupervised. She bossed me around the entire time. But it was a good dinner. I used to never care about cooking. Only eating. Now I can cook. I'm not a great cook. I can't make a lot of things. But I can cook traditional salmon."

"Really," Rayanne said, realizing she was more impressed than she should be. "Okay. You can be in charge of the food."

"Wait a second," Henry said.

"No take-backs. You'll do fine. I'm sure there are clips for that and you can bring your mom to boss you around. She boss Arnie around?"

"Of course," Henry said.

"She's invited. So what happened with your great concert event?"

"Pepe knows more about promoting music shows than I do. He said an unknown band isn't going to draw enough people to make us rich and famous, or even pay for us to use the spot. I guess I'm a moron. I did research but not enough research. My friends are going to be disappointed."

"What's the goal?" Rayanne asked. "Play in front of an audience?"

"Yeah, you know. Have people discover them. Develop a following. Tour the world."

"Could you plan something smaller? What if you could find a small venue with a stage? Do they have a mailing list? Do they know other bands? If you could get enough friends together to cover a smaller place, it would be fun and they could see what it was like."

"You know a lot about this," Henry said.

"I know about event planning," Rayanne said.

"So I've heard," Henry said. "I guess I should talk with them and figure out what we want to do."

When they arrived back at the office, Rayanne said, "Thanks for helping me find a new spot. You do the menu planning and I'll get the agenda together. We can meet again and figure out how to put the meeting materials together. Sound good?"

They stayed in the van, sitting next to each other like it was the end of a date. A strange vibe bloomed between them. Rayanne was aware of each breath he took and a coil of heat unwound inside her.

"We could work on it now," Henry said.

"Thanks," Rayanne said. She gathered her things, wanting to get away. "Day is done. I have a bunch of other stuff to do before I go home." She couldn't miss the disappointment on his face. Without meaning to, she reached over and put a hand on his forearm. "Thanks for your help. Finding this place was great. I appreciate it." His arm was solid and warm. She wanted to slide her hand up and squeeze his bicep. He eyed the place where she touched him and she warmed-up right where you would expect. She avoided his eyes and snatched her hand back. "I'll see you tomorrow morning."

6

_L_inda tried to help Margie up the front steps, but the elder reached for the railing and pulled herself up to the front door, one precarious step at a time. She opened the front door and stepped inside. Linda braced herself for what was coming.

"Where are my rugs?"

Linda followed her inside. "We had to move them."

"But I love those rugs," Margie said, her voice weak and trembling.

"I know," Linda said. "I love them too. But the fringed edges are too easy to trip over. You break your hip and that's it. You're off to assisted living." Margie's face was pale and her thin, gray hair needed styling. How long could Margie stay in this house like she wanted to?

"I could be very careful," Margie said. She shuffled along with her cane to demonstrate. Her feet scuffed along the floor as she walked.

"You could," Linda said, "but I would be more comfortable if you could live without them. I worry about you." Linda found that if Margie thought she was being bossed around, she would argue. If Linda appealed to her common sense, she might get somewhere. "Have you thought more about the medical alert system?" Linda may as well have asked Margie if she'd thought about growing a horn on her head.

Margie brushed the question away. "I got a little sick and I'm a little worn down. I'm not going to fall down and become helpless."

A little sick. That's what she called pneumonia. She'd been feverish and couldn't communicate for days. The doctor had warned them her condition was serious but she bounced back. At least if Margie was crotchety, it meant she was on the mend.

"Merely a suggestion," Linda said.

"You know what you can do with that suggestion."

Rayanne arrived and charged through the front door. "Good news! I have a place for the retreat." She went over and gave Margie a hug. "You look great, Auntie. Are you feeling better?"

"This one is taking away my rugs," Margie said.

"We're trying to keep you in one piece," Rayanne said. "When you can do a cartwheel, we'll bring your rugs back."

Margie made a face and shuffled out of the room.

Linda gestured at Rayanne. *What more can we do?*

Rayanne gave a weak laugh, quiet so Margie wouldn't hear.

"Tell me about the retreat location," Linda said.

"It's great. It's called Milk Creek Farm. There's a little meeting house surrounded by trees with a view of a pond. A handful of picnic tables. Some walking paths."

"Good work," Linda said. "How did you manage that?"

"Henry," Rayanne said, like she was sorry to admit it. "He gets one point so far."

There was a crash in the kitchen. "I broke a little cup," Margie called. "Don't run in here."

"This is depressing," Rayanne said quietly. "No matter how smart or kick-ass you are. No matter how many times you speak before Congress or save treaty rights, you end up all old and feeble. You know it was a major revelation for me, when I sat in a room full of old people, and realized that at one time, they were all young and hot and trying to get into each other's pants."

"We still sometimes get into each other's pants," Margie said, making her way back into the room, one creaky step at a time. Her new cane had padded feet at the base, keeping her moving.

34

"I don't know if I like the images popping into my head," Rayanne said.

"Why not? Never too old to have fun," Margie said. "I could teach you a thing or two."

Linda made a joke of covering her ears to block out Margie's bragging, but really she was thrilled with her sass.

Margie stopped and leaned against a chair to catch her breath. She pointed to the handle of her cane. The tassels were strings of shells and beads. "My granddaughter made it for me. She called it my bling."

"No one ever said you weren't fancy," Rayanne said.

Linda found it hard to reconcile this breathless woman with the powerhouse she had met ten years earlier.

"Could one of you girls bring me a cup of tea?" Margie asked.

"Always," Rayanne said, and went to the kitchen.

Margie sat down. She pointed to her wall of books. "One day you girls are going to get all of these."

Linda loved these books. Margie collected books about tribal history, culture and art. She had a shelf of mythology books. She had poems and memoirs. How many rainy afternoons had Linda visited Margie, and ended up sprawled out on the couch flipping through her books?

"What are we going to do with them?" Linda said.

"Create a library at the center."

Linda could picture it. There would be one room devoted to the books. They'd fill it with comfortable chairs and couches. They'd put a big study table where people could do research. They could look for grants to get it organized. Maybe they could even find a librarian who could help them put it together.

"What a generous gift," Linda said.

Margie waved off the comment. "What am I going to do with them?"

"Thank you. When we get to the new building, we'll find a special place for them."

Rayanne returned with the tea, and set it on the little table next to Margie.

Margie peeked into the cup. The corners of her mouth turned down. "Did you put honey in it?"

"I can put honey in it if you want," Rayanne said.

Margie shook her head. "I can drink it like this."

Rayanne made a face at Linda. "Later I'm making a dinner that will no doubt be a terrible disappointment. You joining us?"

"Don't be smart," Margie said with a small smile.

"Can't make it tonight," Linda said. "I gotta go meet with Arnie."

"Oh, really," Rayanne said.

"For work or for fun?" Margie asked.

"Both of you stop," Linda said. "We are friends and now colleagues. That's it. And if things continue like they're going, he's going to have to fire me. That's not the basis for a great date."

"I've always thought you two would make a good match," Margie said. "You don't feel a little sparkle? You have a lot in common."

"Yeah," Rayanne said. "Sparkle. I see it too. You like an Indian in a suit."

Linda forced a laugh. "I have known him forever. We are not dating."

"It's okay to change your mind," Margie said.

"Just because people are unattached, doesn't mean they should be together. We are friends."

That's how all the great romances begin," Margie said.

"Yeah, maybe all this working together and you'll change your mind," Rayanne said.

"Why are you after me? You've been making lovey eyes at Henry since he walked through the door."

"I can't lie," Rayanne agreed. "He is fine on the eyeballs. He's also ruining my job. But I'm dealing, as I was instructed."

"Good. These guys don't get what we do. Arnie wants to charge in, make changes, and boss everyone around. We need him to do what we want him to do, and we need to make him think it's his idea."

"You understand everything I've taught you," Margie said with a smile. "It's official. You don't need me any longer."

"Yes, we do," Linda and Rayanne called out together.

"You're going to tell him to keep his hands off the festival," Rayanne said.

"Sweetie, you need him on your side." Margie spoke with her eyes closed, her head propped up on her hand. "You need to woo the board into continuing to support your plans. You need them if you want the center to exist."

"I will do everything I can to make sure he understands us. I'll try to keep Henry out of your hair." Linda got up and put a wool blanket over Margie. She smiled but didn't open her eyes.

Linda followed Rayanne to the kitchen. "Thanks for making Margie dinner. Is she going to be part of your rotation?"

Rayanne nodded. "Good luck with Arnie. Maybe if you two had a thing it would help our cause."

"He doesn't see me like that. Things might work better for the center if we both keep our pants on."

"That won't be a problem," Rayanne said.

Linda headed out to meet Arnie. It was strange to think of them working together again after all this time. They'd always kept in touch but he was back and forth to the rez and traveled around the region to government meetings. They'd barely seen each other in years. She might have been happier about it except her job was on the line.

When they first met in college, she'd been smitten. She didn't meet a lot of Indian men, and the ones she did meet did not appeal the way Arnie did. He was so single-minded on leading in Indian Country. He wanted to go back to the rez, and make a difference for his own people. He was handsome. A little shorter than she would prefer but, as Rayanne pointed out, he looked damn fine in a suit.

He also made clear his lack of interest in her. Arnie enjoyed dating a wide variety of women. But not women like her. He learned to play the exotic boy from rez to his great advantage. He always had pretty girls lined up after him.

Time to stop thinking about that. She had a job to do and he was the boss.

7

---

*A*rnie spotted her before she came through the door. Time hadn't just been kind to her, time had been magical for her. In college she'd always been so serious, striding around campus with her single braid and a giant backpack. Now she was long legs and graceful motion. Her dark hair curled around her shoulders.

If he were asked to summarize her back then, he would have described her as a woman of too many ideas and too little direction. Somehow there was always a piece missing. She would have a great idea but they should have been working on it six months earlier. She wanted the Native Students Association to host a treaty rights conference but she couldn't convince any of the Native Studies professors to sponsor them in time. She was always on the short end of a crisis, either searching for her coat or chasing after a lost phone. But she was also a loyal friend and made time for him whenever he needed to talk to someone who reminded him of home.

She was the perfect person for this job but she was having such a hard time with it. She was brilliant with whatever budget she could get. She found great people and brought them together. Why weren't they fulfilling any of their goals?

Arnie stood when she approached the table. She wore jeans and a T-shirt smudged with dust.

"What did you do, clean out a barn?"

"That would have been more fun," Linda said, leaning over for a hug. "Helping Margie stay independent as long as she can. No more rugs. Did you know that's one of the top injury hazards for elders?"

"I never thought about it," Arnie said. "How is she doing?"

"Moving slowly, but she's tough. She's not going to go down easy."

"Good." Arnie pointed at the chalkboard menu. "Do you want me to grab something?"

"Decaf, sugar and milk. Thanks."

When he returned, she was paging through the folder of notes he had put together for their discussion.

"This the dossier you've compiled on me?" Her tone was light-hearted.

"Something like that," Arnie said. He set down the coffee and two cookies.

"How did you know I needed this?" Linda said. She broke one of the cookies in half, and ate it in three bites. She took a swig of coffee and sighed. "I'm having a hard time with everything. Part of it is about Margie. Losing her as a colleague but also watching her slow down and give up this work she loves. But that's not all. I'm fretting about the future of the center and this building we're getting into. What do you think? Is there hope? Are you going to have to axe me? You can be straight."

The woman had not changed on the inside. She worked hard to the point of destroying her ability to do things well. She was the person who stayed up for two days to study for an important exam, and then was so sleepy she could barely finish. She was always the first one to arrive and the last one to leave at every demonstration. Then she would have to write a ten page paper in one frenzied sitting.

"I am straight with you. Hope isn't the issue. There's always hope. The issue is making things work. Everyone wants to see the UIC succeed but no one wants to keep throwing money at something that's not working."

"What's not working?" Linda said. She circled the stirrer around the cup a few times. "The retreat foul up was all my fault. The deadline got past me. But the delays on the building purchase are outside my control. We had a structural inspection. Then an environmental review. We've met every deadline. We've done everything they asked us to do. Once we get that piece taken care of, everything else will slip into place. Replace me if you have to, but my mistakes are more about trying to do too much, and not about being a complete idiot."

"No one wants to replace you."

"But you aren't denying thoughts that I'm a complete idiot."

"We haven't used those exact words."

"That's a relief."

She searched his eyes like she was expecting to find something there. She'd always had a direct gaze that would disrupt his train of thought if he weren't careful.

"The way the board views it..." What was the best way to put it?

"Are you differentiating your opinion from the board's?"

"I'm not the only person making decisions. We have to report to the tribes funding you. Those tribes are asking about actual on-the-ground services. What they see is planning for services more than providing services."

Linda sighed with frustration. "I don't know what to say if that's what they think. We're working toward more services. I think they underestimate our value. Am I doomed?"

"No one is doomed," Arnie said, failing to laugh it off. "A year ago Margie convinced the tribes she needed another year. What's happened since then? Not a lot."

"You sound like a government official. You want to know why we don't do more, and you don't want to give us enough money. You can't have it both ways."

Arnie nodded. "I am a government official. That's what we do. We'll go over all the numbers at the retreat, then we'll have a better idea of the big picture."

"There's one piece of good news. Rayanne found a place for the retreat, thanks to your nephew. Didn't take long to sneak one of your relatives on the staff. Is he there to check up on us?"

"Henry's a good kid. Can't you use the help?"

"I'm sure he is but why not make Rayanne a project manager and let Henry answer the phone? I don't need a person without experience. I need a grant writer. I need a fundraiser. I need the ability to offer services. Like how about making sure our elders can vote? With the new laws, some of them don't have whiteman birth certificates. They need help navigating the system. We could do basic medical care instead of referrals. That's what we need to be talking about. How am I supposed to pay him?"

Arnie cleared his throat. He wasn't sure how Linda was going to take this bit. "I have a small fund that can be used to keep him on staff for now."

"Ah, you have a fund for your nephew," Linda said. "Of course you do. Do I even want to hear the story?" A burst of temper flashed in her eyes. "Does he have a juvenile record? A little drug dealing? Petty theft?"

"Of course not," Arnie said. "He's a perfectly good kid."

"You already said that. Fess up. What's going on with him?"

Arnie took a moment to figure out what to say. "He's a little lost. My sister wants me to help. I'm trying to keep her off my back."

"I could threaten to be the worse one on your back but since you're my boss, I'll cooperate."

"He doesn't want to do it anyway. Maybe he'll give up and move on. I can say I fulfilled my familial duty."

"Terrific. An underachiever who might not even last. Here, ladies, do your best. When was the last time someone expected a room full of competent men to fix some halfwit female?"

"He's not a halfwit. Look at this a different way. You have the opportunity to inspire another young Native to our cause." Arnie was trying to be funny but she wasn't buying it.

"Why does he have to be in charge of something?"

"He's not going to do it if the job is answering email and stapling documents," Arnie said. He should never have brought Henry in but now it was done. They'd have to deal with it.

"Do you hear what you're saying? We don't just have to take on the reluctant apprentice, we have to make it fun for him?"

"He has the job," Arnie said. "Can you please tolerate him for now? Can I at least hold out hope that he'll appreciate the role models and maybe it will rub off on him? I've always admired your stubborn persistence, that's why I like you in this job. I guess we have to focus on getting the small things right."

"We are getting the small things right," Linda said through her teeth. "We're doing everything right. Have you ever tried to use specialized funding to purchase property for a nonprofit? They need paperwork. Then a narrative statement. Then a tour. Then an appraisal. Testing for a million toxic substances. Then, when the deal is supposed to be done, I can't get anyone to return a phone call. The people that I do get on the line give me vague responses like, 'It's on someone's desk. We'll get back to you.' I'm not sure what else we could be doing."

"I'm not articulating myself well and you're misunderstanding my concern. Why don't you tell me what the property is like."

"It's great. We should go out there," Linda said, her tone lighter. "It was built to be an elementary school, and later repurposed into an administration building. There's room for a playground. There's a big room with a kitchen adjacent so we could plan a huge range of activities. Rayanne could get her elder club going. Maybe some sort of daycare. Cultural activities. Classes." Linda sighed. "Room for more employees. It will be miraculous to have a space like that as our own. How about your connections? You're a big mover and shaker. Don't you know someone you can call?"

"City politics and Indian politics, not the same thing." Arnie took the folder back and scribbled some notes. "I'll see what I can do. Listen, I'm not going to lie. There are some who have lost confidence in you. I know Margie is a big fan—"

"I'm good at my job," Linda said. "It was not some special favor Margie did keeping me in there."

"You misunderstand. You have my complete support, Lulu." She smiled when he used the old nickname. "Truly. I want this to succeed. Too many of our people end up in the city but completely lost. Believe me, I know. Every time I see a native person living on the street, I want to do something. I want them to have a place to go when they are away from home, and I think you are the one to do it. That's part of the reason I agreed to do this."

"What's the other part?" Linda asked. Her tone was playful; he could tell her the truth.

"You know how I am. Strategic planning for my own future. Raise my profile in the community with an eye to running for state office and, someday, to Congress. We need more representation at a higher level."

"I should have known. If anyone can do it, you can." And when she said it, he believed he could.

8
―――――――――――――

*T*he van made a new sound. Henry hadn't heard it when he was out with Rayanne, so either he'd been so crushed out he hadn't noticed, or it had just started. The scrape and hum sounded at comforting intervals. The van was another in a long line of almost fixes that Henry had going on in his life. He had a problem, he needed transportation. Someone at one of his job sites had a friend who was selling a van for cheap. He'd asked all the right questions. He checked under the hood, and examined the hoses and belts. He made an informed opinion. Besides, at his budget level he didn't have a lot of choices.

Later Arnie told him he was supposed to take the van to someone who could inspect underneath for him.

It didn't matter now. The van was his and the band's only form of transportation so he was stuck with it. He'd replaced two tires a month ago. What next to empty his wallet?

He kept going back and forth on Uncle Arnie's great job opportunity. He didn't get what was so important about those programs. He wanted a job where he was wanted, not a job where his uncle made the people take him. And he didn't know the first thing about managing projects like that. He didn't mind helping Rayanne with the retreat, but the minute that event was finished he would be out of there. Rayanne would be happy about that.

Inside the apartment, his roommate, Jack, banged cupboard doors open and closed, working his way through each one. They'd known each other since they were kids when their moms became friends taking local parenting classes for Indians. When they were younger, they thought their moms took the class because they had problems. Henry was a teenager when his mom explained that she'd joined the group for companionship. She wanted to meet other native moms who lived off-rez. Jack's family was Blackfeet from Montana. He spent a couple weeks a year there, but he was a city Indian too.

"What happened?" Henry asked.

Jack waved his arms over his head like he was trying to stop cars on the highway. "I can't find any food. Also, we gotta get out of here."

Henry separated the conversation into two statements. "If you can't find any food, it's because we don't have any."

"Did you bring something?"

"No," Henry said. "I had lunch with my uncle. He wants me to take a crazy job I could never do. What did you mean about getting out of here?"

"We're losing this place," Jack said. "Someone left a note on the door. We're evicted."

More difficult days ahead. Another setback in a long line of setbacks. "By a note on the door? Was it real?"

"It was a real note on the door."

"They can do that?"

"For an illegal squat?" Jack went back through each cupboard, this time taking time to slide things aside and reach to the back.

"This isn't a squat." They had thrown rugs over the uneven floor, and put up posters to hide the patchy drywall.

"It's a dump," Jack said. "We're not legal so they can do what they want. That's the tradeoff for too-cheap-to-believe rent."

They'd ended up in that place purely by luck. Jack's brother had lived here first. He was a friend of the owner or something like that. Someone needed the extra cash so they'd turned their garage into an apartment. The place had never been finished. There were plywood dividers for privacy. The cupboards had been salvaged from two different remodel jobs so they didn't match but they worked fine. There was a stove and a small but adequate bathroom.

Henry didn't mind. The place cost half as much as a real apartment that size. Plus he was out on his own. This news cemented the already pitiful uncertainty he had about where he was in life. He pictured Rayanne in a swank decorated apartment with pictures on the wall and a set of dishes that matched. She hosted dinner parties and used cloth napkins. He ate all his meals out of the same bowl.

"How long do we have?"

"End of the month." Jack reached the last cupboard that held nothing but a can of water chestnuts, whatever those were. There had also been a can of pumpkin pie filling, but Henry ate it one night for a snack.

"That's it?"

"That's it." Jack yanked his arm out triumphantly. "Can of chili. Split it?"

"You have it," Henry said, glum now. "I'm full from lunch."

Jack opened and closed drawers until he found a can opener. He dumped the chili into a bowl, and fired up the microwave. "What was the job?"

"Project manager at an urban Indian center," Henry said.

"What?" Jack drew the word out into a three-syllable song.

"That's what I said," Henry said. "They provide Indians with services like healthcare and transportation. Rayanne thinks she should have the job."

"Who's Rayanne?"

"She works at the center. She's a hot, sexy native woman. She's got a lot of plans and ideas about Indians that live in the city. She says people who grew up on a rez miss being around Indian people. I never thought about it."

"How much time did you spend with this girl?"

"All afternoon." Henry grinned. "Took her out to Milk Creek Farm."

"Like a date?" Jack pulled the bowl out of the microwave and stirred before he tasted it.

"No. They need a place for a retreat." Henry pictured her in the passenger seat, her hand floating out the window. In this imagined memory, she traded bashful smiles with him.

"What are they retreating from?"

"I don't get it either. I guess it's a meeting that lasts all day. I'm going to cook for it."

"This sounds better than a lot of jobs you could have. I would do it. What about the band? Beat Braves going to headline a gig out there?"

"The owner told me we would never attract enough people to make it pay. We're not the first to suffer this delusion."

"It's not a delusion. What does he know?"

"He's hosted shows that were a bust. I'll scout out some other places. Maybe we should get on the housing situation first."

"Sooner rather than later," Jack agreed. "I think I could stay with guys in the band if I get desperate."

"I can stay in the van," Henry said. "Wasn't this moment inevitable when I bought it? We knew this day would come."

Jack scraped the bottom of the bowl. "I'm still hungry. Why don't you take those jars to your mom for a refill? She'll pity us and give us something to eat." He was referring to a box of canning jars that had once been full of jam, smoked salmon, and tomatoes. The jars had been sitting in a box in the corner of the kitchen since they finished the last item.

"I don't want to deal with my mom right now," Henry said. She would want to know about Arnie. She would ask a bunch of questions about the job. She would make comments that were intended to sound like supportive mom-talk, but under the surface she was cutting him down, because he wasn't a successful college grad doing meaningful good-paying work, and dancing for joy about it every day.

Jack stuck out his hand. "Give me the keys. I'll do it. I can tell her about the job and Rayanne."

"Forget it," Henry said. "I'll go talk to her."

"Bring me back some food," Jack reminded him.

HENRY'S MOM still lived in the same two-bedroom bungalow that he grew up in. When he went through the front door, the house was quiet.

"Mom?"

"I'm in here." Mom sat at the kitchen table. She had a bright desk lamp shining on a small disk she was beading. "I thought this would relax me, but instead it forces me to confront how bad my eyes have become."

"Why aren't you relaxed?" Henry asked.

"My son has surprised me with a visit. What is it now?"

He put the jars on the kitchen counter. "You want small talk, or should I get to the point?"

Mom laughed and made a let-me-have-it motion with her hand.

"We're getting kicked out of our apartment."

Mom sat up and pushed her glasses up on her head. "What did you do?"

Tildy was the kind of mom who could take almost anything. Not murder and nothing bad against a woman, but anything else she could deal with. That didn't mean she wouldn't inflict suffering, but nothing surprised her.

"Nothing," Henry said. "The place is illegal. The owner wants us out. Maybe he has his own deadbeat kid who needs a cheap place to live."

"That's the lesson. Things that sound too good to be true, probably are. What are you going to do?"

"Find another place, eventually," Henry said.

"And until then?"

Henry gave her his prettiest pleading smile.

"You're suggesting living here again? In this...what was that you said as you stormed out the door when you moved out?"

"I said, 'Thank goodness this is my last day in this hellhole,'" Henry said. "I meant it with love."

"What was the rest of your speech as you stomped off into independence? 'I don't need you or any of your stuff'?"

"I may have spoken too hastily. I was also very angry. Insults were thrown."

"They were," Mom agreed. "As long as you have a place to stay, you don't need me. I'm sure you can find another apartment. Or a room to rent. You have to get off your duff, and go look for it."

"I know how to find an apartment, Mom."

"Congratulations. When I see the family, I won't have to hang my head in shame. Did you see Arnie yet?"

Henry had hoped to avoid the subject. "We had lunch. I took him to that great burger place."

"That's why I was asking. Because I wanted to hear where you went for lunch. What did you guys talk about?"

"I know you asked him to get me a job. He wants me to be a project manager at this urban Indian center."

Mom smiled so hard she was in danger of breaking her face. It was like he had an offer to run the UN.

"I can't do a job like that. I don't even understand what they do. And there's already someone there who's way more qualified. Arnie is giving me a job that should be hers as a favor to you. It's totally embarrassing."

"Family giving you a job is the Indian way," she said.

"Then why don't you do it?" Henry said.

"Because I'm already employed in the high glamour world of government contracts. I can pay the bills. Last time I checked, your rock-band idea hadn't gone anywhere."

"It's a native rock band with a hip-hop influence. It takes a while to get things going."

"I'm not clear on the difference, and you don't have to make me a song list. I will use my imagination."

"It's called a playlist."

"Whatever you say. You're capable enough. This is a terrific opportunity for you."

"You sound like Arnie."

"Arnie gets to be right for once. Be sure to tell him I said that, he'll be happy to hear it. How is he doing?"

"He does nothing but work all the time like you want me to." Henry eyed the refrigerator door. There had to be something in there that she would love to hand off to her son and his hungry roommate.

"I didn't raise you to be a leech. Do you want to be broke for the rest of your life?"

Henry abandoned that plan. "Don't start with that. It's not like I don't want a job. I don't want that job."

"That's not how life works. You don't sit around waiting for some perfect job with lots of pay to appear. Sometimes it's good for you to do something you don't want to do."

"So life works by insisting you take the job your family wants you to have?"

"You can't expect to fall back on me every time something goes wrong. You can't—"

"That's enough lecture for today. I'm out of here."

He left empty-handed. Jack was going to have to go hungry.

9

*R*ayanne picked up Ester at seven, and they headed out to Milk Creek Farm. Traffic was tight in town, but they were driving against the flow and made good time.

"Why are we doing this so early?" Ester wore sweatpants and a sweatshirt. She carried her work clothes in a backpack that she hugged on her lap.

"So we can be ridiculously organized and prepared and impress everyone with our initiative and fortitude."

"Fortitude? We need to demonstrate fortitude? In a movie, you would be the army captain making us do the obstacle course in the rain and mud before we'd had our coffee."

"And you'd thank me at the end."

"What's the scoop with Mr. Dreamy Face?"

"I don't know what you're talking about."

"Our new project manager, Henry? Remember, the guy who's been hanging out with us in the office? If you don't want him, can I have him?"

A surprising pang of jealousy struck her in the chest. Rayanne shook it off.

"He's not mine to give away. And he's not that great."

Ester ran her fingers through her messy hair. "Really? He has a terrific haircut and struts around like a huge slab of delish bronzed warrior with his big shoulders and—"

"Enough," Rayanne said. "I may have noticed those things and possibly even admired them. We're working together. Working. It's working."

"Whatever you say," Ester said.

Henry had suggested they drive to the retreat together, but Rayanne didn't want to deal with him and his sexy smile, and big, brown man hands. Whenever he was in sight, her eyeballs couldn't stay away from his hands. Today, her job was to sell the board of directors on the future of the center. Henry would be in the background dealing with the food, and staying out of their way.

When they pulled into the parking lot his old decrepit van was already there.

"What, did he sleep here?" Ester said. "How ambitious. If your dream guy is another overachiever you may have found one."

"I don't get the sense this guy is an overachiever, and he's not my dream guy."

They made their way into the meeting lodge. Henry was in the kitchen.

"What are you doing?" Rayanne asked.

"Why the cranky face?" Henry had on an apron over nice slacks and a dress shirt with buttons. He grabbed a couple of mugs, and poured coffee from a steaming pot. "How do you ladies like it?"

"If I had a dollar for every man who asked me that," Ester said, taking one of the mugs, "I would have one lone dollar. Black is fine."

Rayanne took the mug from his hands. "I can do it." She ripped open two sugar packets, and poured some milk into the coffee.

"You're not morning people," Henry said.

"No sane person is," Ester said.

"I can be," Rayanne said. "I wasn't expecting you."

"What is that incredible smell?" Ester asked.

"I'm glad you asked." Henry pointed at the giant bowl on the counter. "I'm baking muffins."

"Are those what I think they are?" Rayanne said, spotting little blue dots in the batter.

"Huckleberries," Henry said. "Harvested during the summer. My mom donated to the cause. This was her idea. She wants me to make a good impression." He smiled. "How am I doing?"

Rayanne wasn't about to gush. "Not bad, I guess. Someone is bound to approve."

"Like me," Ester said. "Call me the minute those are done. I have to change into my professional retreat clothes."

Linda called out from the main room. She was wearing a cute yellow sundress and long turquoise earrings that dangled almost to her shoulders. She held a takeout coffee cup, and tipped her head back to get the last few sips.

"How did you manage to get here so early?" Rayanne said.

"It's easy when you don't go to bed. The bags under my eyes have bags under their eyes." She pointed to her face but, other than a little puffiness, she looked great.

Henry called from the kitchen, "How do you take your coffee?"

"Sugar. Milk. Thanks," she called back. To Rayanne she said, "He's bringing me coffee."

"If you want him as an assistant, he's all yours."

When Henry brought in the coffee, he had a plate of muffins too.

Ester returned from changing. She wore a short-sleeved blouse and a skirt. She moved fast when she saw the muffins. She had her mouth full when she told Henry, "These are the things that make life worth living."

Rayanne tried one and agreed, they were amazing. Maybe Henry wasn't so terrible to work with after all. He'd shown up, done whatever they'd asked, and been charming and polite.

"These are good," she said.

"I'm glad you like them," he said. "I'll be in the kitchen if you need me."

Linda had a little notebook out and paged through it. "We need to go over our plan."

"You're cute when you try to be organized," Rayanne said.

"Gee, thanks," Linda said. "Cute is what I was going for. Ester, can you deal with the projector stuff?"

While Ester unraveled cables and set up the equipment, they reviewed the agenda and major points they wanted the board of directors to hear.

"I miss Margie," Rayanne said. "She always supported everything we did."

"We all wish Margie were here," Linda said. "But this is the board and Arnie is the man now. We need to impress these people."

On cue Arnie arrived, blustering through the door like the star of the show.

"Smells like Grandma's huckleberry muffins." His voice boomed across the room. Here was a man incapable of making a quiet entrance. He wore a nice suit and a bolo tie fashioned with a huge polished stone.

"Not Grandma, but next best thing," Rayanne said.

Henry came out of the kitchen with another plate of muffins. "Hey, Uncle Arnie."

"Don't call me that. It makes me sound like I'm a hundred years old." Arnie took a muffin, and ate half in one bite. "Not bad. I need a word." He nudged Henry back toward the kitchen.

ARNIE GAVE HENRY A DISMAYED ONCE-OVER. "Why are you in the kitchen wearing an apron?"

"To keep my clothes clean," Henry said.

"I need you out here listening to what's going on so you understand how the place works."

Arnie took another muffin. "This is a terrific idea. Baking to get everyone on your side."

That was Henry's reasoning when he decided to go through with Mom's idea, but now that Arnie mentioned it, the move felt transparent, like *hey, look at me over here baking and being helpful.*

"I'm in charge of the food all day," Henry told him. "That's why I'm here."

A single huckleberry bounced off of Arnie's shirt, leaving a pale purple dot.

"Shit." Arnie went to the sink, and used a wet paper towel to blot at the mark. "You can drop the BS. Your mom told me you lost your apartment."

"It hasn't happened yet. And I can figure out how to pay my own bills." Arnie needed to return to the main room and leave him alone.

"Pay attention to what they're doing. We'll find a project that you're interested in," Arnie said.

"Don't get me wrong, I appreciate that you did this. I've learned a lot. Mostly that I'm not cut out for this. I want to get through today, and then go back to my own plans."

Any levity in the conversation vanished. "Here are the stakes Mr. Do-my-own-thing. Your mom wants me to get you a job out on the rez. She's convinced your Uncle Mike to give you a room at their house. If I were you, I'd jump at the chance to live out there, but I'm not and I'm guessing that you prefer to be here, close to the fancy restaurants and rock clubs. Consider taking this more seriously."

Arnie went back into the main room and made an announcement. His voice rose above everyone else's. Henry couldn't make it out with the anger boiling inside. Now they were making plans for him, even arranging his housing. And he was supposed to appreciate all this? He put together another plate of muffins and joined the others.

By this time everyone had arrived and settled in the main room. The chairs and couches had been arranged in a big U. A projection screen hung from one wall. Henry recognized the four other board members who joined Arnie and the staff. There were another half dozen people who he assumed were the attorneys and consultants that Linda and Rayanne had talked about during planning.

Tommy waved him over and pointed to the chair next to his. He handed over a familiar-looking binder. Henry had been the one to put them together. It contained the agenda, an assortment of charts, and lists of talking points.

"What about you?" Henry asked, noticing that Tommy didn't have his own binder.

"I don't need it," Tommy said. Moments later he made a face because Rayanne stuck another one in his hands. She gave them each a pen too.

"Be sure to take notes," she said. She returned to her seat at the table with Linda. Together they looked like students, bent over their pads of paper. Ester sat close by, typing into a laptop.

Linda prepared to open the meeting, but Arnie waved her off and went to the front of the room. "There going to be a microphone?"

Linda's face had gone rigid. Arnie may have had numerous accomplishments under his belt, but he had no clue how to read people.

She said, "Do we need a microphone? This is a little ol' retreat, not a revival meeting."

Arnie smiled. "You know best. Who's going to do the opening prayer?"

One of the older board members, Lou, shot out of his seat, moving fast for a big guy with a bum leg.

Both Linda and Rayanne flinched. They'd discussed this, and chose another board member named Pauline to do the prayer.

"Get comfortable," Tommy whispered. "Lou is going to talk as long as no one stops him. And that's before he starts the prayer."

"I'm not going to say much," Lou said. "But before I start talking, I have a few things to say." He had a kind face and laughed a lot although Henry couldn't follow his story. He spoke about his grandfather, who had served in the war, and how he'd come home to hunt but the government came in and took all the water. His grandfather also played basketball, like so many kids today. Why wasn't there more basketball? The story lurched from topic to topic.

Rayanne would check her phone, and then tap her pen on the agenda in front of her. She tried to attract Linda's attention, but Linda kept her eyes on Lou.

Tommy leaned back in the chair and closed his eyes.

Rayanne had planned the day's activities to the minute. By Henry's estimate, they were already behind and they hadn't started yet.

Arnie had remained at the front of the room next to Lou, his hands clasped together in front of him, his eyes lowered to the ground. He reached over and touched Lou's elbow. "There a prayer in there somewhere, Uncle?"

Lou laughed, his scratchy voice ringing out. "I talk a lot."

"I don't think anyone noticed," Arnie said in a false whisper. Everyone laughed.

Lou sang a song, and it was a long one. He held the final note, reluctant to be done. When he finished, he shuffled back to his seat.

"I want to thank you all for this opportunity," Arnie said.

Now Arnie was doing a speech? Rayanne made a face as she scribbled across her agenda.

"I'm looking forward to working with you all to make a difference with urban Indians. My attention has always been on my rez, and I want to make a difference here too. We have big goals." He gestured at Linda, who gave him a tired smile. "We're going to raise our profile in the community. Find sponsors and partners. Grow this thing into something big. Now I turn the floor over to our talented executive director, Linda Bird."

Rayanne and Linda exchanged a surprised glance. They must have expected him to talk for a while too. Rayanne nudged her and Linda went to the front of the room.

In the office, Linda came across as a person who brought disorder to everything she touched. It was tough to imagine this was the same person. She was an energetic speaker who could make the most mundane topics interesting. Arnie could learn a thing from her. She talked about the issues that Indian families in the city faced. She told stories of people that the center had helped. They had connected individuals with medical care. They'd acquired bus passes and helped with job applications. She spoke of her long-range dream to buy an apartment building where they could provide affordable housing.

The board had lots of questions, but she was prepared. Henry flipped back and forth through the binder, taking notes. The morning flew by and before he knew it they were talking about lunch.

He jumped to his feet. "We're having sandwiches. I'm saving the good stuff for dinner. Give me a minute and I'll have everything set out."

~

RAYANNE SET her plate down next to her laptop and reviewed her presentation. If her time ended up being cut short, she didn't want to leave out any key points.

"It's a retreat," Linda said, coming up beside her. "You should be out there building relationships, improving communication, and most importantly, kissing the boards' brown fannies."

"You might want to lay off the coffee for the rest of the day, boss."

"Come along," Linda said.

Rayanne closed the computer and followed Linda outside.

The midday sun was warm, and the sky a cloudless blue. A breeze came off the pond, and brought the quiet chatter of birds.

Once everyone had a plate, Henry joined them outside. He picked the spot next to Rayanne, his elbow brushing her side when he sat down. The contact added an extra, sweet warmth to her day. The success of the morning session had washed away the cloud of worry. Already the future of the center was improved. Henry's presence turned out to be a calming force rather than a steady aggravation.

"You're right," he said.

"About which thing?"

"I am learning a lot."

"Thinking of sticking around?" She tilted her head, surprised that she wanted to hear that he was.

He took his time finding an answer. "If there's a project that makes sense for me, then maybe."

The lunch break went quickly. As they were picking up their plates, ready to head back in, Arnie called for everyone's attention.

"Let's do a short walk around the place before we go back in."

"But we've got a full agenda for the rest of the day," Linda said.

"I don't know about you, but eating makes me drowsy. It's gorgeous out here. We're surrounded by beauty. A ten-minute walk in the sunshine will wake us up for the afternoon." Arnie pointed to the path that led around the pond.

"Can you believe that man?" Linda said to Rayanne.

"You sound like my mom," Henry said.

Linda hid behind her hair. "I shouldn't have said that. I meant—"

"We know what you meant," Henry said. He jumped up to chase after an errant napkin picked up by the breeze.

"I'm going to help clean up, and then run back in so I can review my presentation," Rayanne said.

"You're leaving me to deal with this?" Linda said. The others had already taken off down the path.

"To walk around the pond? Yes. Those are your friends. Remember?" Tommy and Ester had paused at the pond's edge to skip stones.

"I remember." Linda followed the others.

Henry returned with a garbage bag, and held it open while Rayanne tossed in the stack of paper plates she'd collected. They gathered the rest of the trash and carried everything back to the kitchen.

"Let's go join them," Henry said, nodding toward outside.

Rayanne shook her head. "I need to prepare. I'm on when we get back."

"We know you. I bet you've been preparing for this since January."

"Not quite that long," she said, pushing her hair back.

"Come on," Henry said. He touched her shoulder and then slid his hand down her arm and lightly grasped her wrist. "Fresh air is good. You can practice your presentation on me."

Rayanne pulled back but there was no force in it. He didn't let go.

"I need to do it with a screen," she said, her voice quiet.

Henry took a half-step closer. He smelled like vanilla and huckleberries. How did he do that? He'd been setting out sliced cheese and cleaning salmon, yet he smelled terrific. He leaned closer. "You'll deal with the screen later."

The attraction manifested everywhere at once. She needed to be touching him, and the hand on her wrist was not enough. Her other hand hovered while she determined the most efficient way of conveying her meaning with the least amount of risk.

Everything was quiet except for a distant shushing noise, like air leaking from a hose, followed by dismayed cries in the distance.

"Something's happening," she said.

Henry changed his grip so he was holding her hand. Whatever trajectory she had implied, he was ready to complete. In the haze of attraction she identified the sound.

"Sprinklers?"

Linda hollered her name.

They dropped hands and ran to the door. All across the meadow, jets of water whooshed out in overlapping arcs. The retreat participants beat a hasty trail back to the house.

"I'll find Pepe," Henry said.

Linda helped Pauline, who struggled through the wet grass.

"Help Lou," Linda shouted. Her hair was already limp and straggled around her shoulders. Her gorgeous dress had gone sheer, and clung to her skin.

There was no way to avoid getting wet. The water hit in cold, forceful spurts. Rayanne ran to Lou, who was disoriented by the water.

"What's going on?" he asked, grabbing her arm for support.

"Come on," Rayanne said, trying to blink the water from her eyes. "Let's get you out of here."

Her clothes were soaked in moments. Lou kept listing toward the source of the water. Rayanne had to pull to keep him on course for the house. The sprinklers lost intensity, and then went off with a squelch.

Pepe came running down the slope. "Sorry! We were testing our timer system and I messed it up. I didn't realize you would be outside." Pepe moved from one guest to the other, his distress so genuine it was hard to be angry with him. "There are towels in the house."

"It's okay," Arnie said. "Wasn't my best suit." He'd taken off his jacket but his shirt was wet and clinging to his skin, as well.

Ester had a muddy patch on her skirt from falling down. "Best retreat I've ever been to," she said. "I don't know why we don't do this more often."

"I'm glad I'm not the one who suggested a walk," Rayanne said.

Henry came out of the house with an armload of towels. Rayanne helped Lou find a seat, and brought him a towel. She made sure everyone who needed one had something to dry off with.

Henry found her and draped a towel over her shoulders.

"Thanks," she said. "Where did Linda go?"

"She had to change." He made a gesture as if to brush off his front. "Your shirt."

Rayanne glanced down and hurried to pull the towel more tightly around her. She had worn a white knit blouse with a bralette, and the water had plastered everything to her skin. She'd been concerned about Linda's revealing outfit, and it didn't occur to her to check her own. No imagination was necessary, the material clung around the curve of her breasts, and her nipples pointed up like they were trying to break free.

Henry kept his eyes averted. "Do you have something to change into?"

"I can get by like this for now."

"I have a T-shirt you can wear."

Rayanne bit back a tart remark. She could imagine what kind of shirt Henry would want her to wear, but she dreaded the idea of sitting in a wet blouse all afternoon.

"Meet me in the spare room. You can look at it and decide."

Inside he handed her a beige T-shirt.

"Beat Braves?" The image was a cartoon of three Indians. Two held guitars, the other, a microphone.

"The band."

"Of course," Rayanne said. "Thanks."

"We were going to spell it B-R-A-V-E-Z but people might think it's pronounced *bra-vehz*."

"Can't have that."

Henry stood there.

"I'm going to need you to get lost while I change."

"You sure?" he said with a smile.

"I am." She grabbed him by the shoulder, which was warm, firm, and difficult to let go of, but she pushed him out the door.

She peeled off her wet shirt, and after a moment of consideration, left the wet bralette on. She pulled on Henry's shirt. The material was soft. She couldn't help it, she took a whiff but it smelled like fresh laundry.

She went out and hung her wet shirt over the back of a chair and rejoined the meeting.

10

*H*enry listened from the back of the room. The tone of the room shifted after the sprinkler fiasco. The morning session had been serious and fast-paced. The afternoon was more of a drowsy affair. Henry wanted to stay where he was, but Arnie's gestures escalated until it looked like he might hurt himself. Henry returned to his seat next to Tommy.

Rayanne had talked about her presentation all week but he still didn't know what it was about. When she finally got up there, her voice was pitched higher than usual, and the words came out in a rush. After the first few slides Linda asked her a question, which must have been a signal they'd worked out in advance, because Rayanne closed her eyes and took a deep breath.

She returned to an earlier slide.

"As you already know, in our tradition we value our elders. Their experiences are invaluable to our lives." Her voice came out thin even as the message was clear. "Here in the city it's tougher to get around. There is no common place to meet. Back home we have senior lunch right in town at the elementary school. I would like to create that here. I am proposing an elder program that would include regular transportation, activities and meals for elders."

"Elder daycare?" Lou joked.

"Exactly," Rayanne said. Henry caught her eye and gave her an encouraging smile.

She returned to her slides, setting out her ideas for funding and the sort of support that would be needed.

"Tommy acquired a bus for the center. How many passengers can it hold?"

Tommy held up a hand showing five fingers.

"Five people?"

"Fifteen," Tommy clarified.

"How often would you conduct events?" Arnie asked.

"Ideally, all the time. We could do the meals during the week and extra activities on the weekend. It wouldn't have to be anything fancy. And all this could be integrated with youth programs. Right, Tommy?"

Tommy made a vague gesture. Henry got the idea that where Linda and Rayanne did everything with notes and planning, Tommy went with the shortest path to accomplishing what needed to be done. Tommy just told them what they wanted to hear. This could be his role model.

"I like the idea," Arnie said, nodding thoughtfully. "A lot. But as presented, it's too ambitious for where we're at right now."

"When we get to the new space, we'll have a big room and a kitchen. It will be like a community center."

"We'll grow into that," Arnie said. "It's a big commitment. We're not ready."

Pauline nodded, doing a poor job of hiding a yawn. "We're not going to be ready for such a demanding program right away."

Lou had his own remarks along the same vein. Linda kept her eyes on her notes.

Rayanne nodded, a stony expression on her face. Henry expected her to interrupt with more data or another anecdote. Instead, she packed up her things and returned to her seat while they were still discussing it.

Henry excused himself and went outside to get the fire started.

Rayanne showed up later while he was threading salmon onto long, hardwood sticks.

"Done?" he asked.

"Nope. A few more miles to go. Last break before dinner."

"How are you holding up?"

She offered a tired smile. "I'll get over it. Where did you get the sticks?"

"Arnie brought them." His hands worked easily, keeping the flesh side up and securing the fish with smaller cross sticks.

"At home we use smaller sticks and cut it more like a salmon steak." She made the shape of a rectangle with her hands to show him how big.

"You'll have to show me sometime. I'm not much of a fisherman, but I can cook salmon in the traditional way. My entire family made sure of that. Don't tell anyone I told you, but the Indian secret is the butter and lemon, like our ancestors did."

Rayanne smiled. "It smells good."

Lou came over to the fire pit.

"Salmon again," he said. "I was hoping for elk. I'm not one of those fish-eating Ind'ns."

"You are today, Uncle," Henry said, "Or else I can make you another sandwich."

"I'll take the fish," Lou said.

"Only in Indian Country does a man complain about salmon," Henry said.

"I'm not complaining," Lou said.

"You're going to like this," Henry said, grinning.

"How you plan to get them stakes in the ground?" Lou asked, stubbing his toe in the hard dirt.

"It won't be easy. Pepe didn't want me to dig a new pit out where the ground is softer." He looked around to make sure Pepe wasn't close by, and then got a shovel from the van. "Don't look so surprised. I came prepared. You ever been to a get-together where you couldn't get the stakes in the ground?"

It took some muscle but he chopped at the ground around the fire pit until he'd loosened enough to get the stakes in. When he set the shovel aside he caught Rayanne staring at him with heat in her eyes.

He waggled an eyebrow at her. "What are you thinking about?"

Rayanne stood up straight. "The usual. Budgets, pie charts, funding line items."

"Yeah?" Henry said. He worked the sticks into the dirt and angled them toward the fire.

"Yup. That's it. I'll meet you in the kitchen at dinner and help serve."

"I'll be there," he said, his eyes never leaving her until she disappeared into the house.

ESTER WAS UP. Rayanne worked to keep her attention focused on business. Her mind kept drifting back to the sight of Henry and his manly arms driving that shovel into the ground. She rubbed her eyes and forced herself to concentrate on the presentation.

They got through two more items before Arnie rubbed his hands together and said, "Let's eat. We can wrap everything up with dinner."

Henry had brought the salmon in from the fire, and cut it into pieces. The rectangles of pale orange flesh were fanned out on a platter.

Rayanne fixed a plate for Pauline and brought it out to her.

"I know you're disappointed," Pauline said, grabbing Rayanne's hand and giving it a squeeze. "It will happen. Be patient."

"I know," Rayanne said, unable to express why the urgency. "I'm going to get Lou a plate, then I'll bring you a soda."

But by then Henry was setting a plate in front of Lou and getting instructions for more bread. "Yes, Uncle," Henry said.

Back in the kitchen, she and Henry stood side by side, fixing their own plates. "You did great. Thanks for cooking." She forced a cheerful note into her voice.

"I like your idea. My mom isn't an elder, but she would like a community center. She does beadwork, and she says it's more fun with family around. Everybody visiting and kids everywhere."

"That's my vision too. I hate to think of our elders being lonely."

Henry nudged his arm against hers. He lowered his mouth to her ear. "You look good in my shirt."

Rayanne didn't move. Every cell in her body was buzzing, unsure whether to pull away or press into him. He moved his hands to her waist. She let him spin her around to face him. Henry had his mouth on hers but their feet got tangled. While he was regaining his footing, she leaned back and his hand scraped over her breast.

"*Oof*, sorry."

"Don't be sorry," Rayanne said, exhaling into him. Her fingers ran down his chest to his flat belly. His breath caught and he buried his face in the crook of her neck. His lips were warm and soft. They brushed across her skin, making her shudder.

"I wanted it to be less clumsy," Henry whispered.

She slid a finger through a belt loop on either side and pulled him closer. "Clumsy is fine." She put her head on his shoulder and purred at the back of her throat.

When she opened her eyes she was staring through a narrow opening into the main room where everyone was eating. Her hands dropped to her side.

Henry ran his fingers along her spine, his lips trying to work their way to her collarbone.

"Stop," Rayanne said.

Henry's hands stopped. "Really?"

"This is a terrible idea."

Henry stepped back and took a second to collect himself. "It's a terrific idea. Sure, the time and place aren't ideal. Who cares? No one is paying attention." He drew her close again.

"What are you guys doing in there?" Arnie bellowed from the other room.

Rayanne pushed Henry back. "See?"

Henry handed her a plate of brownies. "Later, then," he said, his face close so she could feel his breath on her face. That clouded her head for another second before she grabbed the plate and carried it out.

"Dessert," she said, waving the plate.

"Have you two eaten dinner yet?" Ester asked.

Rayanne did not know she was capable of blushing so intensely.

"We're working on it," Henry said, carrying their plates out.

"Sorry, gang. We gotta wrap this thing up," Linda said. "Great job, you two." She came over and put an arm around Rayanne's shoulder and gave her a squeeze. For a paranoid moment she thought Linda could tell something was up.

"It was Henry," Rayanne said. "He's the one that found this place. And he did the food."

"My nephew, the cook," Arnie said. "Who thought we would see the day? Remember that time you made spaghetti and burned the noodles? Who burns noodles?"

"Remember who was supposed to be taking care of me and instead was off trying to impress some girls?" Henry said.

"I don't remember that," Arnie said, but his smile suggested differently.

"That sounds like the Arnie I know," Linda said. "This is last but definitely not least. Rayanne, you're on."

Rayanne was more confident on this idea. "When we move to the Chief building, we're going to do an Indian arts festival. We'll have booths with artists, serve food, and we'll have a stage with dancers and music. It would be like an open house."

"For Indians?" Arnie asked.

"For everyone," Rayanne said. "Urban Indians are invisible. What a great way for people to see us and learn what we do. We raise our profile in the community. In the long run, it will help us raise money. Maybe we could develop partnerships with existing programs to help tribal people with housing and education."

"That's a great idea," Arnie said. "It would improve our brand. Don't make a face. That's the lingo. I know Crooked Rock Urban

Indian Center isn't about being a brand. A festival like this would draw attention to what we do. What do you think, Henry?"

Henry smiled. "It's a great idea."

"Good," Arnie said. "You're interested in music. This is the perfect project for you. You're in charge of this event. Show them what you can do."

11

On Monday, Henry wasn't sure what was more cringe-worthy, finding himself with an office job, or his uncle handing him Rayanne's job. A job he had no idea how to do and with people who didn't want him there. Once again, he had good intentions, and events managed to conspire against him. He would have quit right then, except the need for food and shelter beat out proving something to Arnie. Not to mention avoiding getting shipped out to the rez. He needed time to come up with his own plan.

Back when they'd been cleaning up the retreat house, Rayanne ignored him other than to fire furious looks his way. Ester had offered a sympathetic shrug when Rayanne was out of the room but didn't help try to smooth things over. The minute they'd signed off with Polly, Rayanne took off, her car bouncing down the uneven road in a cloud of dust. He found his Beat Braves T-shirt folded up on the driver's seat of the van.

He spent all weekend rehearsing his speech for Rayanne, aiming for contrite but not pitiful. They were stuck working together so they'd better make the best of it. He understood the arts festival meant a lot to her. She might be mad now, but he could talk her into a collaboration. He would defer to her. It was her idea. She'd made the plans. She could boss him around. Arnie wouldn't know the difference and besides, Henry didn't have the slightest idea how to run an arts festival.

The more he practiced the conversation, the more confident he became. She would understand. There was no reason to be nervous. For now, he would pretend the whole kissing thing never happened. That perfect, incredible moment when she pulled him against her, like she'd been suffering the same attraction all day. Their bodies fit together with a jolt of recognition, jarring but also sweet and comfortable. He would earn another chance.

When he arrived, the front room was empty and the center quiet. He went to get a cup of coffee and passed Ester's office. She leaned back in her chair with her keyboard on her lap. Her typing style bordered on violence. She cleared her throat by way of greeting.

Henry tried to imagine this as a permanent job. Could he become someone like Arnie? He'd wear a suit and travel from meeting to meeting day after day. He'd have to learn all this goofy vocabulary, like cost sharing and nonfederal entity, not to mention a blur of acronyms. Nothing about it appealed.

No one had given him a work station, so he returned to Rayanne's desk with his coffee. The amount of paperwork stacked onto that one surface was almost comical. She kept everything in neat piles with notes stuck on top. The biggest stack said, "Need Money." Another stack said, "Need Reading." Two other stacks were labeled "Future Projects" and "Far Future Projects." He picked up a short pile that said "Elder Support."

"I'm going to find you a desk so you don't have to sit on mine," Rayanne said. She had on a blue blouse and snug jeans, and as soon as he saw her face he forgot all the things he had prepared to say. Even in the state of subdued fury she took his breath away. The heat in her eyes this morning was not friendly and his heart ached for a look like the one she'd given him the night of the retreat.

He jumped off her desk, causing his coffee cup to wobble. A few drops splashed over the rim and left a damp brown semicircle on the top paper.

"Sorry."

"It's just coffee." She pulled a napkin from her drawer and blotted at the spot with exaggerated patience.

"What's elder support?"

She pulled the papers out of his hand and put them back in line with the other piles. "My special project that got shot down. Remember? Don't you have your own job to do, or are you only interested in taking over what I'm doing?"

"I...uh—"

Rayanne handed him a binder. "This is the work I did. Everything you need to know is in here. Baking muffins. Planning arts festivals. It's all the same thing."

"I don't know what to say. I'm sorry," Henry said, his voice low. "You don't understand everything—"

Rayanne held up her hand. "I don't need an explanation. You need a job. Someone got you one. I've got plenty of other work to do."

"It's not like that." Henry lowered his head. "Do you want to talk about..." He gestured meaningfully between them.

"About?" Her facial expression was pleasantly blank but her eyes dared him to continue.

That was a definite no.

"About the festival planning."

Rayanne shrugged. "You're in charge now. You figure it out." There was no room for negotiation in her voice.

Henry exhaled in one long audible breath. It was like a canyon had opened up between them since that moment in the kitchen when he could taste the skin on her neck and smell her hair.

"It says here you have an appointment to visit the site."

She nodded. "And now you have an appointment to visit the site. Do you need directions, or can you find it yourself?"

"I can find it, but I don't even know what I'm looking for. What's the purpose of the visit?"

Rayanne tapped on the notebook and dismissed him. He had no place to sit. No computer. He had a binder filled with lists and notes. He stayed where he was.

72

"Would you please join me? I could use your input."

"I'm sure you could," Rayanne said, "but there's no point in the center paying two people to do the same job."

"Be mad at Arnie," Henry said. He didn't mind pleading. "He's the one who made this happen. We all need for this to succeed. Can you please find it in your heart to work with me? At least help me get off to the right start."

Rayanne's glare lost some of its intensity. She threw up her hands in surrender. "Let's get this over with."

IN THE VAN, she sat back in her seat, her arms folded across her chest. As he pulled out of the parking lot she sat up as if to say something but changed her mind.

"What's the quickest route over there?" he asked.

She shook her head, although clearly she had an opinion.

Henry headed for the freeway. "Can you tell me about the building?" If she wasn't going to volunteer information he would coax it out of her. "Why do you call it the Chief?"

"One of the city's founding fathers was named William Chief. The building is named for him. Not an Indian chief."

"Whose idea was it to buy it?"

"It was something Margie cooked up. The organization has needed a bigger space since its inception. Margie was acquainted with a guy who works for the city, and quizzed him about potential facilities. He suggested it. It's been two steps forward, three steps back ever since. Supposedly everything was finalized and ready for signature, but the date has been pushed back twice. We've offered to lease it until the purchase can be worked out but no word on that either. We're anxious to get in there. The landlord in our current place has been letting us extend month-to-month as well but he's hinted he needs to make future plans."

"And today's appointment?"

"They said a custodian could take me around, so I could get

another look at the layout. I have a diagram and I've been out before, but I wanted to double-check the power supply. Things like that. Have you even asked yourself what this festival is about?"

"You said it was about bringing people together to celebrate Indians in the city," Henry said. "Raise the center's profile in the community."

"I guess you were listening," Rayanne said.

"Yes, I was listening. Are you bummed about that?"

"No. But it's also about us. Indian people celebrating our own people. Giving artists a chance to be seen."

"I get that," Henry said. "I want this to work for you."

Rayanne didn't say anything. She glared out the window while twisting the ends of her hair. They drove in silence until Henry pulled into the parking lot. There were about a dozen cars in the lot.

"I expected this place to be cleared out by now," Rayanne said.

The old brick building was streaked with moss. Two floors of dirty windows looked out over the parking lot. The plant beds were empty except for a couple of rhododendrons that needed pruning. They got out and headed inside. The double glass doors at the front entrance were locked. Inside, there was a deserted reception counter and no sign of anyone waiting for them.

"We'll have to get everyone out here for a clean-up and power-wash day. We can plant a few flowers to make it look nice for the event." Rayanne knocked on one of the doors but no one appeared. "Let me take you around back."

In the rear of the building there was another set of double glass doors that opened to a concrete slab. Beyond that, there was a grassy area that needed mowing.

"You can see why it's ideal for us," Rayanne said. The sharp tone and hard edges had melted away, and her eyes were bright with enthusiasm. He warmed to her all over again.

"We have room for a playground and a place for stick game. We can put up a basketball hoop. For the festival I thought we could put the artist and food booths along here and then set up a stage over on that side. I have some folks that are going to loan us tables and chairs."

"Do you think this is enough space?" Henry asked.

"Sure. There's also an auditorium where we could do demonstration dancing. There's a kitchen. We could prepare traditional foods."

"Cooking sounds like a lot of extra work. I had a tough time at the retreat and that was only a handful of people. What about food vendors?"

A series of emotions registered on her face. Her enthusiasm dipped and faded from her eyes. Her shoulders slid up and down. "Right. This is your show."

"We're working together," Henry said. "I can't do this by myself."

The dark frown returned to her face. The smile disappeared. Whatever window had opened was closed again.

"When I hear festival, I think bands," Henry said.

"Of course you do," Rayanne said. "If Linda approves, do what you want."

*R*ayanne checked the time on her phone. There were cars in the parking lot so there had to be someone here. Why hadn't anyone come out to meet them?

She searched the windows facing the back. Most of the rooms were dark. On the second floor someone sat at a computer, but he or she never took their eyes off their work.

Henry needed to knock off the desperate attempts to smooth things over. He was a bundle of earnest questions and forlorn glances. And yet, every time he stood close to her, the heat of him unbalanced her again.

He moved to stand next to her again and followed her gaze to the windows. "Did you talk to someone in the building?"

Rayanne took a deep breath. "I left a follow-up message last week, and another one this morning. Someone should be expecting us."

Henry pulled up the binder and flipped back and forth through her notes. Her eyes traced the line from his shoulders to his forearms where his shirtsleeves were folded back. He described himself as a city boy but he had working hands. He found her diagram of the lot and tapped a finger on it.

"Did you have a question about that?"

He smiled. "I have so many questions, I'm not sure where to start. I'd like to get inside."

"That would be nice."

They approached the back doors and knocked on the glass. The hallway was dark, but light shone from more than one open doorway.

"Anyone in there?" Henry called.

"There's a bigger sketch of the floor plan in there." Rayanne nodded at the binder.

Henry shuffled through the pages until he found it.

Rayanne pointed to the drawing. "We could use some of these rooms to share information about what we do. Ester loves to make movies for us. We could do like a museum and have a couple of short films on a continuous loop. We could print out some fact sheets."

As they talked, the hall lights flickered on. A man wearing a suit and tie came to the glass doors and crouched down to unlock them. He opened the door but didn't invite them in. He had thinning hair and had to be close to retirement age.

"Can I help you?" he asked.

"We're doing a little recon for an arts festival," Rayanne said. "I've been talking to a couple of people on the custodial staff about getting a tour today."

The man did not let down his chilly bearing. "Who are you?"

Rayanne introduced herself and Henry. "We're from the Crooked Rock Urban Indian Center. The center is in the process of purchasing the building. We're planning an arts festival to celebrate the opening once the transfer takes place."

The man shook his head. "I haven't heard anything about that or any future events here."

"Oh," Rayanne said. "Is there someone else here who might know?"

The man offered a thin smile. There was no mistaking the tilt of the head and the patronizing tone. "I've been with the Office of Education for thirty-five years."

"Then I'm surprised you're not aware of what we're doing." Rayanne was accustomed to dealing with this type of administrator. "We've been working on this deal for over a year."

"Any sort of transaction to turn over this facility to an outside organization would be put on hold right now. We've got economic considerations and an election coming up. Any sale that might have been in discussion certainly won't be happening now, if at all."

Rayanne swallowed a stunned expression. "There must be a mistake. Would you be involved in the selling process? Maybe this is taking place outside the work you do."

"When were you expecting to have your event?"

"In a few weeks when we move in here. The deal is done. We're waiting for the last details to get ironed out." Rayanne could sense something was off. This wasn't a person out of the loop. This was a person who wanted to ease them on their way without giving up any information.

The man pressed his lips together and looked upward, then shook his head. "If you're making plans, you should make them for another location. This won't be available."

"Is the sale off? Have you been involved in the negotiations?" Rayanne asked.

The man held up his hands. "I'm afraid I can't discuss it with you. I'm going to have to ask you to leave the grounds."

Rayanne took a step forward. "You're asking us to leave? We aren't doing anything. Isn't this a public building?"

The man tilted his head again. Did he think this made his delivery more bearable?

Henry put a hand on her arm but she shook it off.

"We're allowed to be here," she said. "If we weren't Indian would you ask us to leave?"

"Let's go," Henry said, his voice calm and steady. "We have the information we need."

Rayanne inhaled, her mind working through everything that had happened. They'd met with the city, hadn't they? She'd sat in on one of the meetings. What was that woman's name? Maybe the sale wasn't final, but this man was making it sound like it didn't exist.

Henry put his hand on her back. His nudge was insistent.

"I *am* going," she said.

At this moment, Rayanne understood the expression blind rage. She needed to talk to Linda and get this addressed right away. Whatever was happening was unfair, and the sooner they talked to the right people, the better. Everything they'd been working for wasn't going to go away on account of one cranky old guy who probably hadn't laughed in—how long had he been in education—thirty years?

"I'm going to drive." It wasn't a request. She held out her hand until Henry gave her the keys. He might have said something but she didn't hear it. She stomped all the way to the van, got in and drove away.

~

"RAYANNE? HEY! WAIT!"

Henry chased after the van, hollering and waving. He managed to bang his hand on the back window a couple of times before it pulled out of reach. His van heaved out of the parking lot. The tires squeaked when they hit the street, and the vehicle sped out of sight. This was the second time since he met her that Rayanne exited the scene with her pedal to the metal.

He should have been surprised but instead, there was a sense of inevitability, as if from the moment they'd met they'd been on a course that ended with him standing alone in a parking lot while she zoomed off in his van, going to save the day without him.

He reached for his phone and checked all his pockets several times. He'd left his phone in the van. Figures. She wouldn't have answered his call anyway. How many times had he dealt with a woman with that look on her face? She was on a mission and nothing was going to stop her.

He'd expected to spend the day reconvincing her that he was on her team. He would show her that he could solve problems too, and that he was part of the solution, not part of the problem. The suit in the building helped out by becoming the bad guy. But Henry had gone from a problem to forgotten. Maybe this development would work in his favor. He could go back and talk to the guy. Maybe he had more information. It's not like it was private. There had to be a misunderstanding. That old guy couldn't know everything.

The man had moved to the front doors and kept his eyes on Henry. He held a cellphone in his hands and made his meaning clear.

What a dick.

Fortunately, as a person with a long history of unreliable transportation, Henry knew his bus routes. He walked several blocks to a busier street. The closest stop was at least a half mile away. Rayanne had a pen in the binder, and he stopped to make a note to learn about creating or relocating bus stops. When they sorted out the problems and completed the building purchase, they would need a more convenient bus stop.

While he waited for the bus, he read through everything in the binder. There were no words capable of describing how comprehensive her planning notes were. There were lists of her lists and reminders printed on different-color paper. She had zippered plastic pockets to hold receipts and other scraps. The volume was overwhelming and reinforced every doubt he had about his ability to do this job.

By the time the bus came he was ready to quit again.

13

---

*R*ayanne took surface streets back to the center because the back way was faster. That man's pissy *who are you?* looped through her head until she wanted to ram something.

She pulled into the parking lot and hopped out of the van. Someone had propped the door to the center open with a chair. More chairs and stacks of boxes lined the front walkway. Linda ran out the front door carrying a box. Were they moving without her?

"What's going on?" she asked.

"Flood," Tommy said, hurrying out the door. He dragged a bag of basketballs to his car.

"What do you mean a flood?"

Tommy opened the trunk and hefted the bag in. He already had a box of books, a blanket, and what appeared to be a chainsaw in back. He had to shove it around to get the trunk closed again.

"Can you help over here?" Linda called as she went back into the building. Rayanne ran to catch up with her. Inside, she stepped into a puddle.

"It's water, right?"

"I sure hope so," Linda said.

The front room floor was shiny with wet spots. She expected to find water gushing from a pipe she'd never noticed but instead it was more like a creeping seep moving through the building. All the boxes they'd stacked against the walls for moving were being carried outside or stacked on tables and desks.

"Did anyone find the shut-off valve?" Rayanne asked, grabbing for one of the boxes behind her desk. She had many of Margie's books and files stuffed in with her own. The box was heavy and an awkward shape. She struggled to get a good grip on it.

"I don't know," Linda said. "Do you know where it is?"

"No," Rayanne said. "I heard it's a thing to look for." She staggered outside and put the box down in the parking lot.

"Are we cursed?" Linda's face was shiny with sweat and she had a dusty smudge across her cheek. "Did we anger the gods or unknowingly do something to bring wrath upon ourselves? Maybe it's the fate of our people. Maybe we're not supposed to have a good life. It's always got to be adversity. That's how we know we're alive."

"I think it's a tad dramatic to equate our tragic history with malfunctioning plumbing," Rayanne said. They returned to the building and carried out another awkward box together.

"It is," Linda agreed. "But this wears me out. Especially now, when we're supposed to be demonstrating what a well-tuned machine we are. I would like to cry but I'm not sure if it fits into my calendar."

Ester strutted out of the building with a smile on her face. She swung one hand over her head like she was preparing to rope a steer. "Water to the building is off!" She sang the last word with a high note, like a pop star.

"Bless you, dear woman," Linda said, sagging with relief.

"Shut off the power too, for safety."

"How did you know what to do?"

"While I'm tempted to keep it a secret, I will add 'how to handle various building emergencies' training to our never-ending to-do list. Right after 'write grants we have no time to fulfill' but before 'find cute furnishings for office.' We're moving soon, aren't we?"

Linda sighed. "That's the plan." She turned to Rayanne. "How are things going over there?"

Rayanne offered a noncommittal shrug. "Fine, I guess."

"Did you talk to anyone? Are they all moved out?"

"It was quiet over there," she said. It wasn't a lie.

"Henry is cute," Ester said. "I thought you two were hitting it off at the retreat."

Rayanne shot her a look. Ester couldn't resist the urge to be a loudmouth. Rayanne said, "Is there a plumber on the way? Shouldn't you be checking the computers or something?"

Ester feigned innocence. "I said we'd meet him right here."

"Where is Henry?" Linda asked. "Didn't he come back with you?"

Rayanne spun around, as if he'd been there a second earlier and she was surprised he was missing. His van was parked in the parking lot and...

Uh oh.

She grabbed her phone and stared at it, realizing she didn't even know how to call him.

"Do we have a file on him? Or a résumé or something?" Rayanne asked. "I need to find him."

"We don't," Linda said. "Remember? We didn't hire him. Arnie gave him to us. Did you lose him?"

"I guess I sorta left him at the Chief."

"You drove off in his van and left him behind? What did he do?" Ester said. "I can't wait to hear the rest of this story."

Fortunately, Rayanne was saved by a gray truck with an anthropomorphic wrench painted on the side.

"Plumber is here. Let's go." Ester danced across the parking lot in long strides, her arms pumping the air as she went.

Linda smiled. "I want to be like her when I grow up. I give you points for trying to get rid of him, but the board gave him the job. Leaving him somewhere isn't going to change that."

"I didn't do it on purpose," Rayanne said. She took the keys from her pocket and climbed inside the van. She let down the window and drooped in the seat, trying to hold back the crushing sense of futility. Her anger had vanished and in its place was an exhausted sadness.

The van smelled like Henry, wood smoke and boy sweat with an added cherry tang of air freshener.

"Ma'am, you're under arrest for grand theft auto."

Henry stood at the driver's window. He didn't even have the decency to be pissed.

"Is that what a cop would say?" Rayanne asked. "Wouldn't they yell, 'Get out of the car! On the ground! Hands where I can see them'?"

"How would I know that?" Henry said, smiling. "Besides, you look like someone ate your puppy."

"You Plains Indians and your puppy-eating jokes," Rayanne said, shaking her head.

"Not Plains, Plateau. But I learned the joke from a Plains Indian." Henry nodded his head back to the activity in front of the center. "What's going on in there?"

"A pipe burst or something. Water everywhere. Stuff ruined. Business as usual."

"Sheesh, what sort of end-of-days operation has my uncle gotten me involved in?"

"See?" Rayanne said. "You guys thought we were incompetent. It's Coyote times eleven."

"First of all, I never thought you were incompetent. Second, bad luck runs in streaks. It'll turn around. Or that's what I keep telling myself. You wanna give me my keys?" He reached through the window and leaned over her, the heat radiating off him. His arm brushed over her chest and she felt it in every part of her body. When he turned, his face was inches from hers. "Don't expect me to give these to you again anytime soon." He had a teasing smile on his face.

"I won't," Rayanne said. "I've got my own car."

"Good. Let's go mop."

14

---

*H*enry grabbed a water scraper from the back closet, and scraped water out the front door.

"Where'd you get that, man?" Tommy asked. Tommy was busy rearranging the boxes stacked on the tables and chairs to fit more in. It was too early to see how much damage had been done.

"There's a closet in the corner of the meeting room."

"The one with the locked metal doors?"

"Yeah. It's not locked."

"Good to know. Any other cool things in there?"

"I'm not sure what you consider cool. Something on a long handle like a trash picker." Henry mimicked a crab claw with his hand.

Tommy's face lit up. "That's what I'm talking about. I'll have to go check. Listen, how does your van run?"

Henry laughed. "Barely. I've spent more time with my arm inside its foul-smelling innards than I care to remember."

"You're like a poet," Tommy said.

"That's what I'm known for. What's going on with the bus?"

Tommy growled unhappily.

"Still not running?"

"Between us," Tommy said, "not really. Don't let the ladies find out."

"I got a buddy who's a mechanic. I could connect you two. He's from up Colville."

"Really? One of them Colville mechanical Indians?"

"Normally that's a well-kept secret."

Tommy smiled. "I could use the help. The boss is coming this way. Time to look busy." He motioned for Henry to hand him the water scraper, and then disappeared into one of the offices, dragging it behind him. The person Tommy referred to as boss, was Rayanne.

"Let me guess. He wants your van. He saw me with the keys and he figures it's a free-for-all." Rayanne had an old beach towel in one hand and a mop in the other. She offered him a choice.

Henry took the towel. "Something like that." They worked side by side mopping up the last traces of water.

"I complained about not having carpeting under my desk, but now it turns out to be a good thing." She went outside to squeeze out the mop. "Sorry about earlier," she said when she returned. "You don't know what all we've done to get that place. Reports and assessments. Standing in front of groups begging for money. We're so close and we've waited so long. That guy's smug face was so infuriating. The thought of disappointing everyone causes me physical pain. I was not thinking clearly."

"So, we're even now?"

She laughed. "Not even close. One stolen arts festival for one stolen, but quickly recovered, van. Who do you think won that deal?"

"I didn't steal it, Arnie did. And I'm telling you, be the boss. Besides, that van isn't worth its value as scrap and I'm still driving it. I'm giving the edge to you."

Rayanne nodded. "A fragile truce."

"Not fragile," Henry said. "A truce."

Rayanne let him shake her hand. He tried to squeeze in a way to convey the depths of his crush on her.

"What did Linda say about mean old Mr. Suit?" he asked.

"I didn't tell her. I hate holding back, but now we're in the middle of this giant disaster. She can't take any more bad news or her head will pop off and roll away. We can't have that. Besides, it's got to be a mistake. Maybe that guy is new and so accustomed to intimidating people, he didn't pay attention to what we said."

"Arnie knows lots of government people. He can find out what's going on." Henry tried to sound reassuring.

"Maybe," Rayanne said. She took out a bright green sticky note and scribbled on it. "If we ever get power again, we'll research the property and look for something in the public records. Maybe we can get an answer that way." She stuck the note on her computer screen.

"We've mopped up. Now what? What do you do at work when there's no power?" Henry threw the wet towel into a bucket. Rayanne added the mop and leaned it against a wall.

"Good question," she said. "Kill time? You said bad luck runs in streaks. What's your bad luck?"

Henry took a deep breath, not sure about revealing the most incompetent parts of himself to a person who redeemed herself every fifteen minutes with an act of miraculous competency.

"I lost my apartment," he said.

"Kicked out? Bummer," Rayanne said. "You're moving. We're moving. I sense a theme here."

"Relocation is in our DNA," Henry said.

"Some relocations are better than others. What part of town do you want? Rents are nuts all over. Well, unless you don't mind a commute. I heard there are good places on the east side."

She even had more information about moving than he did. He could learn a thing or two from this woman.

"I'm keeping my options open."

"When do you have to be out?"

"End of the month." Maybe it was fortunate his mom told him no. How humiliating would it be to tell her he was living with his mom and sleeping in his old bedroom?

Rayanne didn't hide her pity. "What a pain. Are you using one of those apartment finder apps? I helped one of Linda's friends find an apartment that way."

"What's it called?"

"May I?" Rayanne nodded at his phone.

He hesitated before he handed it to her. "Can I trust you not to run off with it?"

"You can." Her dark hair swung forward as she bent over the device, her fingers moving swiftly across the screen. She tossed her head and her hair tumbled back over her shoulder. She smiled when she caught him staring.

"Sorted by proximity to the office," she said, handing him back the phone.

He scrolled through the results. "Do you want to check out apartments with me?" It was an accident that he said it out loud.

"Not even a tiny bit," Rayanne said. "Besides, I have big plans tonight."

"Oh," Henry said. "You, uh, seeing someone?"

"I am," Rayanne said. "It's not what you think."

"What do I think?"

"Guys?" Linda came out of her office. She made a noise that was a cross between a sigh and a groan. "Plumber says it's medium serious, but will cost some money. He can't do anything until he gets an okay from the landlord. Landlord is MIA. Insurance is sending someone over. I don't know what good that will do. The damage is limited to our old moldy files and the bottom of our furniture. What happened out at the Chief?"

He expected Rayanne to break it to her slowly. Instead, she said, "Gruesome. Some guy with a mopey face said that there was no sale, no one is moving and it was a big mistake. Then he told us to leave." Rayanne's voice cracked on the last bit. He had underestimated how upset she was.

Linda stared up at the ceiling, her lips moving silently as if in prayer. Then he heard a whispered, "Eight...nine...ten."

"Mopey didn't give you his name?" she asked.

"I stole Henry's van and drove off before he had a chance." Rayanne glanced at Henry.

"He nonverbally indicated I should get the hell out of there," Henry explained. "Given my limited options, I did."

"Okay," Linda said with false brightness. "I'll put this on my list of giant problems that can't possibly be worse than getting knocked up at seventeen and living in a trailer. I'll get to it as soon as I can."

"Sorry," Rayanne said.

"Don't be sorry. It's probably a misunderstanding. I'll handle it."

Linda returned to her office and closed the door.

Arnie handled problems like this all the time. Out on the rez they had fires and traffic pileups in icy winter weather. Why wouldn't they just phone him?

Henry nodded back at Linda's door. "Did she get knocked up at seventeen? Not judging. My mom did something like that."

"No, that's the path she thinks she avoided by busting her ass in high school and going to college a year early. But when things are grim here she weighs it against the road not taken. It's supposed to be funny. She knows this is the much better choice."

"I get it," Henry said.

"You could use a better understanding of what's going on here," Rayanne said.

Henry stared at the chaos the flood had caused. "You think I don't understand?"

"I'm speaking of another level."

"I have no idea what you're talking about."

"You curious what I'm doing tonight?" Rayanne asked.

"I am," Henry said. What was she up to? Creating a study scheme for her native language? Spending hours in the rock-climbing gym? He couldn't imagine what it might be.

Rayanne hesitated before giving him her address. "Don't be late. We gotta schedule to keep."

"What schedule?" he asked.

"Wait and be surprised." She smiled at him, a welcoming smile. After all this time fighting him, maybe she was warming up. A trend he wanted to continue.

"Is it illegal?"

"Not even close," she said.

15

Ten measly minutes without any new disasters and Linda could figure it all out. It was a matter of prioritization, and determining who to contact, and figuring what questions to ask. Normally the familiar chaos of her office offered comfort but now the floor was wet, and her desk was covered with boxes and stacks of paper that needed to stay dry. The room was dark and she flicked the light switch several times before she remembered the power was off.

She sat down in the dark and immediately stood again. Coffee and something sweet would save her. There was always a cookie or a half of one of those red velvet donuts that no one would ever finish in the break room. She picked up her coffee mug and was halfway out her office door before it occurred to her that, without power, there was no coffee either.

There was nothing fun about a burst pipe. The office smelled like wet dog and already a whiff of mildew fogged the air. Too bad a lit match wasn't an acceptable solution. She'd be sorry to lose all her stuff, but she smiled at the vision of flames roaring through the windows of this terrible building. They could get office chairs with seats that weren't permanently indented and filing cabinets that closed without a well-placed kick. She could be free of the clutter she wasn't able to part with voluntarily. Knowing her luck, the center would be the beneficiaries of a new wave of worthless donations and shabby furniture that other organizations wanted to get rid of.

She propped her office door open as wide as it would go and used the feeble light to attempt to clear a spot on her desk big enough to work. She heaped the folders and books into even higher teetering stacks. She grabbed a couple of binders before they slid from one pile to the floor. A single page came loose and floated to the spot in front of her.

"Of course," Linda muttered. Margie had given her a line drawing of Coyote in the Pacific Northwest style of thick, curving lines. She propped the picture up against a box. "Maybe lighten up on me, could you, pal?"

Ester bopped into her office, not smiling but a bundle of motion and energy. She spotted Coyote. "Oh, that explains a lot."

"About today or my entire existence?" Linda said.

"Get it together, boss, we need you."

"I haven't run screaming from the building. Isn't that good enough? What news have you got?"

"As your quasi-IT gal, I need to ask, should I turn the power back on?"

Linda shrugged. "I don't know. Is it safe now? Who would know? Rayanne's been itching for more responsibility. Why don't you put her in charge?"

"Because you're the leader now, and you're doing great." Ester came around and gave her a hug. Ester was a slender person but her surprisingly strong arms gave a good squeeze.

"Thank you," Linda said.

"Have you talked to the landlord yet?"

"No. Do you know that technology trick where it would look like the call came from a prize center? Maybe if he thinks he won a sweepstakes, he'll answer the phone."

"Not like I'm on his side," Ester said, "but it's only been a few hours. He may legit be away from his phone."

"In my next life, I want to be born as one of those optimistic Indians."

"No need to wait that long," Ester said. "What can we do in the meantime? Can we move into the Chief now?"

"Ugh." Linda shook her head. "It's still full of other people. They told Rayanne they weren't moving. I don't think the city could pull the plug on this and not tell us about it. Until I'm in a better position to investigate, I'm assuming it's a communication misunderstanding that will be cleared up soon. But we're stuck here for now."

"Have you called Arnie?"

As it turned out, Linda had considered and discarded the idea several times. Arnie had insisted she had his support at the same time he emphasized he answered to the board. The board that had lost confidence in her. Ester didn't need to know all that.

"No. We don't need him to solve our problems for us. But we're going to have to tell the board about the flood eventually. We'll wait until we have a more complete picture of what's going on."

Ester eyed her with skepticism. "Don't call it a flood. Call it a 'modest liquid disturbance' and see what he says."

Linda shook her head and laughed. "That sounds like we had an incontinent alien in here."

"Maybe we did. Tell him we got carried away with a floor rejuvenation project. Refer to it as a fractional spillage event. We barely noticed. We carried on with a little damp on our shoes, but if he has some ideas he could share them."

By this time they were both cracking up.

"The problem was so minor, we flipped off the power and carried our stuff outside and called it a regular Monday," Linda said.

"You got it," Ester said. "I have a fully charged, old laptop you can use to get through the rest of the day."

"I'll come get it," Linda said.

Out in the front room, they found the landlord talking to Tommy.

The landlord was an older man with watery eyes and hunched shoulders like he hadn't heard good news in decades. Linda could never be certain whether he was a man who lived with terrible sadness, or if it was a natural look he'd been born with.

"I've called insurance. Sometimes these things happen," he said. He could have been talking about anything.

She took him through the building to show him the damage. The carpet was already drying out and they'd rescued the things that had been on the floor.

"How soon can you be out of here? I can prorate the rent you paid for this month if you're out by the weekend." His calm tone indicated he had no idea what he was asking.

"Where would we go?" Ester said.

"Do we have to get out?" Linda asked.

"You planned to move anyway. Can't you make arrangements?"

"Not that quickly, no. In fact, I was going to ask to extend our month-to-month."

He offered a noncommittal shrug. "It's going to be tough for you to do business during the cleanup. We're going to get dehumidifiers set up around the suite. The machines are the size of a suitcase, meaning the old-style, big suitcases. Not these things on wheels that everyone takes on the plane. The machine will suck the moisture out of everything. Even the socks on your feet. Helps prevent mold. A little noisy but you might get used to it."

"Cool," Ester said. She and Tommy high-fived.

"And the extension?"

"I thought we agreed this was the last extension," he said. "It's easier if you're out of here. I'll get back to you." The landlord studied the floor. "You did a good job. Probably minimized the damage. Good work."

At least one person thought she did something right.

16

*W*hen Henry arrived at Rayanne's, she barely opened the door before she turned and hurried back to the kitchen. Her apartment was smaller than he expected, but at least she had one. It was tidy and contained real furniture like a couch and a TV stand. A dining room table big enough for four was half-covered with paperwork. There was a Pendleton blanket thrown over the back of the couch. The kitchen was a nook with room for one and enough counter space for a toaster oven and a cutting board. The room was infused with a delicious meaty smell.

"What is that? Are we having dinner?"

"Meal delivery. We've got meatloaf, mashed potatoes and gravy, green beans, and cornbread. Come over. I'll show you how to assemble it. Wash your hands."

Henry squeezed in next to her. She had a stack of containers on the counter. She put a generous square of meatloaf into one. "I use bison," she told him. She added scoops of vegetables and a drizzle of gravy. "You do the cornbread. Slice each square in half and put a little butter in the middle. Then do the plastic wrap."

"How many are we making?"

"Six tonight but you and I will eat with my grandpa. We need eight, counting the two of us."

She was inviting him to meet her grandpa. When he didn't move, she added, "You don't have to eat with us if you don't want."

"I do." Henry got to work, taking his time to cut the pieces the same size. "Who else is this for?"

"Elders I know. Either from the center, or I know them from my grandpa. I started doing this for him. He's never been much of a cook, and I saw how he was eating after my grandma died. A cheapo can of soup or a peanut butter and jelly sandwich. I wanted him to have a hot meal when I'm not around. That's why the portions are so big. Most of them can get two meals out of this."

"Do you get donations or do this yourself?"

"Myself," Rayanne said. "This is my main project I want for the center when we move. I want to have a senior lunch, at least during the week. Or if we can raise the money, lunch for anyone who could be there. People who don't have family in town could meet other Indians and have a place like home. When Tommy picks up the bus, we can help out with transportation. Grandpa doesn't drive anymore. I take him around when I can, and Tommy has taken him to the doctor."

Rayanne put the last piece of meatloaf into a container and licked her fingers. She dropped the pan into the sink and ran the hot water.

"How come it took the center so long to get a bus?"

"The usual," Rayanne said. She brought out a padded box and packed the dinners into it. "Time, money, insurance. What the pros refer to as technical assistance. Too many things for too small a staff. We'll get there." She gave Henry the box, then went back and loaded plastic bottles of juice into another padded bag.

"Let's go."

He was prepared for her car to be a junker, but it was an older model with a few dents. The kind of dents anyone with an old car would end up with. Once they got going, she said, "Be prepared for questions. There are very few things elders like more than talking about the love lives of young people. Say we're friends or colleagues and steer the conversation in another direction. The ladies will love it if you flirt with them."

"I'm familiar with that," Henry said.

"I bet you are," Rayanne said. "You close to your grandparents?"

"Gram on my mom's side. She lives on the rez," Henry said. "Grandpa died while I was at college. Dad-person is out of the picture. His family lives in Montana. I have a little contact with them but it's awkward. I got their name but that's about it. They aren't Indian. You?"

"Grandpa is from my mom's side. He's my favorite person. That's why I do most of what I do. My mom wasn't the best. She, uh, tried but you know...alcohol. That whole deal. Same as you, sperm donor out of the picture so my grandparents got stuck raising me. We moved up here when I started high school. They thought I would have more opportunity if we lived in the city. Then Grandma died, and she's buried in the cemetery. Grandpa doesn't want to leave her."

"That's so sad," Henry said.

"Yeah. He's very loyal."

Rayanne parked the car in front of a small blue house. She took a box from the padded container. "Get one of those drinks. Have you met Margie?"

"I've heard about Margie," Henry said.

"She's amazing but also a piece of work. Be ready."

Rayanne let them both in. "Are you decent?"

"No more than usual," Margie said from her chair. She hadn't turned on any lights. The house was dark and smelled like burned coffee.

"What are you doing in the dark?" Rayanne said, turning on a lamp.

"Thinking," she said. When she spotted Henry she said, "You recruited a helper. He's tall."

"Nice to finally meet you, Margie." Henry took her hand, surprised to find he was nervous. "I'm Arnie's nephew, Henry."

"I heard about you. Getting into the business?"

"Not by choice. This one is trying to teach me the ropes."

"You know how it is," Rayanne said. "The board wanted us to work together."

"After hours?" Margie said doubtfully. She gestured for the container. "What's the menu?"

Henry handed it over. "Meatloaf, vegetables, and cornbread."

"Rayanne makes the best cornbread." She unwrapped the plastic and broke off a piece.

"Do you want to eat now, or should I put it away for later?" Rayanne said.

"I'll hang on to it. I'll eat after you two leave."

Margie's house was too warm. He wanted to open a window. She had a series of small framed drawings and paintings on the walls and propped up around the room.

"Are you an artist?" Henry asked, studying one of the drawings more closely.

"When I was younger. For fun." She held up her little brown hands with twisted fingers. "Not any longer."

"These are beautiful," Henry said.

"Pick one out, you can have it," Margie said.

"That's okay. I don't want to take your lovely art to the sorry excuse I have for an apartment."

"Nonsense," Margie said. "I can't enjoy them all. Pick one."

Now that he was paying attention, he saw a number of gaps on the wall where a picture had been taken down.

Rayanne came to his side. "If Margie wants you to have one, there is no use trying to stop her. Pick something you like. It will make her happy."

Henry was familiar with curved lines of native art in the Pacific Northwest and Alaska. He touched the frame of an illustration of a bird with a huge beak and outstretched wings.

"Raven," Margie said. "Good choice."

"Thank you," Henry said. "I'm honored. It will be the one pretty thing in my hovel."

"If you hang out with this girl you can have two pretty things."

Henry blushed on the inside.

"Good night, Margie," Rayanne said in a cheerful, let's-wrap-this-up voice. "You were our first tonight. We got more hungry folks to feed." Rayanne gave her a kiss on the cheek. "I'll be back in a few days. Call me if you need anything."

"Goodnight, kids," Margie said. "You look cute together."

Henry nodded in agreement but Rayanne was already out the front door.

"I told you," she said, when they got back to the car. "We need to get Linda and Arnie in the same room with her so she can embarrass them to death."

"Linda and Arnie? I'm not sure—"

"Relax. Margie wants to turn everyone into a couple. She even tried to match Tommy and Ester. Don't get me wrong, I love those two like siblings. And they love each other like siblings. Together, they aren't suited for romance."

They dropped food off at the rest of Rayanne's elders. All of them lived alone. All the places had reminders of home. There were photographs of landscapes, and strings of beads or shells on the wall. Everyone was anxious to talk. Henry understood why she did this.

"Last one," Rayanne said. "You get to meet Gus the grandpa."

"Should I be nervous?"

"What for?" Rayanne said. "You're bringing him meatloaf."

GRANDPA HAD A BIG, round face with eyebrows high on his head, like he was always in the process of hearing surprising news. This was the expression he wore when Rayanne came in with Henry. She'd never brought anyone with her before and wasn't sure how that was going to go for him.

Grandpa's apartment was a studio in an older building. The kitchen had coral-colored tiles that Rayanne loved but Grandpa called silly. He insisted he didn't mind having his bed in the same room as the kitchen, but Rayanne had put up a set of curtains to screen that part of the room from the rest. As they walked in, the curtains were open. She crossed the room to pull them shut.

"You don't have to do that," Grandpa said. "He don't mind seeing an old man's bed."

"How do you know what he minds?" Rayanne gave him a big hug. "That's Henry."

Grandpa kept his place tidy, but there was a whiff of stinky trash even with the windows wide open. She made a mental note to take it out when they left. He had trouble carrying it down the stairs.

"Nice to meet you, sir," Henry said, offering his hand.

"Hello, Henry." Grandpa tottered toward him to shake. He was a big man and he didn't take care of himself. It had gotten worse since Grandma died. He moved stiffly, sometimes grimacing but never complaining. He hesitated to call her even when she insisted he was no trouble.

"You can call me Gus. What have you got for us, Rayanne?"

"Meatloaf. I'm going to give this a quick blast of heat," she said, going into the kitchen. She opened a drawer and pulled out placemats and silverware, and gestured that Henry should set the table.

"How was your day, Grandpa?"

"I'm still here, aren't I?" he said. "Did some puzzles. Watched a ball game. Walked to the park. Let me make you kids a drink."

"I can get it," Rayanne said. She looked at Henry. "Soda or water?"

"Whatever you're having is fine." Henry pointed at the table. It was barely big enough to fit two placemats.

"Squeeze them in."

He overlapped them as best he could.

"Come over here, Henry. I want to show you something." Grandpa held out a pretty, light-brown basket decorated with a pattern of triangles and lines. "You ever seen anything like it?"

"No," Henry said, inverting it when he picked it up, so that he held it like a bowl. "This is so different from the baskets out our way."

Grandpa indicated he should flip it back over. "It's a work hat. This one is pine root and bear grass and what's the other one?"

"Maidenhair fern," Rayanne said.

"It's beautiful," Henry said.

"Ceremonial hats is fancier," Grandpa said. "This is for doing chores."

"Fancier than this? The weaving is so fine, it's hard to believe it's handmade."

"Belonged to my wife," Grandpa said. "It's going to be Rayanne's but I'm not ready to give it up yet."

"I wore it for college graduation," Rayanne said.

"She looked real pretty too. My daughter sold it once but we got it back."

Rayanne was old enough to remember that terrible incident. Grandma was alive then. They'd discovered the loss almost immediately, but there had been days of frantic phone calls before they could find out what happened, and who had ended up with the heirloom. The buyer was in the Bay Area and agreed to let it go back, for a price. They'd had to sell the lawnmower and Grandpa's hunting rifle to get enough cash for gas and the money to buy it back. After that, Mom wasn't welcome in their home any longer. It broke everyone's heart but they couldn't trust her. Back then they'd discovered other things missing, like Grandpa's nice watch, and pearl drop earrings from Grandma's wedding day. But the work hat had been made by Grandma's grandmother. They couldn't bear to lose it.

"Dinner is ready." Rayanne transferred everything to plates and put them on the table. She poured everyone soda from a big plastic bottle. The drink no longer fizzed but Grandpa had no trouble drinking it so she didn't mention it. Rayanne dragged a footstool over since there were only two chairs. They crammed around the little table.

"*Ta'ávahiv*. Time to eat," Grandpa said.

"*Ta'ávahiv*," Rayanne said.

Henry gamely repeated after them.

"That's pretty good," Grandpa said. "She tell you about where we're from?"

"A little bit," Henry said. He'd taken a bite of his meatloaf and closed his eyes for a moment. "This is great."

"She's a good cook," Grandpa said.

"We're not trying to sell me," Rayanne said.

"Nothing wrong with pointing out something that's true. Cornbread is good too. That's my favorite," Grandpa said.

"That's why I brought you two pieces," Rayanne said.

Grandpa was so busy talking, he hardly touched his food. "We come from a beautiful place. You hunt?"

"Not very much," Henry said. "I went with my uncles when I was younger, but then I went away for college and got out of it. I like being out in the woods, though."

"Good," Grandpa said. "I was out hunting with my brother and we seen a beautiful buck. We have a camp up in the mountains."

"When was this?" Henry asked.

"Been some time," Grandpa said with a laugh. "Haven't been hunting in a long time. Harder to hike and I'm no good to carry out. What do you do, Henry?"

"Nothing that interesting," Henry said.

"Tell him about your band," Rayanne suggested.

Henry gave her a look, *you're kidding me.*

"What kind of a band?" Grandpa asked. Rayanne loved how curious he was. She could tell him she was learning to juggle rattlesnakes, and he would want to know the rattlesnakes' names and where they came from.

"Sadly, I'm not musical," Henry said. "My friends have a rock band with a hip-hop influence. I help them out."

"Which kind of music is hip-hop?" Grandpa asked.

"You know, rapping, sampling. Heavy beats. These guys are all native so they make it their own thing. I'm helping promote them. We're trying to find some places where they can play. It's not easy."

"Grandpa has a band, too," Rayanne said.

"I play drums," Grandpa said.

"What's your band like?" Henry asked.

"We got an old man intertribal drum group," he explained. "Anyone can join. It's not part of my tradition but they let me in."

"Oh, a drum circle," Henry said. "Where do you play?"

"One of the guys has a house and we meet there. Eat some pizza. Talk about the old days. It's hard for me because I don't drive anymore. I don't see so good at night."

"I'm his driver," Rayanne said.

"I don't like to bug her all the time," Grandpa said. "She might like to get out and do other things."

"You never bug me," Rayanne said, leaning over to give him a kiss on the cheek.

"I'm always telling her she should go back home. She misses it," Grandpa said.

"I have a great job, and I'm doing things for Indian people," Rayanne said. "That's what I want to do."

"Are you going to do your arts and crafts show you told me about?"

Rayanne gestured at Henry. "Not me, him. He was hired to do it. I do what he tells me to do." Henry smiled but she could tell he was uncomfortable.

"I'm helpless without her knowledge. I'm doing the best I can but I'm new at this," Henry said.

"She's a smart one," Grandpa said.

"I knew that the minute I met her," Henry said.

Rayanne wasn't going to be charmed so easily. "The foundation has been laid. You'll do fine."

"She's stubborn, too," Henry said.

"You got that right, son," Grandpa said.

17

*H*enry snuck glances at her the entire ride back to her place. She didn't say much. Instead, she focused on the road, almost like she was avoiding him. They drove past the city's indoor arena.

"You a sports fan?" he asked.

Her head snapped up as if startled by his voice. "Not really. Sometimes basketball or football. I'm not a diehard fan, but I enjoy watching games now and then. You a sports nut?"

"Maybe a little more than you," he said with a smile. "For sure, basketball. Sometimes football or hockey. Occasionally baseball."

Her attention went back to the road so he let the silence stretch between them.

When they arrived back at her place, Rayanne went to the trunk to get out the padded boxes they'd used to transport the food. Henry helped her carry them and followed her inside to set the stuff in the kitchen.

A warm tension flared between them, but if she felt it, she wasn't showing it. His desire grew from a spark to a flame. He didn't want the night to end. "Can we hang out for a while?"

Rayanne wouldn't meet his eyes. It took so long for her to answer, he expected an angry reply.

"It depends on what you're asking. You can stay for a few minutes. But no—" She motioned with her hands in front of her like she was rolling a big ball of dough.

"No pizza making?"

"No hanky-panky. Sit in your own chair. No bumping or brushing against me. Everyone keeps both feet on the floor at all times."

Henry pointed at his feet. "How about when I walk?"

"You know what I mean. You want a glass of wine?"

"I'm not a big wine drinker," Henry said. "Plus I heard you say a few minutes. You're sending mixed signals." The couch looked invitingly cozy, but he chose to sit in one of the dining room chairs.

Rayanne poured herself a glass and sat down across from him. "I'm not sending any signals. We're colleagues. We're being collegial. How are you feeling about everything?"

Henry pointed at her wine. She got back up and poured him half a glass.

"Are you asking how I feel about you giving me a bunch of no-touchy instructions before inviting me in for a few minutes? Or do you want to know how I feel about your one-woman meal delivery service?" The wine wasn't too bad.

Rayanne gave a little laugh. "I don't care about the first one. What about the second one?"

"I understand why you do it. It's not just bringing them food. It's making a connection. I would have hung out with any one of them."

Rayanne took a sip of her wine and made a thoughtful face. "You get it. I should have expected that. Perhaps I've misjudged. I was expecting you to be more of an apple."

"Red on the outside, white on the inside?" That was like a stab in the heart even though it was half true.

"No, green on the outside. Tart and crunchy on the inside," she said. Was she flirting with him or not?

"Your grandpa said he encourages you to go home. Do you miss it?"

"Every day," Rayanne said. "Growing up, when we lived down there, life wasn't perfect but you wake up every day surrounded by mountains and trees. The city sometimes feels alien. I'll be waiting in traffic so I can move a few miles. Back on the river, heavy traffic is three cars on the road. That place is in my blood. Do you have a place like that? Where you close your eyes and you can smell the air?"

"I do. Huckleberry picking. When I was younger I went every year. I'm not good at describing things, but it's the same kind of memory. The color of the mountains and everyone's voices. And yeah, it smelled like woods. Fresh. My gram had a special little red bucket that only I was allowed to use. I bet she still has it."

Rayanne's hands were on the table and he wanted to hold one. Except he'd agreed to her instructions. "I'll take you sometime," he told her, as if they were the kind of people who planned things like that.

She made a noncommittal sound. "I'm staying here as long as Grandpa is around. I have so much to learn from Linda. You guys might have your doubts but she is great at her job."

"I don't know enough to have doubts about anyone except myself," Henry said. "I could use your continued help on this festival thing."

"*Thing?*" Rayanne snorted out the word.

"Prestigious event," Henry corrected.

"I help everyone." Rayanne frowned at him. "That's my destiny apparently. To help everyone else with their stuff but never be in charge of my own stuff."

"You haven't been there that long," Henry said.

"Neither have you!"

"Okay. That didn't come out right. My impression is that everyone needs this event to be a success."

"We do." Rayanne finished her wine and got up to put the glass in the sink. She remained standing. "Do you even want to do work like this? It's not all rock-star like your band."

"I don't know." Henry didn't want to explain his shortcomings to her. "I don't think I'm cut out for a day job. It makes me a little, I don't know, anxious? That's not the right word. Don't get me wrong. I admire the hell out of Arnie, and when I was in college, I thought about what he does. He's so into it. But he's a good leader. He likes meetings. He likes talking in front of people. He grew up out there and understands things like timber and treaty rights. I don't know enough and I don't see myself doing that day after day, week after week. I'm afraid of waking up and finding a bunch of time has passed and all I did was endure it."

"I have news for you, buddy," Rayanne said. "No one thinks they're cut out for a day job. No one likes meetings. No one wakes up one day and says, I only want two or three weeks off until I'm too old to enjoy having time off. No one starts out knowing how to do this. But there's work to be done, and we're the ones to do it. There are lots of nonnative people who will do work like this. But they don't understand it in the same way. We need people like you."

"I hear what you're saying," Henry said, "but—"

"This is how things get done. Think of the most pie-in-the-sky dream jobs. Rock star. Actress. Professional athlete. They have to put in the time. Learn the skills. Chase down the work. Prepare. Practice. Promote. You decide to do it and then you do."

"It sounds like you've surrendered to adulthood," he said. He sounded whiney even to his own ears.

"I sure have." She came over and pointed at his glass. He tipped the last sip into his mouth and handed it to her. She nodded at the door. "And I need my sleep. See you tomorrow."

This was not the good night he had hoped for.

*R*ayanne arrived at the center hoping to find that the flood problem was history, and they could get back to work. In one corner, there was a machine on a dolly humming like a leaf blower. Another one sat in the hallway outside Linda's office. They had to yell to hear each other over the din.

"Dehumidifier," Linda said. "If I understood the cleanup company correctly, it will be here for days. And by the look on your face I know what you're thinking and I thought the same thing, but the crew said we will avoid mold and who doesn't want that?"

"How about retaining our sanity? What are our goals with respect to that?" Rayanne said.

"That monkey left the cage days ago." Linda pointed to the piles of boxes. "We're going to have to go through all the stuff that got wet and inventory what can be saved. The rest gets tossed."

"Less stuff to move," Rayanne said.

Linda smiled. "You and I think alike. Why don't you get Tommy to help you with the boxes out front?"

"Tommy is taking a couple of elders to doctor appointments."

"Do it when he returns. Ester and I will work on the ones in back."

"Will do. Did you find out what happened with the Chief? What are we going to do about the festival if we can't move? I mean, what is Henry going to do about it?"

Linda shook her head and gestured for Rayanne to follow. It was quieter in the break room. Linda poured herself a cup of coffee.

"As far as I'm concerned, everything is on schedule, full steam ahead. You guys work together to make the event happen and make it good. I'll get the Chief sorted out."

"Arnie said Henry was in charge," Rayanne said.

"Get over it and do what needs to be done. This is what we're dealing with, and it is critical that the event succeed. Help him," Linda said.

"I am," Rayanne said.

Ester came in and sagged theatrically against the counter. "I can't live with that sound. It will turn me inside out. I checked and we didn't lose any equipment, that I can tell. Everyone is plugged back in and, at least in terms of our electronics, we're working."

"Can you get Henry a computer?" Rayanne asked.

"Done," Ester said. "I found a working model from the Hoover administration. I set it up on your desk."

"My desk? There's no other place to put him? What about the meeting room?"

"Not possible," Ester said. "That room is already double booked. Are you worried his cute face will be too distracting?"

"No one is too distracted by his face," Rayanne said, frowning at her.

Ester laughed. "If you say so."

When Rayanne got back to her desk, Henry had found a chair and worked at his computer directly across from her seat.

"This is handy," he said.

"Isn't it."

Ester had stacked up all of Rayanne's neatly arranged piles of projects to make room for Henry. She dug around to find her current tasks.

"You don't mind sharing?" Henry said.

"I don't have a choice," Rayanne said, "what with this end-of-days operation we have going."

"Okay, what do we do first?" Henry held up her binder of festival tasks.

"I know I agreed to help you, however"—she indicated the mess that Ester had made of her work—"I have to catch up with my stuff first. You can figure some of that out on your own. We can work together this afternoon."

Henry nodded and flipped through the binder. He moved his attention to the computer screen and tapped on the keyboard a few times.

Rayanne tried to keep her attention on what she was doing. She wanted to finalize her notes from the retreat and translate them into a document they could use for planning. Instead, her senses were filled with Henry. Even with her eyes averted, the sound of his breath and the movement of his body so close to hers pulled her mind away from her work. He wore plain old business casual and still managed to look sexy and dangerous. Well, he was not going to win this one.

She fixed her attention on her computer screen and focused on her revisions. Out of the corner of her eye she saw him get up. He returned a few minutes later with Ester.

"Why didn't Rayanne help you?" Ester said, a notch louder than needed.

"She's busy." Henry conveyed the air of a neglected small animal when he said it. Rayanne continued to ignore him.

"She could show you how to navigate the directories," Ester said. "Here. Festival stuff. Did you hide anything from him?"

Rayanne quit the document she was working on and went around to stand beside Henry. He smelled minty fresh and the view of his neck inside his collar was inviting. Damn him and this number he was doing.

"Fine. I will work with Henry this morning, but when Tommy gets back we have a project to work on," Rayanne said.

"Tommy isn't going to be back any time soon. Have you ever taken elders to the doctor? It's work for saints. I'll leave you two." Ester patted Henry's shoulder. "She'll help you. Be patient."

"I sent you my bookmarks this morning," Rayanne said. "There are a lot of contacts. There are permits to follow up on. Artists to track down and invite. Make a program. Make a press release. Make an update for the website. Get listings in events calendars—"

"Whoa," Henry said. "Can we slow down? I have read through the binder, and gone over the calendar. I need help prioritizing."

"Fine," Rayanne said. She brought her chair over so she could sit next to him. "Show me how far you've gotten."

"From reading through this," he indicated the notebook, "you envisioned this as art and food in support of cultural events on a stage."

Rayanne was impressed. Linda once told her that she underestimated people and that it was a poor way of forming good working relationships. Maybe there was some merit to that.

"It's all in there," she said. "There's a list of artists I invited. Not everyone replied so you need to follow up on that. I talked to some food vendors. As you pointed out, it would be tough to do a traditional salmon feed so maybe get the word out for food booths. We need some performers for the stage. I talked to a poet who was interested. Maybe a cultural speaker to talk about local history? I didn't get too far on that."

"Musicians? What about a native rock band with hip-hop influences?" She was about to laugh until she saw his face. He was serious. "No one wants to come for your friends' band."

"Believe me, someone does," Henry said. "Give me a good reason. Why not something more contemporary?"

"This isn't a show for your friends' band," Rayanne said, irritated now. "There's a sheet with a budget in there too. You're going to need some sponsors and donations. I need to finish my report and then work on the flood damage. You have enough to keep busy."

HENRY DIDN'T ENJOY the work but he kept at it to prove to Rayanne that he could. He familiarized himself with all her lists and notes. She was a marvel of practical ability. Her notes had the answers to questions he didn't even know he had.

She sat at her desk, absorbed in whatever was on the screen. She shot down the Beat Braves idea in a second. Well, she wasn't the final word on that.

He texted the idea to Jack and confirmed their plans for apartment hunting.

injun rawkstarz yesssssss! Jack replied.

According to Rayanne's notes she was hoping at least five hundred people would come through. If even half that watched the Beat Braves that would be a huge debut. His phone buzzed again, but this time the text was from Arnie.

NDN youth dancers Armstrong MS Check for festival?

No thanks, he texted back. Rayanne's notes didn't say anything about youth dancers and if she didn't like his suggestions, she wouldn't like Arnie's either.

Ask R, Arnie texted.

Rayanne was at her computer but she stared into the far distance.

"Quick question?"

"Another friend need a boost?"

"Kinda. Arnie said there's something going on at Armstrong M.S. Do you know where that is?"

"Armstrong Middle School? Yeah, we did a youth program with them once. They're interested in teaching accurate local Indian history. We'd love to develop a curriculum with them but—" She gestured to the center in its disarray. "What's going on there?"

"Nothing big. A native youth dance group Arnie knows. He said I could check them out."

"What did you tell him?"

"No thanks," Henry said.

"Are you nuts? That's exactly the kind of performance group we want. When is it?"

"After lunch. Do you want to go over there with me?" Henry

understood his instincts for this were non-existent. He wanted her to make sure it all went right.

"You think we can drive up to a middle school and watch a youth dance demonstration?"

"No?"

"Not these days. Does Arnie have a contact or anything?"

"I can ask."

She made an exasperated sound. "Don't bother. I have cultivated relationships with local educators. Let me get permission for us to visit for the dance."

Henry sat back, overwhelmed by the layers of knowledge a person needed to do things. Could people learn to be competent or were they born that way?

Rayanne was on the phone a few minutes before calling over to him, "We can pick up a couple of visitors' passes and go to the gym at one o'clock."

"Do you want to go get lunch before we go over there?"

"Sure, why not? I'll tell Linda what we're up to."

She met him at the van. "You firm on not letting me drive this thing?" She gave him a sly smile.

"I don't have a problem with you driving it. I have a problem with you driving off in it without me." Henry pulled out of the parking lot. "I was going to take you to a food truck that makes these amazing barbecue sandwiches. Does that sound okay?"

"You're taking me? We're not on a date. We're eating lunch on the way to a work activity. Got it?"

"Loud and clear," Henry said.

The sandwich truck was parked in a lot with three other trucks.

"All these trucks have good food," he said. "There are benches in the shade if you want to sit down. I will be sitting down. You're free to make your own plans."

Rayanne sighed and got out of the van. He couldn't keep his eyes from her as she moved between the trucks, stopping to check each menu. Every so often she would run her fingers through her hair and hold it back from her face before releasing it again.

She came to join him in line. "I'll trust you on this one."

Once they had their food, they found a place to sit. She took a bite and worked her mouth for a few moments, and then gave him an enthusiastic thumbs-up.

"It's the perfect balance of chewy, spicy, tangy, creamy," he said.

She finished her bite and nodded. "Perfect balance? Are you a foodie?"

"Only in the sense that I like food."

"Me, too," she said. "Good suggestion. I begrudgingly give you a point for this."

"A point? A whole point? Did I get any points for the retreat?"

"Did I not make that official?"

"Great. Two points. What's the max? When can I redeem them?"

"Points are infinite," Rayanne said. "I'll let you know the rest, as needed. What's going on with apartment hunting?"

Henry laughed and shook his head. "What apartment hunting? I'm too busy. I want to ignore it until it goes away."

"That's an interesting strategy. I'm no expert on the details of your life, but I don't think that will work out well for you."

"My roommate, Jack, and I have got some places to see tonight. We're using that app you showed me so thanks for that. You get a point too."

"Oh, goody," she said, returning her attention to her sandwich.

"I'm dreading it. I hate dealing with things like that. First you have to figure out what you can afford, which is nothing. Then wait for someone to return your email. Deal with their all of forms. Credit check. I'm going to live in the van."

"You could leave it in the parking lot and you wouldn't have to commute," Rayanne said.

"Wouldn't that be handy?" Henry said.

HENRY PAID attention to the way Rayanne talked to the school officials. The principal gave them both visitor badges and explained that the assembly was a part of a cultural studies program. They sat in the gym bleachers with the students.

The dancers were middle-school age too. They bounced around the gym floor in their bright-colored regalia, waiting for their performance to begin.

"I always like the jingle dancing the best," Henry said. "I even like saying it. Did you ever dance?"

Rayanne shook her head. "This kind of dancing isn't part of our tradition."

The music rang out over the sound system, a steady drumbeat with singers rising above it. The kids' faces were intent, their bodies moving with the sound. The combination of the music and the jangle from the dancers was familiar and comforting, and brought a sense of peace that he couldn't articulate.

"It's a shame they have to use recorded music," Henry whispered to Rayanne. "We should have a live music group if they dance for us."

Rayanne had a blissful expression on her face. "Look how happy they are. It makes you want to jump up and join them."

"Why don't we do something like that? Everyone would be invited to dance with the kids at the end. I mean, if the kids want to."

"That's a good idea," Rayanne said.

After the dance, they introduced themselves to the group's teacher and told her about the arts festival.

"You're Arnie's family," the woman said, nodding at Henry. "I can see it. Bet he wishes he had your height, eh?"

"I don't know. I don't think I'll ask him, though," Henry said.

The woman laughed. "Maybe not. We love your uncle. He's doing a lot of good work. Nice to see you follow in his footsteps."

Henry cringed on the inside but didn't correct her.

"I'll talk to our group and get back to you, but I'm sure we'll want to do it."

On their way back to the center, Rayanne said, "That's what I'm talking about. Traditional performances. That's how we want to connect to the community. Not a big loud thing."

"Beat Braves are more than a big loud thing. I would like to change your mind about this," Henry said. "They're going to play at a party this weekend. Let me take you." Before she could start, he added, "Not as a date. For work-related information gathering. You can even meet me there if you don't want a ride with me."

"I'll think about it."

19

*H*enry drove while Jack used the apartment-hunting app to give him directions. They drove up and down a busy street lined with strip malls and fast-food spots.

"This should be it," Jack said.

"What should be it? We aren't anywhere," Henry said. "I see asphalt, telephone wires, and a mini-mart with bars on the windows."

"Maybe that's it. Maybe there's a little room over the mini-mart," Jack said. "Make a right at the light and pull around into that alley."

Henry followed his instructions and stopped adjacent to a rundown building. "The peeling paint is a nice touch."

"This says they have a one-bedroom in our price range. Updated appliances, bike parking, and close to public transportation. Do you want to go in?"

"Not really," Henry said. "Is there anything in a less desirable location in our price range with two bedrooms?"

"Less desirable than three steps off the main drag, and within spitting distance of a mini-mart and a fried-chicken stand? We're here. Let's look."

"Those things might be amenities," Henry said. "We might like having immediate access to beef sticks and cheap beer."

Henry hoped once they saw the inside they would change their minds.

"I don't think this will work," Henry said, staring at the freshly shampooed maroon carpet. Even the windows seemed too small. It would be fine for one guy but not for two, even the two of them who were accustomed to less living spaces that were less than optimal.

Back in the van, Jack said, "There's a place another nine miles east of here that has a gym and a pool."

"Nine miles? Is it the same time zone? How does it look if we cut back on eating and put a little more toward rent, what does that get us?"

Jack reset the app and directed Henry to another neighborhood. They drove up to a shabby building with dirty windows and faded paint. The door to the laundry room was off the hinges and leaning against a wall.

"Easy access to laundry in well-ventilated space," Jack said.

"I wouldn't be surprised to learn someone has been murdered there. Is it too much to ask to find an affordable place that isn't tiny and grim? What are your ideas?"

"Being born into a family with more money comes to mind," Jack said. "It won't help you, but the guys said I can stay with them. The couch smells like farts, and I have to wait until everyone goes to bed before I can sleep on it. But they said I can have it as long as I throw in for groceries and utilities. That might be the best I can hope for at the moment."

Henry studied his friend and tried to think of a time when they weren't stuck between a terrible option and an undesirable choice. "I can't afford to live by myself."

"I don't know what to tell you. We knew we were riding on borrowed time in the current hellhole."

"No one told me that," Henry said.

"It wasn't obvious?"

"No," Henry said, even though it wasn't true. He wanted to kick himself for not being prepared for something like this.

"I have no financial solutions," Jack said. "I have to go back to the pizza delivery thing as soon as I can get the green car running. I don't even have money for that. I'm kinda stuck here. My family can't get me a fancy-pants job like yours can."

"Don't start that. I didn't ask for the fancy-pants job. I didn't have any choice. As you know, we need the money. It doesn't make sense to turn it down. I can give you a couple hundred bucks for your car if it helps."

"That didn't come out right," Jack said. "I'm not fishing for your money and I'm not mad. I don't have the same choices you do. You're better off trying to find your own place without me. How is the fancy-pants job going, anyway?"

"I don't know. I'm not a good fit."

"I thought it was all Indians," Jack said.

"What does that have to do with it?" Henry said. "It's an organization that figures out things that need to be done and then does them."

"You don't plan to be there forever, right? At least you're meeting a bunch of people. Networking. Maybe this will lead to something you want? Isn't that how it works?"

"Maybe. Everyone who works there is about as excited about my uncle giving me the fancy-pants job as you are. This other woman is super smart and hardworking and Arnie comes along and hands me her promotion."

"You don't have to impress her. She'll get over it."

"I thought I was networking. Besides, I want her to like me. She's pretty fine."

"Is that why you took the job? Because of a girl?"

"Maybe. She has her shit together in a way I can only dream of, and she knows how to figure things out. I like being in the same room with her."

"Good luck," Jack said doubtfully. "You're known for your smooth way with the ladies. No reason to think this will go differently."

Jack was being a smartass because Henry was known for his mannered approach to meeting women and the subsequent failure. He could get almost anyone to go out with him once or twice. There was that exotic factor. But forming relationships remained elusive.

"Thanks for the vote of confidence, man. I invited her to the party this weekend. She says you guys aren't a good fit for the arts festival so we're going to show her that she's wrong."

"Why wouldn't we be a good fit? You said it's for Ind'n performers."

"You can ask her that question when you meet her."

"Cool. We all going to truck over there together in the van?"

Henry cringed. The band would have a front-row seat of his non-date with his beautiful crush. "Yeah, I guess. She hasn't said yes yet."

"I promise we won't make it awkward. Have you found any other potential gigs for us?"

"Gigs? You're thinking gigs? At this point wouldn't a singular gig be a victory?"

"How you doing booking us any number of gigs?"

Henry hadn't done anything since he talked to Pepe and Polly. "Doing this and that. It's coming together."

"Sounds like you're full of it, as usual," Jack said. "Let's go hit the dollar menu for dinner and go home."

20

*A*rnie wished Linda would have called him sooner. He wasn't sure what he could have done but if they were working together, she should have wanted him to know right away. He made a special trip into town so he could go to the center. As he came through the doors, Rayanne and Ester were following a couple of men rolling out unidentifiable contraptions.

"Hallelujah!" Rayanne said, high-fiving Ester. They high-fived Arnie too. Henry watched them carry on.

"Those things are dehumidifiers," he explained. "They make a sound like giant bugs zooming next to your ear."

"I heard that droning sound in my sleep," Ester said.

"You here about the Chief?" Rayanne asked.

Arnie nodded. He had expected more disorder but, other than a more-than-usual number of boxes stacked around the front desk, the office was running as usual.

Linda came out and herded them all into the meeting room.

Arnie followed last and took the chair at the front of the room.

"Flood, famine or pestilence. What do you want first?" she asked him.

"Do we have all those things?" Arnie asked.

"Very well, I'll start with flood. Remediation is finished. Damage to our stuff is minimal. The bad news is that the landlord needs to undertake some major repairs and wants us out. Thirty days maximum. Then we need to be over at the Chief."

"And what do they say?"

"We're getting nowhere," Linda said. "Everyone I talk to transfers me to someone else until I end up in voice mail. No one has returned my calls. All email is either unanswered or I get a reply that has one of those mealy mouthed non-answers like, 'First, let me apologize for any inconvenience you have experienced.' Like they equate blowing off a building purchase with mishandling a noise complaint."

Arnie typed notes into his phone. "Who was your original contact on this?"

"That's the kicker. I found out he retired. I wondered if he wasn't supposed to sell us the building so they got rid of him. No. Everyone knew he was retiring. Why didn't they pass this information to us?"

"I agree. Do you have other names or any sort of documentation that might help?"

"Fortunately, I have documented everything within an inch of its life," Linda said.

"What do you think is going on?" Rayanne asked.

"I don't know. It sounds like you've done everything right," Arnie said. "It's got to be a communication error due to the retirement. We'll set it right."

"So we can keep preparing to move and plan for the festival in a couple of weeks?" Rayanne asked.

"Keep doing what you're doing," Arnie said. "We can always come up with an alternate site as a last resort."

"Alternate site? Have you ever planned an event?" Rayanne asked.

"I thought Henry was in charge," Arnie said.

Rayanne didn't try to hide her scowl. Henry sat next to her and patted her arm in a familiar way.

Way to go, nephew.

Arnie turned to Linda. "Pull together any information you have. Let's go to City Hall."

"Right now?"

"Sure," Arnie said with a grin. "Some of my most effective work has been accomplished by showing up where I wasn't expected. It's easy to ignore email and calls. Not so easy to ignore a friendly face at your office door."

"The building has security. We can't wander around from door to door."

"Where is that unyielding woman I went to college with?" Arnie said. "Weren't you the one who waited in the parking lot for an administrator who didn't want to meet with you?"

"I did. And I was lucky; that could have gone badly."

"But it didn't, did it?"

ARNIE COULDN'T HELP but be a hundred percent more confident in Linda now that he'd seen all the work she was doing. He should have known better than to doubt her. She carried a stack of paper secured with two large rubber bands. As soon as she sat in the car, she sorted through the paperwork, setting certain items aside.

"Here's my concern," he explained. "These deals start out like this. Everything is positive. Everyone is working together. Then something happens. Who knows? Someone, one of them, asks a question so instead of moving to the next step, the deal gets held up. They need an attorney or an engineer. Then it sits on someone's desk long enough that no one remembers it."

"I'd be lying if I said that I had never been the bad guy in a scenario like that," Linda said.

Arnie couldn't help laughing. "Yeah. Me too. What would you call it? Disruption of the organizational flow?"

"That is some varsity-level jargon right there."

"How's everything else going?" He was curious about her personal life.

She didn't pick up on it. "Rayanne has pulled her head out of her butt and is helping Henry. They might have a little crush on each other and why not? We were lucky we didn't lose anything to the water, but to be honest, there wasn't much to lose. It's hard not to expect some disaster, that we haven't even thought of yet, might be on the way."

"Don't think that thought," Arnie said.

When they arrived at City Hall, they had to wait in the main lobby at security. The guard said they needed a guide to go beyond the barrier.

Linda gave Arnie a triumphant look that said *See?*

"Whose side are you on?" Arnie asked. He dropped the name of someone he knew in the mayor's office. That guy was out but his assistant agreed to come down and speak to them.

"You know what they need?" Linda said. "A tribally trained person. You know? There are so many issues with tribes in the area, and organizations like ours. A number of regional tribal organizations. What if they had someone who understands Indian Country, who could coordinate communication, and help advise?"

"That would be great," Arnie said. "It would be cool if Spiderman were real too."

"I don't get the connection," Linda said, but there was laughter in her eyes.

The assistant who showed up turned out to be a twitchy young woman who, Arnie guessed, hadn't been on the job long. A more experienced assistant would have assured them she'd leave a message with her boss and sent them on their way. He knew how to turn on the charm in situations like this.

He explained the problem and pleaded for additional help. Arnie had seen people get what they wanted by being nasty. And he'd seen people get what they wanted by being nice. He'd also learned that playing up the Indian angle to people who weren't familiar with tribal relations could sometimes work to his benefit.

"This is a critical tribal issue. We're not sure who else to talk to. Is there someone in charge of property issues? Realty? Lands?"

The woman thought for a moment. "There's a facilities manage-ment department. I'll go up there and see if there's anyone who can help."

"Thank you," Arnie said. The woman did know what she was doing. She would send a message back. They would never see her again.

He and Linda sat down on a bench in the lobby. Linda balanced the paperwork on her lap.

"Do you want me to find you a coffee or something?" he asked.

"If I have one more sip of coffee I will explode," she said.

"Don't explode," Arnie said. He took out his phone to check for messages, as if perhaps the mayor's office might respond that way.

Linda looked down the hallway where the woman had disap-peared. "She's not coming back, is she?" Linda said. The fight had gone out of her. Whatever optimism she'd held when they'd set out, had vanished since they entered the building.

Arnie put his arm around her shoulders. "Don't give up, Lulu. I need you not to give up." A short time later, he spotted the assistant coming back out through security. She approached them with a smile on her face.

"Yay, I was wrong," Linda said. "This could be promising."

The assistant handed Arnie a business card. "The meeting to finalize everything is next week. Room 2112. Someone will email you the details."

Arnie took the card. Room 2112 had been written on the back. "Are you Kayla?" he asked, his heart sinking.

She nodded.

"This is great," Linda said. She shifted the wad of papers she dragged around into one arm so she could shake the young woman's hand. "Thank you for your help." She nudged Arnie and gave him an elated smile. "Next week."

"Who's the meeting with?" Arnie asked.

The assistant's bright smile hadn't faded. "All the information you need will be in the email."

"Thanks, Kayla," Arnie said. As they walked out, he didn't point out that they still didn't have a name. They didn't know who they were dealing with. He hoped he was wrong but he didn't think they'd fixed anything yet.

*H*enry cornered Rayanne on Friday afternoon. "You still haven't given me an answer on the party tonight."

Rayanne looked surprised. "I thought evading the question was answer enough."

"Do you have other plans?"

She shrugged.

"Come on. You can't judge until you've been to a show. Visually there's not a lot going on, they mostly stand there and play," Henry said. "But the sound will win you over. I'm already going. It's no trouble to bring you."

"Don't you have to drive the band? Isn't that what the giant party-van is all about?"

"There are people out there who would envy you the opportunity to joyride with the Beat Braves," Henry said.

"How many people?"

"No way to be certain."

"I don't know," Rayanne said. "It doesn't sound like my thing."

"Live music with tasty beats is everyone's thing. And these guys are doing something different. They are one hundred percent native and one hundred percent rock and roll."

"So they're two hundred percent?"

"Exactly," Henry said. "That's the best. I'll take you home early if you hate it."

"I won't hate it. I don't like things where I don't know anyone."

"No one likes things where they don't know anyone," Henry said. "But these are our friends and once the music starts, everyone will be *your* friend."

Henry couldn't stop begging. He wanted to spend time with her and dance with her. He wanted to show her off to the guys. And he wanted her to like the idea of the band at the festival.

"It's not like a date. It's business," Henry said. "In case you were worried about that."

"Now I am," Rayanne said. He could tell he hadn't convinced her. What else could he throw in? "You can give us advice on apartment hunting."

"Well, in that case."

"Really? Will you go?"

"I guess. Don't make me regret it."

"You won't. We'll pick you up at nine." Henry didn't try to hide his stupid grin.

OTHER THAN JACK, there were two other guys in the band. Cody was a big guy from Colville Reservation who played guitar. Cody liked motorcycles and working on his biceps. The bass player, Sam, was short and round and came from Lummi. He did some sort of technology job that Henry never quite understood. The rest of the music came from the computer. That's what Jack did.

On the drive to Rayanne's house, the van shuddered at every red light.

"You using the right kind of gas?" Sam asked.

"I use the kind of gas that comes out of the pump," Henry said. "What would you use?"

"That same kind," Sam said.

"We're picking up Henry's girlfriend," Jack said. "It's their first date."

"Don't call her that, even as a joke. She'll freak out," Henry said. "I like her but we're working together. She says since we work together she only wants to be friends."

"When they say they want to be friends, that means they want to be friends," Sam said. "I should know."

"She's warming up to me. We shared a moment. Don't embarrass me in front of her."

"That's going to be tough," Cody said.

When Rayanne came out of the house, there was a collective inhale.

"You were not kidding," Jack said.

Rayanne wore a short blue sundress with a pattern of feathers stamped at the hem and around the arms. Her hair was up and she had on long blue beaded earrings.

"If you can't date her, can I?" Sam said.

"No. You, get in the back," Henry said to Jack. "The rest of you act normal."

"What is normal for us?" Cody asked.

"Okay, don't act normal," Henry said. "But no farting. No fart jokes."

"Got it," Jack said. He hopped out of the van and held the passenger door open for her. "I'm Jack."

"Rayanne," she said, all business. She took care getting into the van, mindful of keeping her skirt in the right place. Henry tried not to stare at her legs.

"That's Sam and Cody in the back," he said.

She turned around. "Hi, guys. There's a joke about a van full of Indians in here somewhere, but I don't know what it is yet."

"Did you hear the one about the van full of Indians?" Jack said.

No one said anything.

"I guess she's right," Jack said.

Henry wanted to tell her she looked nice but he didn't want to say it in front of the guys.

"How do you all know each other?" Rayanne asked.

"Henry brought this thing together," Jack said. "He and I have known each other since we were kids. He met Sam in college and Cody at his job at the trucking company."

"You sling parts, too?" Rayanne asked Cody.

"I'm a mechanical guy," Cody said. "I'm helping Tommy with the bus."

"You're already doing it," Rayanne said to Henry, nodding in approval. "Bringing Indian people together. That's what the job's about."

"What exactly is this place where you work?" Jack asked.

"Watch out, she'll get you involved, too," Henry said.

"Why not?" Rayanne said. "We can always use volunteers. It's an urban Indian center. We do services for Indians in the community. A lot of healthcare programs. Referrals. Transportation. This and that."

"That's for anybody?" Cody asked.

"The center is for Indians in the city," she said.

"So what's this guy doing?" Sam asked, gesturing at Henry.

"We're moving to a bigger building and, to celebrate, we're doing an arts festival. Henry is in charge. There will be different artists and a stage with traditional music and dancing."

"And that's where we would be playing?"

Rayanne raised an eyebrow at Henry. "Well, the idea for the festival is leaning more toward traditional."

"How do you define traditional?" Sam asked. "Isn't culture evolving? Aren't there traditional things you're doing now that are modern?"

"I'm not going to argue with you on that," Rayanne said. "But this is a small-scale event intended to introduce the community to urban Indians. Not a showcase on evolving culture."

"But you don't think it's a terrible idea to bring in contemporary native music," Henry said.

"Rock and roll, hip-hop fusion is native music?" Rayanne asked.

"It is the way we do it," Sam said.

"Why not bring in more modern music?" Henry said. "We'll attract younger people to the festival. I thought the point was to bring attention to the center."

"Talk to Linda and Uncle Arnie with your great idea," Rayanne said. "Mine's not the final word."

The party was at a house on a large lot screened with trees and shrubbery. The hosts said as long as they didn't crank the sound too loud there wouldn't be a problem. Henry helped the guys haul the gear in. He was disappointed that the party wasn't too big. They were building their fan base ten at a time. He spotted a couple of friends and grabbed them to help with the set up.

From the way she talked about herself, he expected Rayanne might be shy but as soon as she was through the door she was introducing herself to people, and taking a beer that someone offered.

"I'll find you after the guys get going," Henry told her. She barely glanced at him she was so busy talking to a woman that Henry recognized as Jack's on again, off again flame. If she was here tonight, they must be on. Or else she was stalking him. Either way, Jack liked that kind of attention.

It didn't take long to get everything set up. Folks from inside made their way to the yard and filled the area in front of the stage.

"Everybody ready?" he said into the microphone.

The heavy landscaping gave the yard an air of privacy. He spotted Rayanne in the back by the house, leaning against the wall. A guy went to stand next to her and a hot spike of something— jealousy, protectiveness, surprise—hit him in the chest. The guy leaned down to say something and Henry recognized the expression on her face. She leaned up and said something back and the guy moved away.

Henry smiled at her but she didn't see him.

"Everybody get ready for the Beat Braves," Henry said.

"That was a lame intro," Jack said. He worked from side by side laptops that he and Sam had modified. He hit a sequence on the keyboard and the beat started, followed by Cody's guitar.

Henry pushed his way to the back where Rayanne was. She let him grab her hand and pull her deeper into the crowd. He found a place where she could see the stage. He situated her in front of him.

They were using the backyard deck as their stage, and there was little room for the guys to move up there. Jack stood in the middle, a rhythmic shimmy going from his shoulders to his hips. The three of them took turns with the lyrics. The beat made the ground vibrate.

It didn't take long for the party to warm up. Everyone around the stage danced. At first Rayanne didn't move, and he expected at any moment she would tell him she wanted to leave. Or explain why this wouldn't work for the festival. Or announce she would be reading a book inside. But she rocked back and forth on her feet, her movements growing until she was dancing in front of him. Every so often she would brush back against him and, as much as he wanted to grind his entire body into hers, he let her meet the distance. They would brush together and apart. She wasn't that much shorter than him but she had on heels. He leaned his head down to the side of her neck. She smelled amazing, like citrus and summer. He put his hands on her hips.

She turned her face and pressed it close to his ear. "You said this was business." She smiled when she pushed his hands away.

"It is," Henry said. He stepped back.

"I'm glad I'm here," Rayanne said.

FOR THE REST of the night, Rayanne stayed close to Henry but not close enough to touch. Those few moments of bumping together when the music started sent an electric jolt through every part of her body. She wanted his hands on her hips and his body pressed against hers. He threatened all the emotions she kept reined in. She was unaccustomed to this kind of sensation and it made it tough to keep her head.

But she needed to hold it together. Bump and grind was not what this night was supposed to be about. And charming and sexy as Henry was, she did not want to get into a casual thing that was going to cross over in the middle of her work life.

She kept him in her side vision so she wouldn't miss him dancing beside her. His body never stopped moving, rocking side to side. She could tell he was keeping an eye on her too.

The band couldn't play too late and the party broke up soon after they stopped.

In the van on the way home, Jack put her on the spot.

"What did you think?"

"I liked it," she said. And she meant it. "It wasn't what I was expecting. I didn't realize the lyrics would be like that. Writing about home and pride and respect. Issues that are meaningful to Indian people."

"Maybe a good fit for the festival after all," Henry suggested.

"Maybe," Rayanne said, even though she still disagreed.

"Our songs are about boning, too," Jack said.

"I got that."

Jack said it to embarrass Henry and it worked. Henry kept his eyes on the road.

"Anyone getting lucky tonight?" Jack added.

Rayanne laughed. "When I talked to your squeeze, Nicole, she said she was picking you up at your place but she wouldn't wait forever. So, you?"

"Sounds like it," Jack said. When they pulled up to Rayanne's apartment, he said, "Make it quick, you two. No groping at the front door. No long goodbyes."

Rayanne was grateful they had the band there to keep any lingering impulses from taking over.

"It's not a date. I don't need to be walked to the door," Rayanne said. "I liked the show, guys. Thanks for inviting me."

Henry got out of the van and went around to her door. "I'm going to walk you to the door anyway."

All the tension that had diffused gathered up again into a white-hot knot in her center. She wouldn't meet his eyes. The quiet jibes from the back of the van countered the effect. But not as much as she would have liked.

Henry kept a respectful distance but didn't try to rush.

"You're not worried those guys will drive off without you?" Rayanne asked.

Henry held up the keys. "I've learned my lesson on that one."

They stopped at the bottom of the staircase that led to her door.

"I can tell you're not convinced yet," he said.

At first she thought he meant about him. She wanted to see how he would persuade her. He had the power to change her mind.

"We'll talk about it," he said. "Maybe? With an appropriate playlist? No final decisions have been made. Agreed?"

The band. They were talking about the band.

"Agreed."

They both jumped when the van's horn sounded.

"That's my ride," Henry said. "See you?"

"My grandpa wanted you to come meet his drum group. He said they need some fresh blood."

"What do they need my blood for?"

Rayanne smiled. "One way to find out. Would you want to go tomorrow?"

"I would." Henry smiled back. "See you then."

22

The minute she saw him, her desire reignited. How had this guy gotten under her skin? He insisted on driving to Grandpa's. He plugged the address into his phone, and shot across town like a person who had grown up there. He kept one hand draped over the wheel. The other slapped out a nervous rhythm against his thigh.

"Are they going to make me sing?"

"Do you want to?" Rayanne tried to identify a cross street to check their progress but she didn't recognize his route.

"No. I can't sing."

He wore what might be considered a dress shirt. It was made of a shiny fabric in a shade of green that she wouldn't expect him to pick. He had on a pair of well-worn jeans that made it hard to stop imaging tearing them off of him. Dancing together had unhinged something that she couldn't get hinged again.

She let her window down and sucked in a big breath.

Focus.

"You never sang with a drum group?" she asked.

"Not big in our family tradition. I like consuming music. Modern music. I like making playlists. Searching for something I haven't heard before. Checking out clubs. Performing is not my thing. Are you musical?"

"Nope. Can't sing. Can't play an instrument. Grandma wanted me to learn piano but they didn't have one. They made arrangements for me to practice at the church after school, which I never wanted to do. It's hard to get good without practice. I don't like to do things I'm not good at."

Henry hesitated at the intersection. He flipped the turn indicator to the right and then turned it back off. He didn't give her a chance to speak. "Before you comment, I know exactly where I am." One street lined with houses and duplexes blended with the next.

"Have you met Gus's band of musical elders?" he asked.

"Briefly. They're all a bunch of characters. Grandpa has known Earl since we moved here. I'm not sure how the rest of the group got together. They helped inspire me to want to do things for elders. I want them to have a social place."

"But they found each other without the center."

"But who knows what elders are out there who don't how to find each other?"

"I guess." Henry pulled onto a quiet street and took a left turn. He pulled up to Grandpa's apartment building.

Rayanne checked back the way they came. "How did you do that?"

Henry shrugged. "Ancient Indian secret." He came around and opened the van door for her.

He took her hand and helped her from the van, that small point of contact sending a jolt through her body. Her heart sped when she met his eyes. The tension threatened to unsteady her. Two steps and she could be in his arms.

She forced herself to push past him and head into the building.

She knocked on Grandpa's front door, her heart still thudding in her chest. After a minute, she unlocked the door and peeked in. "Grandpa?" She swung the door open. There were signs of disorder. The bed was unmade. A saucepan sat on a burner, and a couple meals' worth of dishes sat in the sink. The bathroom door stood open, and there was a balled up towel on the floor.

"He's usually standing here waiting for me, carrying his giant backpack of mystery. I have never been able to learn what all he carries with him when he goes to visit his friends."

"Maybe"—Henry had to clear this throat—"Maybe he had other plans."

"Like what?"

"I don't know. He's a grown man. He's not helpless."

Henry had a point. But it wasn't like Grandpa to miss a get-together with his friends. Or not to be around when he expected her. She checked the calendar he kept on the refrigerator. He had terrible handwriting and used a system of abbreviations she couldn't make sense of, but the day's date said in shaky block letters, *drum*.

"Does he have a cellphone?" Henry asked.

"I bought him one of those cheap pay-by-the-minute phones for emergencies. He either forgets to charge it or forgets to turn it on. Other times he doesn't hear it. He doesn't know how to check the messages."

She got out her phone and dialed it anyway. A quiet chirp sounded near the door. Grandpa's rain jacket hung from a hook. Henry dug around in the pockets until he found the phone.

"Success," he said, holding it up.

"We want to find Grandpa, not his phone."

"I'm sure he's fine. Maybe he ran to the store, or took a walk and lost track of time. You said he likes to make friends with everyone. He's probably talking some poor guy's ear off right now."

She could picture his face, lit up with joy while he told one of his stories, thrilled to be telling it to someone who hadn't heard it before. He would be careful not to pause too long and give his listener an opportunity to break away.

"You're right," she agreed. "I guess I could tidy up while we wait. And I can make sure his bills are paid."

"Woman, leave the man his dignity. This place is tidy enough. He can ask for help with his bills if he needs it. We can sit here and visit until he gets back."

Rayanne took a deep breath. She walked around to the couch

and picked up a fleece blanket that was scrunched up among the cushions. She folded it up and spread it over the back of the couch before she sat down. She gave Henry a look, daring him to comment.

Instead, he sat down next to her, his leg brushing against hers. Whatever grasp she had on her resolve, it was dwindling fast. Henry came across like a lazy guy but he was working out somewhere. Those thighs were all muscle, flexing against her. He glanced down at the place where they were touching and scooted over.

Her mind flicked to a scenario where she was making out with Henry on Grandpa's couch. She stifled the idea as best she could.

"Has anyone ever said something strange to you about being Indian?" Henry asked, his voice uneven.

Rayanne could hardly think with the desire fogging her brain. "Like what? Some people are taken aback that I don't have an Indian name. What's wrong with the name I have? No one ever says to an Italian, 'What's your Italian name?' Do you?"

"Jack claims that some girl in college begged him to knock her up since her kids would be Indian and could get all the free government benefits. I find it hard to believe any woman would beg Jack for sex but it's too crazy to make up."

"What free government benefits?"

"Exactly. I had someone tell me that I wasn't like a real Indian. I guess he thought I needed to live in a teepee and wear a headdress to be legit."

"That would have made me furious," Rayanne said. "Like if we're not like the Indians on TV, we're not real. I'm also amused when random people tell me they're part Native American Indian. Like we have something in common. I want to tell them there's a difference between Indians with white ancestors and white people with Indian ancestors."

"You can't explain that to most people," Henry said.

"I'm not going to stop trying." Rayanne got up and looked out the window. In the time that they'd been there the light started fading from the sky. The streetlights would be on soon. "He doesn't like to be out at night. His eyes are terrible and he doesn't move fast. Why don't we go look for him?"

"Where would you even start?"

She could only think of all the things that could have gone wrong. What if he got lost, or fell down, or someone drove off with him. Did old people get abducted? Henry was right. She couldn't guess where he might be. But looking somewhere was better than sitting and waiting.

"I'm going to walk to the bus stop and then to the park. I'll come right back. You wait here and call me if he comes back."

THERE WERE two bus stops that Grandpa might use. The closest one was two blocks away on a busy street. She walked as fast as she could while the sky faded to purple. An older woman sat at the bus shelter but ignored her when she asked about Grandpa.

She continued up the street to the park. The basketball courts were lit and one of the groups paused to hear her query before shaking their heads and restarting their game. The dread crept in and shoved everything else aside. What if they couldn't find him? She couldn't make herself think about that part.

She decided to check out the other bus stop on the far side of the park. She rarely felt unsafe in the city but the escalating worry and the growing pockets of darkness increased her unease. She ran until she reached the bus stop, but the bench was empty. She sat down to catch her breath and calm down.

When her phone rang, her heartbeat increased again. It was Henry. "Did he come back?"

"He called here. Tell me where you are. I'll pick you up and we'll go get him."

Grandpa was at a bus stop that was temporarily closed. A big orange notice was fixed to one side of the bus shelter but from where he sat, it looked like a regular stop. A woman about Rayanne's age sat with him.

Grandpa couldn't understand what the fuss was about. As Henry predicted, he was thrilled to have someone to talk to. He was even more mystified when Rayanne burst into tears when she hugged him.

"What's this all about?" he asked.

"We were supposed to pick you up and you weren't there." When Rayanne drew back, Henry rubbed his hand across her back. The warmth and comfort made another few tears sneak out. "I was worried."

"I knew where I was," Grandpa said. "I'm ready to go home now."

"What about Earl's? What about your friends?"

He shook his head. He let Henry help him to his feet and lead him to the van.

"Thanks for helping my grandpa," Rayanne said to the woman.

She smiled. "I have a papa too. I hope people are keeping an eye out for him."

They returned to the apartment and once he was home, whatever force had animated him during his adventure disappeared. He wandered back and forth around the apartment, moving another dish to the sink, picking up and putting down a magazine.

"That was a good idea you had, calling your own phone." Rayanne wanted to cheer him up.

"I couldn't remember your number."

"I'll write it down for your wallet so you have it for next time."

"Next time," Grandpa repeated like he couldn't stand the idea. He made a creaky effort to bend down and waited until Henry went over and helped him pull out a flat storage box he kept under his bed. Henry lifted it to the bed.

Rayanne had seen this box many times. It contained packets of photos and some surviving pieces of her ancient school work. Grandpa showed Henry one of her spelling tests from third grade.

"One word wrong," Grandpa said.

"I still can't spell 'recommend' correctly," Henry said.

"This is what you want to do? Show Henry my old spelling tests?"

"You shush," Grandpa said. "I'm trying to find something." She flinched in surprise.

"This is what I wanted." Grandpa had a map that turned out to be huge when he began unfolding it. Henry helped him move to the kitchen table where he continued to open the document. Grandpa got out his magnifying glass to study it. "I can't remember the place we used to go hunting."

Rayanne recognized what was happening. It was like he needed to regain his bearings by solidifying his old memories. If he could pinpoint something from the past, the comfort carried over into the present moment. He needed an anchor.

"What is this map?" Henry asked him.

"Old forest map," Grandpa said. "Where our people are is forest lands." The map had been folded and unfolded so many times it was breaking apart at the creases. Someone had scribbled across one corner with an orange marker. She guessed it must have been her. His finger followed the blue line of a mountain creek.

"Somewhere around here," he said. "We was up there, me and my brothers. Haven't seen them in years."

She was accustomed to him reliving memories like this but a prickle of worry worked its way in. Had something shifted? Was this dive into old memories different than usual?

Henry read off the names from the map. "Skeleton Gulch? Blue Rock Lake? Buster's Camp?"

These were all the names of places she had grown up with and played a role in his stories.

"Buster's Camp. That's the one. We seen a buck on the ridge. Made a trail to lure it out," Grandpa drew out each sentence in his story-telling voice. "One of my brothers got it. Forget which. Big one too. Our mom was happy to get the food."

"Sounds like a great trip," Henry said.

Rayanne searched the kitchen for a notepad so she could write the story down as part of her family history. She had left some notepaper for him a few weeks earlier so he could keep a list of the groceries he needed.

"What are you doing in there?" Grandpa snapped.

Rayanne stood up and stared at him in disbelief. He never spoke to her like this.

"Grandpa, did something happen today?"

"Nothing happened today. Come away from there."

She left the kitchen and went to stand next to him. "How come you didn't want to go to Earl's?"

Grandpa folded up the map, taking his time and ignoring the original creases. "Earl fell down. Broke his leg."

"Oh no. Where is he now?"

"We told him to watch out. He keeps so many things around on the floor. He's fallen before," Grandpa said. "His daughter said he was at the rehab center."

Something in Rayanne's heart squeezed tight. One of her greatest fears was coming in and finding Grandpa on the floor, unable to move. Or worse.

"I'll find out where he is. We can visit him."

"That's what I was trying to do. I got turned around and then no buses come."

"He'll appreciate the visit when we get you out there," she said.

She tried to gauge Henry's reaction to all this. She expected some show of distress at being thrown in the middle of someone else's family drama. But instead he appeared concerned and willing to help.

"Do you want to try to go now?" he asked.

"I guess not," Grandpa said. "That's the problem with living too long. You lose all your friends."

"He's not lost, Grandpa," Rayanne said. "And you haven't lived even close to too long."

"If you say so," Grandpa said without humor. "Too bad we got no more drum group. Earl's was the only place where we could make a racket with nobody to complain."

"Sorry," Rayanne said.

"I'm sorry for Henry," Grandpa said, doing his best to act cheerful. "Lost his big chance to join us."

"There will be another time," Henry said. "When we get the center moved to the new building, we'll have a place for you."

That was her line. Rayanne would have laughed if she weren't so worried about her grandfather.

"That would be nice," Grandpa said. "I'm just tired. I haven't gone dotty on you."

"I know," Rayanne said. She kissed his cheek. "We'll get out of here. I'll check on you tomorrow."

"Thanks, sweetie," Grandpa said. They left him sitting at the table.

23

The drive back to her place went more quickly than Rayanne wanted it to. Henry parked in front of her building. Rayanne didn't want to invite him in, but she wasn't ready to be alone.

"Would you mind sitting with me for a while?"

"Of course not," Henry said.

Her apartment complex liked to advertise its park-like setting. A concrete path snaked through green grass. Pale yellow light from an outdoor lamp illuminated a bench under a tree. They made their way over to it.

"That made me sad," she said as she sat down. When Henry sat next to her, she held out her hand until he grabbed it, the warm contact calming.

"Me too," he said.

"I'm glad you were there. If I was by myself, I would have missed the call."

"He wasn't in huge danger."

"I know. I can't help it. I worry about him by himself. I don't want him to be unhappy." But even as she said it, she understood old age was its own kind of journey where inevitably someone remained alone. All the elder programs in the world wouldn't make that go away.

The night was quiet except for the distant garble of a television in one of the apartments. The air was cool enough for a jacket. She wouldn't last long out there in her sweater. From where they sat, the garden path was almost a straight line to the stairway that led to her front door.

Sitting next to her, Henry was less like an improbable colleague and more like a person who could understand what was racing through her mind. She could confess her shortcomings and be honest about her flaws and he wouldn't judge or mock. She could ask for comfort and he would be there for her. She let herself imagine what it would be like to indulge in such an ill-considered diversion. He was nice. He would probably come upstairs if she asked. She didn't want him to get the wrong idea about things.

He kept his eyes on the ground but his thumb slid back and forth across her skin where he held her hand, a lazy, absent motion. That point soon consumed all of her attention. He came across as a model of calm and capability. A fire could break out across the way and he would know what to do.

"I'll walk you up to the staircase." Henry used both hands to bring her to her feet but let go so they could walk side by side. A light clicked off in a lower floor apartment. She almost reached for his hand again. She wanted some of that calm strength to carry over to her.

They paused at the foot of the stairs. She could tell he was searching for something to say. She almost talked herself out of it but she turned and gazed up at his face. One of her hands reached up to press against the firm muscle of his chest. She anticipated how his lips would feel against hers as she hooked a finger into a gap between his shirt buttons and tugged him toward her.

His eyes widened and he leaned back.

Oops.

"Sorry," Rayanne said. She whipped her hand out and took a

moment to regain her balance before stepping back. "Sorry," she repeated.

What was she thinking?

She shook her head, willing the moment to disappear. She retreated to the stairs, trying to appear natural. She forced her voice to be merry. "Sorry, Henry. Thanks. Thanks for coming with me tonight. See you at work. Or something."

She cringed so hard it was physically painful. She launched up the stairs and fumbled for her keys, afraid to look back and see what Henry was doing. She couldn't block out the expression he'd had on his face. What was that called? Appalled? What was the word when you were mortally embarrassed for another person?

She bolted into her apartment and shut the door behind her, banging her forehead against it. How many times had she told him to back off? Of course he would have had enough.

She couldn't stop seeing it in her mind, a terrible movie that she couldn't forget. What she wouldn't give to be able to have that moment back. This was more than embarrassment. She'd invented a whole new state of extreme humiliation. That would be her contribution to humanity. Now she had another awkward transition at work to face on Monday. They'd already managed to smooth over an actual kiss and some other weird moments. Maybe this wasn't insurmountable.

She forced a laugh but it sounded pitiful even to her ears. She didn't even wash her face. She changed into her pajamas and crawled into bed. She scrolled through items on her phone without seeing what was on the screen.

She turned out the light and flipped back and forth, the sheet tangling around her legs.

Sometime later, there were footsteps on the stairs and a tap at the door. She got up and checked the peephole. It was Henry. She opened the door a crack. "Is everything okay?"

"Oh, good. You're up." Henry smiled as if there were nothing unusual about this late night visit. "Do you think I could have that kiss now?"

Rayanne's heart pounded a few extra beats. "I guess."

She opened the door wide enough for Henry to lean in. He kept it soft and sweet. It was more like a promise than anything else but it still shook loose a shiver of lust. He backed up.

Rayanne opened the door wider. "What was that earlier?"

"Oh. I wanted to kiss you, too, but after our conversations I wasn't sure. But I thought about it and I was nervous so I'd been rehearsing it in my head. Before I was ready, you moved toward me, which was fine. Great, even. But I wasn't expecting it and you misinterpreted my reaction. Then while I was trying to figure out what to say, you disappeared."

"That was forty-five minutes ago," Rayanne said.

"Yeah," Henry agreed with an apologetic smile. "I wasn't sure what I wanted to say but I realized I would never get to sleep if I didn't fix it tonight. Can I do it again?"

"You'd better."

Henry put his hand on the side of her face this time and pulled her toward him, taking his time kissing her and running his tongue across her lower lip. Her knees trembled and threatened to give way. She wanted to grab a handful of shirt and drag him inside but he had freaked out over an unexpected kiss, so who knows what would happen if she tried something like that. Instead, she took her time backing away, their gazes locked.

"Worth it. Thanks for coming back."

"Me too," Henry said. "Or, I'm glad I did. Whatever sounds best." He stayed in the doorway. She was unsure what he thought might happen.

She didn't want to wait until Monday to see him again. "You want to have breakfast tomorrow?"

Henry's eyes flicked to the apartment behind her and then to her again.

"You mean go and come back?"

Rayanne swallowed. "Yes."

"I would. Make our own or go out?"

"I'm not a breakfast cook unless you like oatmeal."

"Don't worry, I am," Henry said. "I make a mean breakfast hash."

"I don't like mean food," Rayanne said. She couldn't stop staring at his lips and the magical way he formed words. It was bad how lost she was with this guy.

"You'll like this. Do you have eggs, potatoes, and odds and ends?"

"I have eggs and hummus."

"I've heard about you hummus-eating Indians but I've never seen one myself," Henry said. He reached out to touch her cheek. "I'll stop and pick up a few things on my way." He kissed her one more time.

She enjoyed the sight of him walking down the stairs before closing the door.

24

*S*he spent an embarrassing amount of time choosing her shower products, thinking too much about what her hair should smell like when Henry returned. She tidied the kitchen, trying to guess what sort of implements his breakfast dish would require.

He showed up right at ten.

"What a surprise meeting you here," Rayanne said, doing her best to sound breezy. He had on the sexy-fitting jeans and a Beat Braves T-shirt that fit snugly across his chest. How many panties had threatened to drop for those jeans?

She held up a spatula. He had a bag of groceries in one hand and flowers in the other.

"What are you going to do with that?" Henry asked, eyeing the spatula with daring in his eyes.

Rayanne raised an eyebrow. "I'm not sure yet. What do you do with the flowers?"

"Give them to a gorgeous girl." Henry traded with her for the spatula. He leaned down to kiss her. He was fresh shaven and smelled like clean laundry. Her eyes slid shut and she melted a little inside. She was glad she asked him back. There was the easy intimacy of the morning while wisely steering clear of the sweaty gymnastics the night before. And if she changed her mind, there was no reason to assume that opportunity had expired.

"We have to stay out of trouble," she blurted.

Henry held his hands up to plead his innocence. "I mean no trouble."

"Good. I got the kitchen ready for you." She'd put the cast iron pan on the stove, and set out a knife and cutting board. A carton of eggs and a chipped plate with a cube of butter sat on the counter.

"I also had a yellow onion," she said, pointing to it on the counter.

"I'm impressed," Henry said, sounding anything but. "I picked up potatoes and bacon. If you don't mind, I'm going to search your fridge."

"Search away." She swept her hands, indicating the room was his. She pretended to busy herself searching for something to put the flowers in. Instead, she watched Henry from behind as he went through her refrigerator.

"Boy, you weren't kidding. How does such an insanely competent career woman, especially one who bring dinner to elders, get by with a foodless refrigerator?"

"It's not easy," Rayanne said. She stuck the flowers in a wide-mouth jar and put them on the kitchen table.

"I don't know what you've been told but olives can go bad." He set a vaguely familiar container on the counter next to the sink.

"Maybe I like them that way."

"Shall I put them back?"

She shrugged and he dumped them in the trash. He washed his hands and then helped himself to a cup of coffee. He held up the pot and gestured to her with his chin.

Rayanne nodded back and he found her cup and refilled it.

Henry tossed some bacon into the pan and, while it cooked, he got to work on the potatoes. "You want to chop the vegetables I found?"

"You found vegetables?" She went around to work next to him in the small kitchen.

Rayanne couldn't ignore the tension building up in her body. This moment belonged to them. No business. No family drama. No one around to catch them or watch them. No responsibilities until Monday morning.

"What's your Indian astrological sign?" Henry asked.

"Hang on," Rayanne said. "I want to put the plates in the oven to warm. Can you move for a sec?"

Henry moved aside to let her get in the oven. When she got back to her chopping, she said, "I have an Indian astrological sign?"

"Sure, everyone does. I'm buck." He stood up straight and moved to exaggerate the width of his chest. "They have antlers, sorta regal. They're strong but not obnoxious about it. They're smart. It's more than a deer, it's a buck."

"Lots of handy rhymes with that too."

Henry cleared his throat. "Gentle reminder that you are the one who made the statement about staying out of trouble."

Rayanne held her hands up in mock protest. "Duck, truck, cluck, schmuck. What were you thinking?"

"Answer the question. Indian astrology. What's your sign?"

"Does it have to be a mammal?"

"It can be whatever kind of creature you want."

"Then my sign is eagle."

"Every Indian's sign is eagle," he said in an exasperated voice. "You need to pick something else. How about beaver?"

"Hilarious. You see me as a waterlogged rodent ruining trees and building dams?"

"Hm. Maybe not if you put it like that."

"If I get to pick, I want to be skunk. No, buzzard. Turkey buzzard is my Indian sign."

"So you see yourself as a homely beak face with a nice wingspan. They do like to hang out in groups."

"A wake," Rayanne said. "A group of buzzards is called a wake."

"You're kidding."

"No and if they need to defend themselves they barf out partially digested meat. Never know when that might come in handy. Do you think buzzard and buck are compatible?"

"Hard to say. You know how Indian astrology is. But I can't wait to see you do your thing with partially digested meat."

He showed her how he did the potatoes. By then the bacon was done, and he threw the potatoes into the crackling grease. He had more steps with the vegetables, and then the eggs. In the office he acted like collating copies was rocket science. Now he was managing several hot pans without a crease in his brow. It didn't take him long to get the breakfast assembled and ready to serve. Rayanne got out the warmed plates, and Henry filled them up. They carried them to the table to eat.

"Have you ever had a serious boyfriend?" Henry asked.

"My, this conversation turned serious quick. Don't you want to know what I think of the eggs?"

"Sure, how are the eggs?"

She took a big bite and nodded. "The perfect balance of salty, crunchy, greasy, and...chompy."

"Good to hear. Chompy is my favorite too. So, serious boyfriend? Or would you rather not talk about it?"

"Depends on how you define serious. Like, living together or expecting to get married? Not even close. I had a boyfriend my last year of high school but we broke up when I moved to college. I had a hard time meeting people in college. Maybe since I spent so many years living in a small town? I don't know. I made friends in college but I never quite felt...relaxed? I'm not sure how to put it. How was college for you?"

"Not the same as for you. I'm having a harder time with the post-collegiate bit, which you might have noticed."

"To get back to the original question, I haven't been in a good space to meet people. I've been trying to settle other areas of my life before tackling that one. You?"

"I had a girlfriend in college. She was way more serious than me. I thought I was being honest with her, but we had a difference of opinion on that. She gave me an ultimatum, propose or else. So we broke up. Then I was the bad guy. Since then, I have specialized in first dates that don't go anywhere."

"Have you dated any Natives?"

"Nope. I've barely met any native women who I wasn't related to."

"I rarely meet Natives my age. Don't you meet lots of girls, hanging out with a band?" She didn't know why she brought it up because of course he did. They all did.

He smiled. "No one like you."

During the rest of the meal she learned that Henry considered himself a terrible typist, a better than decent basketball player, and he was woefully undereducated on Indian history but said he would try a book that she recommended. In turn, she confessed that she liked dogs better than cats, that she had a special savings account for travel but hadn't chosen a destination yet, and that she hated when people called her Ray.

When they were finished eating, they cleared the table together. Henry rinsed the dishes while Rayanne put things away.

Now that she was full she was sleepy, and the idea that was forming in her head involved calisthenics with Henry, followed by a leisurely nap.

Great idea. Not the right time.

Especially not while they were working together.

Henry saved her by saying, "Much as I love spending a lazy Sunday with you, Jack and I are going out for another desperate and soul-crushing search for apartments. I'm going to take off. Thanks for breakfast." He smoothed her hair away from her face and gave her another kiss before he said, "I'll see you tomorrow."

25

$\mathcal{N}$othing could destroy the pounding exhilaration in Henry's heart when he left Rayanne's. She could say whatever she wanted but there was no denying the sparks when they were in the room together. He already missed her and couldn't wait to see her again.

The front of his place was trashier than usual when he pulled up. There were clothes strewn about and a mattress leaning against the garage door. He couldn't pull into the driveway because Sam's car blocked the way. When he got out to investigate, Jack came across the yard with an armload of stuff that he dumped into the back seat of the car.

"They threw us out," Jack said. Anger blazed in his eyes. He waved at the mess on the lawn. "You'd better grab your stuff."

Henry couldn't process what was happening. A bookshelf had been carried out their front door and tossed to the ground. The cabinet had splintered, and books were scattered in the wreckage. His bedspread and pillows were balled up on the grass. The joy of the morning vanished, and a mixture of rage and humiliation took its place.

Jack picked up a winter coat and a pair of boots and carried them to the trunk.

"This is BS," Henry said.

"It is. They screwed us. They decided they were done having tenants effective immediately, apparently. I was at Nicole's. When I got home, I found it like this." He gestured at the pitiful collection of things that represented what little they owned.

Henry had been gone a couple of hours. That's all it had taken.

The clothes were wadded up in separate piles that appeared to have been kicked across the yard. He recognized some of his shirts covered with dirt and dried grass. Then he recognized the mattress leaning against the garage door. That also belonged to him.

He pulled the van around so it was easier to load and joined Jack, running back and forth, tossing his things in without taking time to check what was ruined.

A heavyset guy without a shirt came out of the house and watched them for a minute before disappearing back inside.

"Don't try to talk to them," Jack said. "Don't even make eye contact."

"What did they say?"

"Nothing. They think it's funny."

Henry stooped to gather up the bathroom towels that were spread along the driveway. Everything from the kitchen had been piled into two boxes that were too heavy to pick up. He grabbed one by its corner and dragged it toward the van.

That's when the *whooping* started. Like the Indian war cry heard in the terrible Western films from long ago. Two scrawnier guys had come out to join the first. They had cans of cheap beer and stood by the front door, taking turns shrieking and banging their hands over their mouths.

"That's not very original." Henry didn't understand why they needed to act so ridiculous. They could have asked them to move. Why all this theater?

He intended to go back for another pile of stuff but found himself on a new course toward the jackasses.

Jack grabbed his arm. "It's not worth it. There are more of them than us. Let's pack up and get out of here."

"But we're such badass warriors," Henry said.

"That'll remain our secret. Come on." Jack didn't let go until Henry changed direction again.

Jack had a point, but ignoring their insults made it worse. Henry went back to work. They managed to get the mattresses and a couple of chairs in the van. The jerks had broken a leg off the kitchen table so they left it.

Henry wanted to check inside the apartment one last time to make sure they got everything, but as soon as he was within six feet of the door, the guys screamed threats. He made do with one last lap around the yard and found a hiking boot under a shrub. Jack had his car running and he waited until Henry was ready to pull out too.

The biggest guy came over and followed Henry to the van.

"Don't want to see you around here again, chief," he said.

"That won't be a problem," Henry said. Before he drove off, he rolled down the window. He had to know. "Why? We never did anything to you."

The guy shrugged. "Time to go back to the rez."

Henry put the window back up and took off.

HE FOLLOWED Jack to Sam's place and they spent the rest of the day rehashing the incident. They tried to cheer each other up, but Henry couldn't successfully dismiss the shame he felt from the stupid spectacle. Sam offered to let him stick around but, as it was, his place was small and already too crowded with three guys. Adding Henry to the mix would take it from cramped to unbearable.

When he left Sam's, he intended to bite back whatever was left of his dignity and go to his mom's. She'd have enough pity to feed him and at least he'd have a roof over his head while he figured out his next move. But when the van came to a stop he found himself back at Rayanne's.

It took some time to build the courage to go to the door.

When she opened up, her hair was mussed and her eyes sleepy.

"You missed an epic nap," she said in a groggy voice. The distress must have been visible in his face because she woke right up. "Did something happen?"

As soon as her eyes widened in concern, the overwhelming unfairness of it knocked him sideways. He collapsed against her, his face buried in her neck.

"Was it something bad?" She wrapped her arms around him and hugged him tight. Her body pressed against his was the comfort he wanted.

The words spilled out in a rush. He described finding his underwear and socks piled around a tree trunk, the pantry items that had rolled into the flower bed, and the ruined furniture and linens.

"Why did they throw you out?"

"Because they could."

Rayanne pulled away. "I have a referral for landlord-tenant issues. We can call them tomorrow."

"No, we can't," Henry said. He followed her inside. "The whole thing was informal, meaning not on the up-and-up. They didn't have to give us a reason."

"They didn't have to be dicks about it. So what happened?"

"They threw our stuff out on the grass like we were deadbeats. They did those stupid war whoops that mean people think are so funny. They told us to go back to the rez. It was stupid and shitty. People are awful."

"I'm so sorry," Rayanne said. "You want a beer or something?"

"The hugging was nice."

Rayanne smiled and wrapped her arms around him again. He inhaled the scent of her hair. He was aware of every place where their bodies met, and tried not to think about how aroused he was becoming.

"Now what are you going to do?" she asked.

Henry shrugged. "I don't know. I need to gird my loins and go deal with my mother. I know I shouldn't have come, but I needed a friendly face."

"I'm glad someone thinks my face is friendly," Rayanne said. After a moment she said, "Would you want to stay here?"

His heart thumped faster. He could feel it everywhere at once. "What do you mean?"

"I mean, you could sleep on the couch tonight. Tomorrow we can figure out a place for you to stay until you find an apartment."

"You're inviting me to stay here," Henry said. He couldn't tell where she was coming from and was cautious not to assume too much. "You sure about that?"

"It was...nice this morning, don't you think? We've become friends, right? That's what friends do for each other. Right?"

Henry heard the words she was saying, but his body was responding in a different way. "Because when I'm close to you, I can barely keep my hands off of you."

"Oh," Rayanne said.

At first he misunderstood the look she was giving him.

"I don't mean...I would never do anything...I'm saying you're so..."

"Well, don't," Rayanne whispered.

"Can you be more specific?"

"Don't keep your hands off me."

26

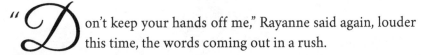

"**D**on't keep your hands off me," Rayanne said again, louder this time, the words coming out in a rush.

So much for staying out of trouble.

He wasted no time. He crushed himself against her and brushed his lips down her neck. The blood rushed every place at once. All she could hear was his breath in her ear. The air around them was supercharged. She couldn't think. His hands threaded through her hair and pulled her face to his.

"I've been dying to touch your hair since the first day I met you," he said in her ear.

She fumbled with the hem of his T-shirt until she worked her hands underneath and caressed the broad muscles of his back.

"I've been dying to do that since the first day I met you," she said.

He grabbed her face again and closed his mouth over hers. His hands stroked up and down her back before reaching down and cupping her ass and grinding his hips against hers. A shadow of doubt passed in some faraway corner of her mind but she sent it away. Doubt wasn't going to play any part of this moment.

"Do we need to get anything?" Henry asked, his voice unsteady. He swallowed.

"Like what?"

"Uh, you know, birth control?"

"Wow," Rayanne said, "your mama taught you well."

"You have no idea."

"I have condoms," Rayanne said. "A vast selection, in fact. You'll be impressed."

"You have a giant selection of condoms? I can't figure out if I should be surprised or not."

"You'll see."

They kissed again and she maneuvered him toward the bedroom. When they arrived, there was another unsteady moment. When was the last time she'd taken her clothes off for someone? Did they need more light or less? She pushed away insecurity over the shape of her body. She'd been denying her attraction for so long and now this was happening. She didn't want to waste time. She moved his hands to her waist again, anxious to avoid any long pauses. Even as a teenager she hated to wait to see if the guy was going to make a move. She liked to keep things in motion.

His hands were warm. He took his time working them over her skin.

"I'm a little nervous," he said.

"Making excuses?"

"Never," Henry said. His lips were soft but aggressive, never letting her mouth get too far from his.

"You taste good," he whispered against her lips. He dipped his tongue into her mouth.

Rayanne's hands slid along his back. Her eyes closed when he worked his mouth along her neck.

He leaned back so he could pull off her T-shirt. He tossed it to the floor and in a split second his hands moved around and her bra sprang loose. He slid the straps down her arms. She inhaled in surprise.

"I've been wanting to do that, too," he said.

"I thought you were ambivalent."

"There was no ambivalence. I act like that because I'm nervous."

"So you're nervous a lot?"

"When I'm around you." He brushed the tips of his fingers across her nipples, and a little croak sounded from the back of her throat.

"You like that?" he said.

"I like all of it," she said, her mind ringing with sensation and happiness that he was here touching her and liked her back. She pressed her hands against his chest until he took a step back. She yanked off his shirt and threw it to the floor. She pressed her skin to his and wrapped her arms around him, stopping him with a hug.

"You okay?" he asked.

"Yeah," she said, backing up and kissing him again. "I'm happy."

"That's promising because I'm not finished yet." He grabbed her hips and pulled her close, grinding against her until she was breathless.

"I like your room," Henry said. "It's nice."

"What's nice about it?" Rayanne turned down the covers and sat him on the edge of the bed. She straddled him and twined her fingers into his hair, pulling his face to hers. She ran a line of light kisses down his jawline.

"The furniture. The decorations. The condoms. Did you find those yet?"

Rayanne pulled back and smiled. "I was busy. Take your pants off, I'll be right back." She went to the bathroom and found the box in the cupboard under the sink.

When she returned, she found him as she had instructed.

Wow, all that for me?

"Should I have waited under the covers?" he said.

"No way. You're gorgeous." She tossed the box on the bed. It was a cardboard box the size of a shoebox and decorated to resemble a wooden chest. Bright yellow letters proclaimed, *Condom Treasure Chest.*

"Already this has been amazing, but I have to say, I'm speechless. Should I ask why you have pirate condoms?"

"I won them at a bachelorette party. I guessed the correct number of penis lollipops in the pickle jar."

"That's my girl," Henry said, reaching for her.

"No, come on. You need to pick one." She tore the plastic off the box and worked the top off. She brought out a handful of foil packets. "Don't worry, we don't have to use them all today." She gave him a sly smile.

"Why would that worry me?" Henry replied. "I'm not moved by glow-in-the-dark right now. Why don't we stick with the standard lubed and ribbed for her pleasure and see how we do?"

Rayanne put the box on her dresser, and dropped a couple packets on the nightstand. He helped her shimmy out of her jeans and yanked off her panties. He held them up for her.

"I love girl panties," he said.

"You love them? Would you like to try them on?"

"No," he said, but he twisted them around in his hands as if he were thinking about it. "They're so small."

"I won't think less of you if you want to wear girl's underwear."

"I don't. You've never seen clothes that you liked but didn't want to wear?"

"Like your sexy-guy jeans. Do you have a shelf in your closet with a little piece of masking tape that says, 'my sexy jeans'?"

"I don't have a shelf or a closet."

"Oh, yeah. Sorry."

"That's okay. You like my jeans, huh?" Henry said.

"I love your jeans. But I like them on you. They wouldn't look like that on me."

"And, you've made my point."

He dropped the underwear and pulled her close. He took his time running his hands up and down her body before he kissed her again.

"Anything I should know before we get started?" Henry said, kissing the side of her head in a surprisingly tender gesture.

"I wouldn't be doing this if I didn't like you," she said, rolling him over so she could slide on top of him. Her hair hung down between them and brushed his chest.

He pulled her face down and kissed her again. "Well, that's reassuring."

~

LATER THEY LAY face to face, catching their breath. Rayanne was sorry she couldn't see his eyes in the dim light. She ran the back of her hand over his breastbone.

"What a day," Henry said. "The lows were low but the highs were high."

"I liked the high parts. I was pretty sure you thought of me like that," Rayanne whispered.

"I thought of you like that. A lot," Henry said.

"I guess we don't have to have a conversation about whether or not you're staying," Rayanne said, curling up against him.

"You don't mind?" Henry said.

She laughed. She reached up and rubbed her fingers through his short hair, massaging his scalp. He made a quiet sound of contentment.

"Have you ever had long hair?" she asked.

"Would you like it better long?"

"I like it now. I'm curious."

"Yeah, I did. When I was in middle school. Our school wasn't like the ones on TV where there were these distinct groups of popular kids versus everyone else, but there were the kids who everyone looked up to. I grew it to my shoulders. Long enough for a ponytail. There was this girl that I thought was pretty. The kind of girl on year-book club and honor roll. We were friends. She told me it was inauthentic, like I was trying to make a statement but not successful in carrying it off."

"What a bitch."

"Yeah, I know that now. But at the time I took it personally, like you do when you're thirteen and you want everybody to like you. I've opted for short and well-groomed ever since. You think I should grow it out?"

She kissed his chin. "I think you should do whatever you want. Listen." She could feel him hold his breath. What was he expecting her to say? "We have to act normal at work tomorrow."

"Are you ashamed of me?" he joked.

"If I could, I would put up a billboard to announce, 'I bagged a hot Indian dude.' But in terms of the office we need to be rigorously professional."

"I like the sound of rigorous," he said, his hands wandering.

"At work. Be cool. Promise."

"Promise," he agreed. "At work. But we're not at work right now."

onday morning, Rayanne ended up in a back room with Henry, searching for supplies they could use for the festival. All that talk about staying professional and now they were tucked out of sight, elbow to elbow in a narrow room. Rayanne held a clipboard and took notes while Henry opened the boxes. They had a black marker to label everything so they could find it again.

She intended to keep it together, holding back her smile, except every time she looked at him he was gazing back with a silly grin on his face. He kept shifting his position so he could brush against her, then apologized and promised not to do it again.

He reached up to pull a box off the top shelf. His shirt rode up to expose a narrow strip of brown skin above his waistband. She'd caressed that spot with her hands and her lips the night before.

Henry tapped the side of the box. "Miss? I'm going to have to insist you stop staring at me like I'm a piece of man meat."

"I don't know what you're talking about," she said with a smile.

Henry pulled the box off the shelf and slit it open with a box cutter. Rayanne helped him open the flaps. Another box of Styrofoam cups.

She found the clipboard and made another mark in the cup category. "We're going to need a coffee booth. Is there a native craft we can do with the kids with Styrofoam cups?"

"Sure, they could make miniature teepees or World's Best Grandpa coffee cups. They could use them as giant beads and make necklaces. They could fill them with fruit punch and put them in the freezer."

"Those aren't terrible ideas," Rayanne said.

"I am gifted that way. I can come up with lots of ideas in a wide variety of scenarios, if you get my meaning."

"I do." She swiped the tape gun across the lid and wrote 'foam cups' across the side.

"I'm not going to let you distract me from the real work," he said. "What's the plan for promoting this thing? Do you guys have social media accounts?"

"For the center? Yeah, Ester keeps track of that stuff. We could probably do more but there's only so much time. I think it's kind of depressing. We'll get comments that say things like 'It's terrible what we did to the Native Americans' followed by comments like, 'Haven't we done enough already? What's with all the special treatment?' It's an awfully simplistic way of looking at our people."

Henry nodded. "I'll talk to Ester about updates on the festival."

He took another box off a shelf and slit it open.

"You know what this reminds me of?" he asked with a playful smile.

"It'd better not be anything naughty," Rayanne hissed.

"It is."

"Then tell me later."

"There's going to be a later?"

Rayanne stopped what she was doing. "I think something later would be nice. Did you have a different idea?"

Henry shook his head. "I think something right now would be mighty fine."

She imagined her back against the wall, bracing her feet against the shelves while Henry held her in place.

Enough of that.

"Right now isn't happening." She indicated he should open the box.

Henry stared down into it. *"Ooh-ee.* Paper plates. We're getting to the good stuff now. If we find a box of napkins, all our prayers will have been answered."

Rayanne handed him the tape gun and labeled the side of the box. Even though they were behaved, she jumped when Ester opened the door.

"Hey, guys, Linda wants us in the meeting room. Urgent," she said. Her eyes flicked back and forth from Rayanne to Henry and back. "You guys doing it?"

"What?" Rayanne said. "No!"

Henry raised an eyebrow.

"All right," Ester said, giving them a thumbs-up as she exited.

"I thought we weren't going to tell anyone," Rayanne said.

"Tell anyone what?" Henry said. "She guessed. She doesn't care that you're diddling the boss's nephew."

"Ah well, when you put it like that..." Rayanne shook her head, still too high from the night before to be truly upset. "We need to get in there. If Linda is calling us all to a meeting, something's wrong."

"Something's always wrong here. Should we guess what it is? The roof falling in? A pack of wild dogs? An extortion plot?"

"An extortion plot would require we have something valuable worth making threats over."

"So roof or wild dogs?"

"You haven't been around long enough to complain." Rayanne couldn't help it, she squeezed his butt as she left the room.

"If you don't watch it, I'm going to report you to your supervisor," Henry said.

"Last time I checked, you were my supervisor."

"Carry on, then," Henry said, squeezing her back.

Linda, Ester, and Tommy were all in the meeting room. Linda was wearing her patented look of strained optimism.

"Gang, the date is closing in. I need an update. Arnie has informed me that this event could be the very thing that will convince the tribes to keep this carnival sideshow going. He says, we do good and the money will follow. He wants me to make sure we are all involved." Linda's tone conveyed something like weariness. Arnie must be trying to manage from behind the scenes. Linda would be impatient with that.

"Where are you at, Henry?"

Rayanne caught herself giving Henry a goofy grin and reset her expression to neutral. Ester caught her eye and made a vague obscene gesture. Rayanne scowled at her and made a production of turning her attention to the clipboard, jotting down notes.

"The booths are ninety percent set. These are all the people Rayanne recruited. We'll have pottery, modern and classic artwork styles, some photography. I've got a few of the higher-profile people giving me some grief. They want estimates of what sort of traffic will be coming through because they don't want to waste their time if it's 'small beans' as one guy said."

"We've never done this before so we have no reliable estimate," Linda said.

"I've been estimating at least five hundred for the day," Rayanne said.

"That sounds optimistic. We don't even have a place for that many to park," Linda said.

Rayanne shrugged. "That would be a good problem to have. There's an art walk event on the west side that gets double that. I thought it was a decent guess."

"We'll soon find out," Linda said.

"Rayanne wasn't having any luck finding someone to come in and cook, but I found a couple of food trucks including a frybread truck from Warm Springs. Those folks would love to participate."

"Here we go," Tommy muttered.

Linda shook her head. "Not the kind of tradition we're looking for."

"What?" Henry said.

Tommy went ahead and explained. "Frybread is traditional in the sense that it came from a terrible moment in history. Plus, giant pieces of delicious fried bread are not good for your health."

167

"You wouldn't know it," Ester chimed in, "but health programs are a big part of what we do here."

"We're trying to show the community that we are more than a collection of clichés," Linda said.

"Couldn't we turn this into an opportunity to inform and at the same time enjoy the fried deliciousness? Isn't that the point of all this?" Rayanne said.

"Aren't you usually the one leading the charge against frybread and all its postcolonial blah blah blah?" Ester said.

"I like fried food sometimes," Rayanne said.

"I'll think about it," Linda said. "What else?"

"We're working on confirming folks for the staged events. Arnie found a great youth dance troupe that accepted our invitation. We have a traditional flute player and a couple of guitar players who sing folk songs. I had an idea for another act that might be considered unconventional but I think would add a fresh dynamic."

Rayanne made a face to try to discourage him from continuing.

"I know of a native rock band hip-hop fusion-y thing," Henry said.

"What does that mean?" Linda asked, a sour turn to her mouth. "Is it that loud music with yelling?"

"It can be," Henry said, pausing to think about it. "But it's more than that."

"I saw them," Rayanne said. "They aren't bad but I'm not sure they are the right fit."

"I think having a variety of music is a perfect fit. It would appeal to younger people who might not come to the festival otherwise," Henry said.

"I don't know," Linda said. "Are they popular? Would anyone have heard of them?"

"Outside of a small group of friends and family, I would have to say no."

"I don't hate the idea but this isn't the time for it," Linda said. "I'm afraid it might scare off more people than it would attract. But keep the suggestions coming."

Rayanne wanted to feel vindicated but the band meant a lot to Henry. It was tough not to feel traitorous.

If Henry was upset, he didn't show it. "Good enough. Everything's on track. Lots of loose ends to chase after but the big pieces are in place."

∼

AFTER THE MEETING, Henry followed Rayanne to their desk. He pointed his thumb to the back area. "Did we have something to finish up back there?" He knew nothing was going to happen at the office but he wanted to keep pretending it might.

Rayanne gave him a distracted pat on the arm, urging him to go work on his own. She sat at her computer and tapped on the keyboard.

"Don't worry, I'm not mad," he told her, and he meant it.

"I'm not worried." She searched her desk drawer for one of her files and tossed it on the desk next to her.

"However, you ladies are wrong about the band. I will make it my life's work to change your minds." Henry waited for her to react but whatever had captured her attention was the only thing that mattered. This woman was intense. Once she was headed in a certain direction, she wasn't going to change course.

"What can I do to help?" He went to her side so he could see the screen and rested a hand on her shoulder like friendly colleagues might.

Rayanne brushed his hand away. "Don't distract me. I just remembered this thing I have to take care of."

"Distract you?" Henry said, his heart a little tender and uncertain.

Rayanne looked up at him. "I like you, okay? We will spend more time together. I need to work on this. You're doing great. The food truck idea is genius. Don't cancel the frybread. Linda won't remember what she decided."

"I'm still not convinced I'm cut out for this," Henry said. He now understood why Rayanne got worked up, and panicked about her calendar and deadlines.

"You're fine. Give me some time here."

"What are you working on that has taken all of your attention?" Henry caught a needy edge to his voice.

"If you must know, I'm trying to get ahold of someone at home to see about elder housing for Grandpa. I think we have to put him on a waiting list but by the time he gets a spot, I'm sure he'll be ready."

"I didn't realize he wanted to go back home. I thought he wanted to stay here."

Rayanne typed into the computer.

"I thought Gus wanted to stay here. Did he tell you he's ready to go home?"

"He needs some help deciding what to do," Rayanne said. "He needs to be around his own people. I'm researching retirement communities around here, too, but I don't think he can afford them."

"Did you even talk to him about it?" Henry asked. "Maybe Gus has something to say about it."

Rayanne's jaw was tight. He'd never known a woman who could flip around between such extreme states, focused then furious, sweet then sexy-dangerous. He was jockeying for a switch to something milder. He attempted to project a calming sense of reason in the midst of a complicated moment.

"You saw how sad he was? And how confused?" Rayanne eyes were shiny. "What if that woman hadn't stopped to help him?"

"I think you're overreacting," Henry said, regretting the words as soon as they left his mouth.

"I don't care what you think," she said. "He's not your grandpa."

"You're right, I misspoke. What I'm saying is, maybe he would like more involvement in this himself."

"He doesn't know how to navigate all this."

Already Henry sensed the futility of this conversation. Rayanne had made up her mind. There was nothing he could do. She had a history with Gus. The best thing to do was trust her judgment.

"Too bad there isn't any such thing as a retirement community for Indians," Henry said.

"There is. It's called elder housing."

"I meant in the city."

Rayanne's eyes never left the computer screen but she lifted one hand and twirled a finger in the air. "That's what this is all about. That's what we're working toward. Or one of the things. That's why we need to impress Uncle Arnie and use his influence to find some check-wielding friends of Indians and convince them that this is the organization to write checks to."

Did she think he could influence Arnie? Did she think he didn't care about the future of the center? The festival would happen and he would move on and find a job he was better suited to and try to get the Beat Braves happening. What would she do if the center failed?

"If Gus goes home, would you go home too?"

Rayanne stopped typing. The silence settled between them. She put her hands to her head like she was nursing a world-class headache.

"I don't know," she said.

Ester beckoned from across the room.

Henry pointed to himself.

Yes, Ester nodded.

He followed her to her office.

"I got the proofs of the programs back from the printer," Ester said, handing him a piece of paper printed on each side. "Program is a generous description. It's more like brochure." She took it back from him and showed him how it folded into thirds. "Tells about the history and goals of the center. Offers a few grim statistics. We can't afford more, but then I don't know how many people would be willing to read a booklet about nonprofit programs."

"Good thinking," Henry said. "Shouldn't Rayanne be the one to check this?"

"She'll review it. I wanted to know what you thought." Henry realized she was waiting for him to say more.

"What about the stage acts?"

"I don't think the performance schedule will be finalized in time. If I do it like this, we can use them again at future events."

"I know nothing about designing programs. I have to trust you on this. How long have you known Rayanne?"

"That was a smooth transition," Ester said.

"That's what I was going for." Henry was startled by the panic creeping in over losing something that had barely started. They hadn't even talked about it. There was an attraction and they'd come together. It didn't have to be a big thing. Yet, already he couldn't bear the idea of being away from her.

"You're into her," Ester said.

"Yeah," Henry said.

"I haven't known her that long. She's super intense about the job. I've never seen her date. I know she had loser parents so maybe she has issues."

"You think I'm a loser?" Henry tried to see himself from Ester's point of view. His uncle giving him this job and him following Rayanne around, and asking for help on the most basic administrative tasks.

"Don't know you well enough to have an opinion on that. I thought that's the sort of information you were asking for. It would be difficult to understate what her work here means to her. She has insanely high standards and she expects everyone else to live up to them too. Don't be surprised if she's disappointed sometimes."

Henry, with no apartment, a crap car, and flimsy ambition. What did he have to offer someone like her? She knew what she wanted and he only knew what he didn't want.

"I guess I'd better get back to her checklists," he said.

Ester smiled in solidarity. "I got a Rayanne checklist of my own."

Henry turned to leave but she stopped him. "In my post-flood cleaning furor I found some video equipment. I'm sure it won't come as a surprise that it was donated and it's not great. But I'm cleaning it up. I thought we could use it to make a little movie about the arts festival. What do you think?"

"I like it," Henry said. "I'll try to come up with some bits to film."

28

Rayanne did the grocery shopping while Grandpa visited Earl in the rehab center. She had walked him in there hoping to find something in the experience she might use to kick-start a conversation about getting him into a better place to live. But the place where Earl was staying was the equivalent of a motel room described as clean and comfortable. There was no getting around it. It was an institutional place that cared for old people. He wasn't going to see himself in this situation.

The common rooms were decorated with light green chairs and coffee tables covered with well-worn magazines. The magazine covers featured either old people playing golf or celebrities that were only old by Hollywood standards, and had a wealthy lifestyle that could accommodate the challenges of aging.

Before she left for the store, Grandpa patted her arm and said, "Don't forget me here."

So how was she supposed to bring it up?

She had two shopping lists. One for Grandpa and one for the week's meal delivery. She put soup, oatmeal, and fruit in the cart. She was planning to make a couple of side salads to go with Henry's idea for elk barbecue sandwiches.

Henry.

Gorgeous Henry with the big strong arms and curious hands that took their time, never rushing. His warm mouth working across her body with endless teasing kisses. His heart thudded against her cheek when she collapsed on top of him afterward. A warm thrill spread through her and into the predictable places. She wouldn't have minded him coming over again but he needed to sort out his living situation, and she needed to keep her head on straight. She was not going to be that woman who took care of guys who couldn't take care of themselves.

She snorted out loud over that one.

But Grandpa was different. Grandpa was family. Grandma and Grandpa had taken care of her and made so many sacrifices. She wanted to do the same for him.

She checked the time and wrapped up the shopping. By the time she returned to the rehab center, Grandpa was waiting out front.

"Did something go wrong?" Rayanne asked.

"No," Grandpa said, his voice bright, "Earl is doing good. He's a tough old coot."

"Your words or the staff?"

"Mine. He said he wants to go back to his house. His kids are telling him it's time to stop living on his own. I don't know what they're thinking. This is the first time something happened. Once he's back on his feet, he'll be good as always. He's doing all the physical therapy and extra if they let him."

"What about you?"

"What about me?" Grandpa's voice suddenly sounded at least four times stronger. She was conscious of not wanting to make him angry. Their relationship had always been smooth because Grandpa had always left the hard parts to Grandma. He was never around when Rayanne sassed back about breaking curfew, or insisted on wearing denim short shorts, or brought home a poor grade because she didn't get along with the teacher. Grandpa never weighed in on those battles. He was the one who watched Westerns with her when she was home sick. He would stick a couple of twenty-dollar bills into her pocket when she went back to college after a break.

Since Rayanne graduated, they shared meals together and they still watched Westerns. But now some serious issues were creeping up and they would have to figure out how to navigate them together.

"I'm worried about you, is all," Rayanne said.

"Not needed," Grandpa said. "I'm slow but I get around. You got years before you need to worry about me."

"Grandpa." Rayanne let a pleading tone creep into her voice.

"You're not putting me in a home."

"No one is talking about a home. You were so sad about losing your friends. I thought you might want to talk about elder housing."

"When you're young, there's something almost magical about elders. They seem so wise and fragile. Becoming one happened faster than I expected and not much fun."

Rayanne didn't know how to respond.

"I wonder if they was all as cranky and impatient inside. Your body doesn't always do what you expect it to do. I get tired."

"We all get a turn," Rayanne said.

"If we's lucky," Grandpa said. "I like my apartment. I like everything the way it is." There was no mistaking the finality of that statement.

"Okay," Rayanne said. "What about other options? A helper to stop by?"

"I don't need as much help as you think I do. I get around fine." Grandpa's voice got louder. "The other night I got a little mixed up and then it got dark. I would have found my way home. Don't treat me like I'm helpless."

Rayanne heard pain and betrayal in his voice. This is not how she wanted this to go.

"Forget I brought it up." Rayanne pulled up to his apartment. Grandpa popped the door open and struggled with the seatbelt buckle. It pained her to do so but, instead of helping him, she got out and grabbed the grocery bags from the trunk.

Grandpa managed to spring himself loose. He headed off for his apartment at a good clip. He could move fast when he wanted to. She followed him and at first he tried to close the door on her.

"What are you doing? I have your groceries."

"Leave them out there, I'll get them later," he said.

"Knock it off. I'm the only family you have left," she said, her voice catching.

Grandpa retreated. He watched her put the groceries on the table. "I can put them away myself."

"I don't mind. It'll take a second." Rayanne pulled a couple cans of soup out of one bag and carried them to the cupboard.

"I said I'd do it," Grandpa said, an anger in his eyes she hadn't seen since her mom was around and making life miserable.

Rayanne set the cans down. "Go ahead. Do it yourself."

"It's time for you to go," he went on. He pointed at the door. "Go on now."

She'd seen this same drama play out once before. But that time it was her mom being shown the door. Only her mom had been an addict and a thief. She was mean, too, trying to hurt all of them. She had accused Rayanne of being a terrible daughter for not wanting to live with her, but she couldn't keep a stable household for herself.

That was a different situation. Rayanne was none of these things.

"I don't want you to barge in here any old time without calling first. I don't want you to go around behind my back thinking you're going to *arrange things*."

She searched for the right words, desperate to fix this now. She couldn't stand the idea of leaving with him so angry with her.

"I didn't mean to—"

Grandpa shook his head. He wouldn't meet her eyes.

"Call me if I can do anything," she said as she left. Her heart was breaking as she shut the door behind her.

29

The entire drive to his mom's, Henry flipped through various versions of the story, searching for the one she would respond to best. She had a low opinion of any deflection of blame. There was no such thing as something that wasn't your fault. A man had to take responsibility for his decisions. Henry should have been searching for a better living situation all along. He should have been better with money when he had a good job. He shouldn't have moped around after he got laid off. He should try to make friends with people who were going places. Somehow he had to guess the future of people around him, if he was going to be truly responsible.

He parked the van but couldn't muster the courage to get out right away.

They'd already had this conversation. More than once. After he finished college, she agreed he could move back while he searched for a job. She even said she liked having him around again. He made dinner for her a couple nights a week, and they would have adult conversations about current events or local politics.

He'd been lucky to find a job right away. He hadn't even known what he was looking for, so parts clerk sounded okay. And that's what it was, okay. He found an apartment. He paid his bills. He went out with his friends. And he didn't hate it but he could sense a little bit of his soul being torn away every day. He was secretly relieved when he'd been laid off, assuming he'd find something better.

She'd let him move back, and the second time was a disaster. He ignored her rules. He left dishes in the sink. He stayed out too late and slept in too long. Then she told him he was turning into a loser like his dad. And the worst part was, she didn't seem surprised or disappointed. When she said the words, it was like she had confirmation of something she had always known.

He simultaneously hated her for saying that and was struck deep in his heart, because the way things were going, she was right. That was when he'd moved into the place with Jack and worked his various odd jobs. He and Mom forged a precarious truce. And here he was, in a rough patch, daring to ask for help again.

Mom made an unhappy noise when he came in. "What's the bad news?"

Henry might have kept it light and even made a joke about it, but Mom was asking for the story. "They threw us out. They took all our things and threw them on the ground. They locked us out." It was as painful to talk about now as it was explaining it to Rayanne.

"This was today?"

"Yesterday."

"Where did you stay last night?"

He should have been ready for the question but it caught him by surprise. If it took him too long to answer, she would figure it out with her special mom-perception.

"With the guys," he said. "But they're already overcrowded. I can't stay there again."

"I'm sorry to hear that."

She waited. She was going to make him ask. She wasn't going to offer.

"Can I stay here until I can find a place?"

She shook her head. "Sorry, sweetie. I know this is a kick when you're down but remember, we had a deal." There was no joy in her voice.

Henry stared at her, astonished. "But this is a special circumstance. They gave us a short warning and then they threw us out. For real. It takes time to find an apartment." He hoped she wouldn't ask how many places they'd looked at because anything less than a hundred would be a disappointment to her.

Mom sat there, unmoved.

"The deal was I had to get a job. I have a job."

"Arnie said you didn't even want the job."

"Well, I'm doing it, aren't I?" Henry said. And to think not long ago he was scheming to get out of it.

Mom didn't say a word. This was one of her tricks. He would have to speak first.

"What do you expect me to do? Live in the van?"

She leaned against the kitchen counter and flipped through her bills. She didn't care what happened to him.

"Fine. I will. Can I park near here so I can use the bathroom once in a while, or should I go to the park with the other homeless people? I guess I can use paper towels to bathe in the restroom at work."

"You may stay here."

Henry sagged with relief. He wasn't ready to be the guy who lived in his car.

"Tonight. Like a house guest. Tomorrow you figure something out. That includes living in the van. You're a grownup now, a fact you have reminded me of on numerous occasions."

He should be grateful but having a place to stay for one night wasn't a big help. "How about until the weekend? I can't apartment hunt while I'm at work." He understood why she was doing it but it's not like he wasn't trying. He kept his anger hidden.

"You need to be out of here next weekend," she said.

"Thanks, Mom."

"Before you 'thanks, Mom' me, here are the rules. You go to that job every day. You tidy up everything. I don't want to find even an eyelash in the sink. No guests. Exemplary consideration during any hours I might be sleeping."

"I got it," Henry said. "You won't know I'm here."

"I need you to remember you're living with your mom, not a roommate. But that doesn't include meal or laundry service."

~

HE BROUGHT his stuff into the back yard and shook it out. Almost everything needed to be washed. Mom clarified she wouldn't do the laundry for him but she didn't mind if he ran the washer himself. There must have been a crumb of mom-ness left in her because she came out and helped him sort through it.

"People are terrible," she said. She shook the towels out over the lawn.

Earlier, when he was desperate for her sympathy, he'd thought about telling her about the whoops and the slurs. But now he was glad he left that part out.

He threw in the first load, then they worked together, sorting out the rest. A few things were torn or smeared with grease and needed to be tossed.

"I have a bedspread in the linen closet you can take," she said.

"Thanks, Mom."

She made easy small talk, asking about the job and people he was working with. He told her about all his colleagues, mentioning Rayanne as part of the group. He told her about the meals program, making it sound like something the center did rather than Rayanne's personal project.

"Do they use volunteers?" Mom asked.

"They love volunteers. Why?"

"I've been thinking about getting involved in something. I don't know what. A book group or volunteer at the food bank. Something to keep me from shriveling up here by myself."

He'd never heard her complain about being alone before. "Everything is upside down while we're moving, but once we get to the new building there will be lots of community-type things you would like."

"That sounds nice. You'll have to keep me informed. Good night."

She put an arm around his shoulder and kissed the side of his head before leaving him to work on his own.

He took a load out of the dryer and folded the warm clothes, his thoughts drifting back to Rayanne. The way her skin tasted and the way her hands felt when she reached for him. The shocked noises she made and the sound of her voice in his ear when they were finished. She probably would have let him stay again if he'd asked. But he didn't want to be the loser that mooched off her. He wanted to earn her.

30

*H*enry found Rayanne's stack of elder services information on his side of the desk. Her side of the desk was piled with binders and dividers for whatever today's project was.

Henry sorted through the collection of pamphlets and printouts that listed what other tribal organizations were doing. There were programs for transportation, financial management and family support, recreation, and elder rights advocates. He stopped to flip through a brochure on in-home helpers. The list went on and on. She had bright-colored sticky flags on grants and pilot projects. He restacked everything into a neat pile and set it aside.

Rayanne arrived in a dark mood. He brought her a cup of coffee. There was sadness behind her eyes that he wanted to hug away. He settled for running his index finger along her arm until her look made him take his hand back.

"Things didn't go well with Grandpa?" he asked.

"It was awful," she said, an edge to her voice. "He yelled at me. He never yells at me."

"You two ever get like this before?"

"Not like this, no," Rayanne said. "He told me I can't drop by anymore. I have to call first. Then he told me to leave." A tear slipped out and she wiped it away. "I think it will blow over. You were right. I need to let him make these decisions. I hoped we could figure out something together. What if something bad happens? How will I know what to do?" She grabbed a tissue and blotted her eyes. "How about you? How did things go with your mom?"

"Also poorly. First she said no. I keep joking about living in the van and, for a minute, I thought it was coming true. Mom is tough-loving me hard on this one. I convinced her to give me until next weekend to find a place. I have a bed a few more nights."

"I wouldn't have minded if you showed up at my place," Rayanne said into his ear.

Henry could tell she meant it. "I don't want us to be like that. Me, a desperate loser hanging out with so little to offer. You, having it all together and acting out of pity."

Rayanne tilted her face to him and leaned closer. "It's not like I wouldn't be taking it out in trade. But I appreciate what you're saying."

A surge of warmth flooded an area he would rather stay calm while they were at the office. "We need to stay out of trouble," he said.

"That crow has flown the nest," she said with a laugh. She spotted the elder materials. "Did you go through that? I've got some great leads for funding. Do you want to learn how to write a grant?"

"That sounds super boring."

"That's not the way to look at it. What you're doing is writing a report to persuade someone to give you some money so you can accomplish something. If you decide to stick around here for the long term, we'll get you into a class. Linda and I both want to hire someone full time but, as it turns out, you need money to hire someone to go out and get you money."

"That's a job? Full time grant-writing?" Henry couldn't imagine the kind of person who would do something like that.

"Indeed, that person could coordinate with all of us for what we're planning. Like Tommy developing youth resources and Ester's health stuff. A full-time person can research different kinds of opportunities. Also help with reporting because that's a big piece. Very few organizations will hand you money and tell you to do whatever you want with it."

Linda rushed out of her office and threw her purse over her shoulder. "Margie called. There's a bird in her house. She said it wasn't bothering her but I'm afraid she might change her mind and then trip over herself trying to get it out. I don't think I have it in me to deal with Margie hurt again."

"I can help Margie," Henry said.

Linda didn't hide her surprise.

"He doesn't want to learn how to write grants," Rayanne explained.

Linda laughed. "You think you don't, but you do. That is a terrific skill to have and would be a great addition to your résumé. But since it would help me out, I'm going to take you up on it. You're going to have to make a stop. She said she needs some light bulbs changed."

"Sure," Henry said. "Which kind?"

Linda shrugged. "Get whatever the most common kinds are."

Henry was tempted to tell her that wasn't much to go on but if she didn't know, she didn't know. He could stock up on a variety. "Remind me again her address."

Linda gave him the information and then directions with an alternate route if he wanted to avoid the busy intersection at Branson and 45th.

"So, it's not just my mom. Every Ind'n woman wants to tell me exactly how I should be doing things," he said. "I think I can find it."

"Good, I'll let her know to expect you."

He stopped at the hardware store and then headed over to Margie's.

While she was holding the door open for him, the bird chirped three times and flew out. It was only a sparrow but the flapping wings made him flinch as it went by.

"That was easy," Margie said.

"Glad I could help. Sparrow is my spirit animal."

"You look more like a buck to me," Margie said. "It was a little thing but Linda likes to fuss. Come on in. I got other things for you to do."

Henry held up the light bulbs. "So I was warned."

"Yes, light bulbs. But I got this chair I want moved." She worked her way down the hallway, steadying herself on one piece of furniture before launching herself to the next. "I got my kids coming over when they can, but all three of them live out of town and they got their own things to do. That one there." Margie pointed to an overstuffed chair that didn't look like something anyone would actually sit on.

"Where did you want it?"

Margie waved until he picked it up and then shuffled back out of the room. "My oldest daughter wants me to sell this place and move in with her. That's sweet but I don't know anyone in her town except her family." She used her cane to indicate a steep downward stairway. "Down there."

Henry fumbled for a better grip on the chair and sidestepped down to the basement. The basement had finished walls and carpeting. There was a main room and a smaller room and a tiny bathroom.

Margie tossed her cane down the stairs. She grabbed the arm rails on either side of the staircase and set out down the stairs, one unsteady step at a time.

"Wait," Henry said. "I have an obligation to your children and Linda to insist that you don't need to come down here. I am acquainted with several of the most stubborn Ind'n women on the planet so I realize that you will pay me no heed."

By this time Margie had made it to the bottom of the stairs. She made her way as far as the chair and sat down with some force. "I could tell you were a smart one." She took her cane when he handed it her.

She sighed and glanced around the room. There was a pile of rolled-up rugs and a lamp without a shade. There were a couple of fussy tables with scuffed surfaces.

"This was the kids' place when they were here," she told him. "They watched TV and played games. When they got bigger, my oldest had that room. Can you take that lamp and those tables to Goodwill?"

Henry flipped one over for a closer look. The tables had fancy

185

curved legs but were solid. "I know some poor Indians who could use these."

"Even better," Margie said.

She waited downstairs while he carried them up and loaded them into the van. He went back down and helped her to her feet. "If you don't mind, I'm going to make sure you get back upstairs in one piece. Linda will kill me if you get hurt on my account."

Margie waved him off. "*Pfft*. She doesn't know what I'm up to. You should see the wobbly stool I use to get things off the high shelves in the kitchen." Off Henry's stricken look she added, "It's a joke."

Back upstairs she insisted on giving Henry a jar of canned salmon. As they stood at the door, Margie said, "No pity for me. I'm doing fine."

31

*A*rnie ran from the attorney's office to his rig. He threw the paperwork on the seat beside him and plugged in his phone so he could go hands-free. He dialed the center.

"Rayanne? I need to talk to Linda."

"Did everything go okay?"

"I successfully picked up a pile of paper from the attorneys, if that's what you mean. I would advise against celebrating until the papers are signed. I'm on my way. Does Linda need a ride?"

"But there weren't any problems. The attorneys didn't mention anything that might go wrong?"

"I answered your question. Can I talk to Linda?"

"Hang on."

Rayanne said something he couldn't make out followed by a series of muffled crunches and then more indistinct voices.

"Put Linda on the phone," he muttered.

"Arnie? Still there? She wants to talk to you."

"I want to talk to her, too," Arnie said.

"Hey," Linda said when she got on the line.

"You sound like you ran a road race."

"No. I was on the phone trying to schedule a moving company. No luck yet, but no new catastrophes at this time. Everyone is staring at me expectantly. How did it go?"

"We went over everything. We're good to go."

"Can you pick me up?"

"I should be there in fifteen."

"Fifteen? *Eek.* That's cutting it close."

"I guess it's time to press this little red button on the dashboard that says, 'Super Sonic Speed' and see what happens."

Linda laughed. "If that's what it takes."

"They aren't going to stop the sale because we're a few minutes late," Arnie said.

"I know. But we've worked for this for so long. I want the meeting to be perfect."

"I'll see you in twelve minutes."

"I'll be waiting out front."

Arnie disconnected the call. He wished he hadn't had that last cup of coffee. His hands were jittery on the wheel. He alternated, wiping first one hand and then the other on his slacks. He had no problem navigating in city traffic but now he felt tense and uncertain with the time frame and Linda counting on him. When he'd volunteered to join the center, he'd doubted their chances of success. Now he found himself surprised that everything had come together. He and Linda worked well together. He couldn't wait to see what they could accomplish going into the future.

As promised, Linda waited out front. She had on the same yellow dress and long beaded earrings that she'd worn for the retreat. The same dress that had gone translucent when she'd been caught in the sprinklers. The woman he'd always thought of as bookish had some intriguing curves.

But I'm not supposed to think of her like that.

The strain of the past couple weeks showed in her face. Once they signed the papers, there would be another wave of intense work to do, but maybe the weight of this unsolved problem hanging over her would be a relief.

He pulled into the parking lot and waited for her to get in. As soon as she was strapped in, she pulled the documents on her lap and paged through them.

"Attorneys are notoriously detail-oriented about that kind of stuff."

"I believe you," she said, her eyes never leaving the documents. "It relaxes me to go over completed paperwork."

Arnie laughed. "And people say that I have a pitiful life."

"You know what I mean. I can't decide what I want to do first when the papers are signed."

"Celebratory dinner?" he asked.

"You and me?" Something in the air between them stretched tight. The suggestion took on additional meaning. Now that the invitation was out, Arnie realized he would be disappointed if she said no.

She stopped shuffling through the documents and stared straight ahead. "I had planned to go home, put on sweatpants, and pour a glass of wine to go with my bowl of cookie dough."

"I'd hate to spoil that," Arnie said, feigning indifference to diffuse the situation. The last thing they needed was to be weird during their meeting with the city.

"Those weren't firm plans. I could rearrange for a celebratory dinner."

"Great," Arnie said, his voice a little too loud. "I know this place that has great burgers. All the cool kids go there."

"How did you find out about it?"

Arnie smiled. "To be honest, Henry took me there."

"Ah, Henry. Surprising us at every turn."

"Is he surprising you?"

"So far he's doing great," Linda said.

"Whew. I thought he was capable but I believe you'd tell me if he was a blithering idiot."

"He's not even close to an idiot."

"Good." Arnie pulled into the parking garage at City Hall. "Let's go buy a building."

~

LINDA'S HEART pounded as they moved through the wide hallways of the city building. The floors reminded her of her elementary school, polished to a shine. Their steps echoed in the quiet space.

"This would be like working in a morgue," she whispered to Arnie.

"Why are you whispering?" Arnie whispered back.

They both laughed. "What was the contact name in the email?" Linda asked.

"I don't know. I thought you were getting the email."

A chill went up her spine as if they were on a high wire and the net had just fallen away. "They didn't send an email. They don't even know we're coming."

"Nonsense," Arnie said.

The security gate was open but there was no officer in sight. Linda expected they would wait, but instead, Arnie put his hand on the small of her back and guided her through.

"Should we be doing this?" she asked.

"Shhh. Kayla told us to be here. They're expecting us." He pointed to the stairs.

On the second floor, they searched for the room. No one stopped them or even acknowledged they were there.

"There it is," she said. A rectangular sign said 2112 in white letters. There were Braille letters below and she ran her fingers over them and imagined she could make sense of the bumps.

"No one is here," she said.

"Maybe not *here*," Arnie said. He glanced up and down the hallway. It was close to the end of the day on a Friday so there weren't many people around.

"Maybe she wrote down the wrong room," Linda said.

"We can hope," Arnie muttered. "Do you want to wait here?"

"We're about ten minutes late. Maybe we should find someone to help us."

It took them several tries and they had to go up another flight of stairs before they found an office with an open door and a person inside. The same young woman who had helped them on their previous visit sat at a computer screen with headphones on.

"Is she the only person who works here?" Linda whispered.

"That's what I was wondering," Arnie whispered back, close enough that she could feel his breath on her ear.

Kayla glanced up and saw them, but it took her a minute to finish whatever she was working on. She lifted off one ear pad.

"Can I help you?"

Linda couldn't believe the blank stare. The woman had to recognize them. She wasn't sure what to say.

"Kayla? Hi. Remember me? I'm Arnie Jackson. This is Linda Bird. We're from the Crooked Rock Urban Indian Center. We talked to you last week about a meeting today? We're here to finalize purchase of the Chief building."

Kayla hesitated, then removed the headphones and got up. "I'll be back in a minute."

She walked back to an office they couldn't see. There was a hushed conversation and then the *thump* of a closing door.

When she returned, she looked like a person put in charge of something she considered above her pay grade.

"Sorry no one informed you. The meeting was canceled."

"Canceled?" Arnie said. "How come?"

She took a deep breath. "I was told the City Commissioners voted to terminate the agreement."

"That can't possibly be correct." Linda heard herself say it calmly but blood rushed in her ears.

The young woman shrugged. "That's what I was told."

"But the deal is complete. That's why we're here. We're signing off." She held up the documents from the attorneys to illustrate how serious she was.

"I guess there was a misunderstanding."

"You've got to be kidding me," Arnie said, his voice rising. "This is supposed to be a done deal. Who voted to terminate the agreement? None of those people have the balls to come here and tell us themselves?"

Kayla swallowed and she took a few steps back. "I'm just saying what I was told."

"Could we please set up another meeting?" Linda said. "They owe us that. They offered to sell us a building. They strung us along while we did everything they asked, some of it at a financial cost to our organization."

"I'll ask," she said.

Arnie wasn't having any of it. He didn't know how intimidating he could be when he was angry. "None of those cowards will talk to us? Are they hiding back there? What if we went back there?"

Linda reached for his hand. "Don't," she said quietly. To Kayla she said, "Tell them we asked for an explanation in writing. That's the least they can do for us."

"I know," Kayla said. Her distress appeared genuine.

Linda pulled Arnie toward the door. His hand trembled in hers and she shared his simmering rage. She'd seen him like this one other time. In college, at a Native Students Association meeting. She and Arnie referred to the students who identified as tribal descendants but had no connection with their native communities as box-checkers. The topic of the meeting had been something divisive. A cowboys-and-Indians-themed dorm party or something like that. One of the box-checkers told Arnie he was too serious and to let someone else have a chance to speak. Arnie had lost it, screaming and insulting the guy.

City Hall was not the time for screaming or insults, especially at some poor woman given the task of delivering an undesirable message.

"We're not going to fix it today," she said. "Let's go."

Arnie took a deep breath. She changed the grip so her fingers were interlaced with his and squeezed his hand. At last the fight went out of him and he let her lead him out.

3 2

*R*ayanne waited while Henry passed a menu to Ester. "It's all miniature foods," he said.

Tommy had already grabbed one from the center of the table. Henry inched his chair closer to Rayanne so they could share. Having him next to her was soothing after a long week of work setbacks and family drama.

"They'd have to with tables this small." Ester exaggerated the motion of her elbows sliding off the edge.

The bar was in the rundown part of town in a narrow room with a high ceiling and dim lights. The four of them were crammed together at a table better suited for two. Henry's thigh pressed against hers. He dropped his hand to her leg and rested it there, the weight of it a promise for later.

Tommy kept flipping the menu over, as if the real food options might be on the other side. "Miniature hamburgers? How do you even find out about these places?"

"I like different things," Henry said, "and I'm always broke so I do a lot of research. Everything is good here."

"He's right about the prices," Ester said.

Rayanne scanned the choices. "What's the miniature pizza like?"

Henry moved his hand from her leg and drew a circle on his other palm with his first finger. She was the one who insisted they keep it cool in front of their colleagues and here she was with the starry-eyed gaze. He'd better be coming home with her.

"Does it have tiny pepperoni?" Ester said. "I want tiny pepperoni."

"I think it's ground-up meat for the topping," Henry said.

"*Phoo*," Ester said. "I want to try a bunch of things."

"Each plate comes with four. We can pass it around."

Rayanne folded her hands in front of her. "I can't decide. You pick. I trust you."

Ester handed back her menu. "I want to try different things as long as one of them is pizza."

Tommy shook his head. "I wish I could watch this cook making a tiny burger. Do they use scissors to cut the bacon?"

"It's made from tiny pigs," Henry said.

The server came and took their order. When he left, Henry said to Tommy, "What was your drink order?"

"I believe you would call it a mocktail," Tommy said. He waved a hand in the air in a *you know how it goes* gesture. "I can't stay long anyway."

Rayanne caught Henry's nod of comprehension. When she'd first met Tommy, she'd worried about inviting him to get-togethers like this. But Tommy had been sober since before he was legal.

"What sort of super-secret mission are you up to tonight?" Ester asked.

"Can't tell you," Tommy said. "Gotta keep secrets, you know, due to my dangerous past."

They all laughed because Tommy's easygoing bearing and slight build made him come across as more likely to be a victim than a criminal.

"I remember when I met you, I wondered how they'd transplanted kitten eyes into your head," Ester said.

"I do have adorable eyes," Tommy agreed. "That's why I'm so successful with my crimes."

The server brought their drinks. Henry squeezed Rayanne's leg before taking his hand away. She missed it as soon as it was gone.

"Shall we toast?" she said, holding up her beer. "Three cheers for the new building."

They *hip, hip, hooray'd* and clinked their glasses together.

"Hard to believe this is all coming together after everything we've been through," Ester said.

"What all have you been through?" Henry asked. "Besides living out of boxes and surprise flooding."

"Losing Margie," Rayanne said. "New board members foisted upon us with their pushy ideas and family members who need jobs."

Henry lifted his beer again. "I'll drink to that."

"At one point some folks in the community opposed the center because they were worried about having those kinds of people gathered around," Ester said.

In response to Henry's shocked look, she held up one hand. "Honest Injun."

"It wasn't a lot of people and we were able to educate them on what the organization is about," Rayanne said.

Tommy turned to Henry. "Now that you've hung out with us, for better or worse, what do you think of our ragtag operation?"

Rayanne was curious to hear his response. The two of them never discussed the job in that way. He'd stuck around because he had to; she'd never asked what he thought now that he'd settled in. Henry took his time before answering.

"At first I didn't get what you were all about," Henry said. "Arnie works with Indian people on the rez but I never thought about people in the city. I don't know what I can do. But I think I want to stick around."

He ducked his head as if he'd gotten caught saying something he wasn't supposed to do. An unexpected wave of relief washed over her knowing he wanted to stay.

"As soon as we get in that building, we'll be able to do real things," Rayanne said. "What kind of programs would you want to do?"

"I'm not sure how it would work but I was thinking about

outreach. To people like me and my mom who are so disconnected we don't even know we're disconnected. I guess the more social and recreational things."

"You want the fun stuff," Ester said.

"It doesn't have to be the fun stuff. I want to learn about fundraising and all the dull paperwork too. I have more ideas but I'm getting my bearings for how it all works."

"Not bad," Tommy said. "We were worried you were a worthless mouth-breather when we found out you were getting the job because you were Arnie's nephew."

Henry's body tensed. At some point she should confess that 'worthless mouth-breather' came from her.

"Glad to hear I defeated your expectations," Henry said. He took a long swig from his beer.

"We like you now," Rayanne said.

Ester snorted but before she could say more, the server arrived with plates of miniature food. They passed around hotdogs the size of an index finger and tacos that could be put away with two bites.

Ester prodded the meat flecks on her pizza. "They could get a paper puncher for the pepperoni. Punch out little round holes."

"I think I saw a suggestion box by the hostess station," Tommy said.

The food was a delicious surprise. It wasn't cheap bar-food made smaller; it was delicious food attracting attention to itself by its compact package. The hotdog had a rich, meaty flavor and the relish had a citrusy tang. The tacos were spicy pulled pork with some sort of vegetable slaw.

"This is incredible," Rayanne said.

"I'm glad you like it," Henry said, staring into her eyes with pure lust.

"*Gah!* You two," Ester said. She crammed a taco into her mouth and washed it down with beer.

"Wait, *huh?*" Tommy said, looking from Rayanne to Henry. Rayanne directed her attention back to her food, a warm flush creeping into her face. She could sense Henry's megawatt grin without even seeing it.

"What do you mean, *huh?*" Ester said. "You can smell it coming off them. Look, some shiny bits dislodged and floated to the floor." They all looked to the place that she pointed and laughed.

"Where was I while this was going on?" Tommy sucked the last of his mocktail from the glass.

"You were there," Ester said. "It started about fifteen seconds after Mr. Tall-Dark-and-Flirty showed up at our the office."

Ester's nickname made Rayanne sink into her seat even more.

"No, it didn't," Henry said. "I had some graduate coursework in wooing to do. Still doing it. But she's worth it."

"I don't know how much longer I can watch," Ester said.

"Stop," Rayanne said, not sure why she was so embarrassed. She tried to pull away from Henry but he would shift into the space she vacated.

Rayanne managed to shift the subject and got Ester talking about the short films she was making about the center. They traded stories about college and then talk shifted to apartment hunting.

"Rent in this town has become a joke," Tommy said. "We can afford it but it takes such a hunk of my money."

"Same," Ester said. "I have roommates. Not ideal but until I find my dream cheap studio in the perfect location without bars on the windows, I am stuck with what I have."

Both Tommy and Ester had suggestions for Henry if he stuck with Jack, or if he ended up trying to find a place on his own.

Rayanne glanced around the room. The bar was filled with young people, like them, talking and laughing. How many times had she sat outside a group, like the one she was in, with longing? She had felt like a social outsider since she'd moved to the city. But tonight she was one of them, hanging out with a group of peers, sharing jokes, having a good time.

Tommy got up and threw some cash on the table. "It was fun, guys, but I'm going to go home and be mysterious. Catch you Monday."

Ester shoved the last bite of her burger into her mouth and finished her beer. "I'm not about to be the third wheel. I'm going to go home and be alone. Again." She waved her card at the server. "And by alone I mean with my roommates who are probably at this minute drinking my milk and eating something that no matter what it is, it will get all over the couch."

"If they have friends who need a roommate, don't tell them about me," Henry said.

"Don't worry." Ester flicked her eyes between them. "You two make a good team. I'm rooting for you."

"Thanks, Ester," Henry said with a happy grin.

"Settle down," Rayanne said. To Ester she said, "It would be fun to get some video footage of the Chief before we move in and then again after."

"I'm going to," Ester said. "I want to try to make a short film about the whole thing. Our little gang of four. Five if this guy sticks around." She nodded at Henry. "I'm going to keep working on it and see where we're at in a year or two."

The server returned with Ester's debit card. Ester stuck it in her wallet and then gave them a wicked smile. "I'm out of here. Don't do anything I wouldn't do. But if you do, name it after me."

*W*hen they got back to her place, Henry lingered at the door as if he were dropping her off.

"You coming in?" Rayanne asked.

"Am I invited?"

"Are you a vampire? You can't come in without an invitation?"

"Would you like for me to be a vampire?" He gave her a theatrical come-hither look.

Rayanne took a moment to appreciate the sight of him filling her doorway. The confident set of his shoulders and his arms crossed over his chest. His mouth curved into a knowing half-smile. But beneath the bluster she detected uncertainty. He needed to hear she wanted him.

"Vampires aren't my thing," she said.

"Something else? Fireman? Or maybe you'd prefer a congressman? Don't ask me to be a cowboy." He opened his arms, reaching for an embrace but he didn't cross the threshold.

"Maybe I like cowboys," she said, giving him a sexy smile. She gestured for him to come in.

He came inside and she shut the door behind him. He tangled his fingers through her hair and tilted her head up to his. "You like Indians."

"I do," she agreed. She closed her eyes and let her hands find his waist and rested them there.

He took his time, brushing his lips across hers and along her jaw and kissing a line to the crease in her neck.

She sighed and let him continue another minute before she pushed him back against the wall.

"This okay?" She pulled his head back down to hers and breathed into him before dipping her tongue into his mouth and waiting for him to meet her. His hands hung at his sides.

She let him come up for air.

"I thought I was doing pretty good," Henry said.

"You were doing great. I thought I would do some things." Her hands worked at his belt buckle. She didn't even pull his pants down. She reached in and grabbed him. "I guess you could say I'm process oriented."

His body shuddered with surprise. He closed his eyes and groaned. He managed to say, "I think you've got that backwards. At the moment I would say you're results oriented."

"Oh, is that what I am? I can never tell the difference." She loved the way he leaned against the door, half-helpless. "I like it when the guy makes some noise." She pressed her lips against his and worked her tongue back into his mouth.

He pulled away long enough to say, "It's hard to moan and groan if I think you're waiting for it. It should come about naturally."

"It's not a demand, just sharing what I like." She stroked him until he groaned again.

"That sounded natural," she whispered against his mouth. He stayed slumped against the wall while she worked her way down and went down on him, sloppy and urgent. She was pleased when he clenched her hair in his hands again and she took her time until he urged her back to her feet.

She yanked at his shirt until he pulled it over his head. She paused to stroke her hands over his chest. He put his hands over hers.

"I'm going to do some things now," he said. He moved away from the wall so he could pick her up. She wrapped her legs around him and he waddled a couple of steps toward the bedroom.

"This looks a lot easier in the movies," he said. His pants were tangled around his ankles.

"Put me down before you break both our necks," Rayanne said. "Can you imagine the headlines? 'Freak accident claims the lives of two promising young Natives.' The things people would be whispering at our funerals."

Henry laughed. "About me they would say, 'At least he died doing what he loved.'" He set her down and, after a few ungraceful attempts to kick off his pants, he had to sit down on the floor to take off his shoes. "This getting you going?" he asked from his undignified position.

"It's all getting me going." She helped him up and he stripped off her clothes and picked her up again. This time he managed to carry her to the bed. He found the pirate chest himself and threw a couple condoms on the pillows.

"I got a little trick I'm going to show you called the Chippewa flip."

"You made that up," Rayanne said, her arms reaching for him.

"Did I? Why don't you find out if you like it before you worry about its origins." He put on a condom and lowered himself onto her. She tilted her hips up to meet him and they joined together in a daze of warm friction, their breaths quickening together.

After a spell, she kissed his ear and whispered "I have my own special occasion move. I call it the Seminole squeeze."

Henry sucked in his breath and then gasped in her ear and she along with him. He collapsed on top of her.

"So who was in charge of that one?" he said, when he caught his breath.

"We're a good team," Rayanne said. "Like Ester said."

"Everything I do, I do better when I'm with you," he said. He rolled off of her and spooned her from behind, his arm curled around her and his hand caressing her belly.

"I'll have to come up with some new stuff to try," she said, sleepier than she wanted to be. The events of the week had caught up with her. His chest pressed to her back was pure warm comfort.

"Did you mean what you said earlier?" she asked.

"Which thing are you referring to?"

"About wanting to stick with the job."

"I think I mean it. I never pictured myself doing anything like that but maybe I do have something to offer. Is that okay?"

"That's great," she said. They were pressed tight but she tried to snuggle deeper into his embrace. "What do you want to do this weekend?"

"I have got to find a stupid apartment," he said.

"Oh," she said. "Yeah, I suppose we can't spend all our time doing this."

"I can fit plenty of this in. Don't you worry."

"I need to deal with Grandpa. We did not leave things very well. I'm hoping he's cooled off and will be happy to see me." The angry flash in his eyes and his harsh words echoed in her memory.

"He's your grandpa. Of course he'll be thrilled to see you."

"You can stay for a while," she said, meaning stay at her place. She liked having him here.

"I hope so," Henry said. "I have no idea where my pants are." It went unspoken that he had no place to go. He threaded his fingers into hers. "I know what you meant and I appreciate it, but I promise I will find my own place. I need to find my own place."

"Is your mom going to care if you don't come home?"

"Probably. She doesn't want me to live there but if I do, I have to report in. I'll text her I'm sleeping on a friend's couch so she knows I didn't fall off a bridge or end up in jail."

Rayanne squeezed his hand. "I'm sleepy now but if you wake up later, wake me up too."

He kissed her neck. "As you command."

34

*R*ayanne called ahead like Grandpa asked and was not surprised when there was no answer. She waited an hour and tried again. Still no answer. She waited thirty more minutes and when the phone rang and rang and went to voicemail a third time, she left a message telling him she was on her way.

In the days since they'd argued, she'd come to understand his anger. She had swooped in with her elder care educational brochures, and her experiences with Margie's kids, and she thought she had all the answers. The one person she hadn't consulted with was the grand old man himself. She'd grown up with him and witnessed daily his strong will. Like an idiot, she tried to tell him what he needed. She couldn't treat old age like a flow chart with a single path leading straight to the end. She thought she was doting. He thought she was dictating. She'd messed it up but she could fix it.

She was troubled that he hadn't answered, but she couldn't bring herself to believe that he would ignore her. No matter how angry he was, or how stubborn he was about making a point, he couldn't cut her out. That's what she told herself on the drive over there. Maybe it was the phone. Or maybe worse. She would never forgive herself if something happened and he was by himself because she waited too long to patch things up.

She knocked at his front door, her unease growing as she waited. She was afraid of rejection. Her grandparents were the people who hadn't let her down when her parents turned out to be such disasters. They argued about keeping her and whether or not they could do enough for her. And they had. Everything she had become was thanks to them.

She heard someone moving around inside. She could picture Grandpa and his slow plodding movements.

"Grandpa?"

At last the locked turned and he opened the door.

"Good. It is you," he said. "Did you try to call?"

"No answer," she said.

"I can't find the charger," he said. When he gathered her up in a big hug, she wasn't sure who was comforting whom. "I was afraid I might have made you too mad. You might not come back."

"I was worried you wouldn't forgive me," Rayanne said.

Grandpa let her go and welcomed her inside.

"You want a drink?" he asked. Before she could answer, he poured her a tall glass of pop from one of those big jugs he always had. She could see when he poured that it was flat, but it made her love him that much more.

"We've always been proud of you," he said.

He meant Grandma too. It tugged at her heart that he didn't like to refer to her in the past tense, even after all this time.

"I know that's why you do all these things." Grandpa stirred his hand in the air. "Working that job, trying to help everyone. It's because of your mom."

Rayanne opened her mouth to protest but Grandpa made a fierce gesture so she swallowed her objections.

"Even as a little girl you always did your homework and followed the rules. We liked to take credit, like we screwed up the first one but now we had another chance to do better." He shook his head. "But it was all you. You worked so hard to prove you weren't like her."

A tear slipped down her cheek. "I was always afraid if I was bad you might send me away."

Grandpa lowered his head. "I don't think we would have done that. We talked about whether we should have done something different with her. Maybe it was our fault."

Rayanne ached for her dear grandparents who had a daughter who caused them so much pain.

"We did better with you because we were older then. We could make better decisions with you."

"She was an addict, Grandpa. She was sick and she wasn't strong enough to get better. That's not our fault. We did what we could."

Grandpa let out a long, shuddering sigh.

"That's what I wanted to tell you. You aren't in charge of making everything right. You couldn't fix her and you can't fix everything else. You have to let some stuff alone. The day might come where I do need you to arrange things for me. And I want you to be there then. But that day ain't here yet."

"I understand," she said. She wanted to point out that sometimes elders waited too long and then it was too late to make their own decisions. But if he couldn't come to that conclusion on his own, then she'd deal with it.

Grandpa came around and sat down in his chair. "Some guy came up to me at the park. He said he helps the elderly."

Rayanne's heart surged.

"Don't worry. My feet are slow but my brain works all right. I told him I didn't need help. I didn't say it but I thought he was up to something."

"I hate hearing that," Rayanne said. "That's the main program I'm going to get going when we move into the new building. A community gathering spot. You could come and get a meal and be around other Indians. Tell stories to the kids or sing with your drum circle. We'll have a park there and no creeps lurking around."

"That'll be nice. I'm proud of you." Grandpa offered an apologetic smile. "I guess you didn't bring me any groceries."

"After our last encounter, I was under the impression that you wanted to take care of that yourself," Rayanne said.

"I may have spoken too quick," Grandpa said. "I can do it. But with the stairs and my slow legs, it's easier if someone gives me a ride."

"Did you want my help with a ride?"

"Yes, please. And could you help me figure out what I need?" He studied his hands.

"Could it be that one of the things you need is your granddaughter?"

"Guess so," he said.

Rayanne got up and kissed his cheek. "Good, I need you too." She went to the kitchen and opened one of the cupboards. "Let's see what you have."

35

*H*enry leaned against the van and scrolled through the final potential hovels the apartment-finding app was giving him. He had set out in the morning giddy with optimism. Perhaps he had defeated the downward spiral he'd been in. Life seemed rich with opportunity. Given the rest of the day's creeping despair, he suspected the morning's good cheer had more to do with the top quality naked time with Rayanne.

So far he'd seen two decent one-bedroom apartments he couldn't afford, three studio apartments that he could barely afford and each had an unfortunate flaw. Two were criminally tiny. The third was adjacent to the building's laundry room and in the fifteen minutes he was there the laundry room door slammed shut two times and there had been a loud argument in there.

The most promising studio was a basement unit with a low ceiling but the little bit of outdoor light came from two half-sized windows. When he'd asked for an application, the landlady said she had other applicants and he would be on the waiting list. He couldn't be sure whether it was true or because of his brown skin. He took the application anyway to prove he was making progress.

In a moment of desperation he'd even stopped by a room for rent and it might have been tolerable, even with the humorless woman who owned the house. The room was on the upper level and had a window that overlooked a quiet tree-lined street. It had a big closet and hardwood floors. The price was right. But the lady had so many rules. Rules taped to the refrigerator door. Rules taped to the linen cupboard next to the bathroom. Rules taped under the thermostat. He tried to see it from her point of view. She wanted to run her home her way. But the comprehensive rulemaking suggested a less-than-relaxing living space.

He'd visited everything on his list so he headed back to Rayanne's. If it weren't for her, he would have given up by the second apartment. If he had to, he could sleep in the van at Jack's for a couple of nights. As long as he could produce evidence he was actively trying, he could convince Mom to relent. She talked tough but he was almost certain she wouldn't let him sleep in the van for long.

When he got back to the apartment, he knocked on the door.

Rayanne answered wearing a sexy short skirt and low-cut blouse. A bright-colored beaded clip held her hair back. His heart ached to see that smile for him.

"Darling," she said, pulling him inside. "I will make it official." She tapped his forehead. "You may now freely come and go without knocking."

She leaned up to give him a kiss. She smelled floral and sweet. He'd never been this easy with someone. He never wanted to be apart.

She went back to the kitchen and searched through one of the drawers.

"You're gorgeous," he told her.

Rayanne smiled and held up a key. "I'm glad you think so."

"You want me to have a key?"

She stopped and looked at it, reweighing the implications. "I went back and forth and changed my mind a bunch of times. I agree. It's soon," she said, choosing her words carefully. "But it feels...well, to be honest, abnormally comfortable. Is it like that for you?" She held up her hand before he could answer. "Forget I asked that. You're in a situation. It's easier for you to have one. How did it go today?"

Henry wrapped his fingers around the key, as if to keep her from taking it back. "Awful. Frustrating. Killing me slowly from the inside out if you must know."

"It's hard to find a place by yourself," she said. "And to be clear, that's a visiting boyfriend key not a live-in boyfriend key."

"I'm your boyfriend?"

"Something like that." Her dark eyes met his.

"No. I'm all yours." He tried to pull her into his arms.

"Good." She pointed at his pitiful duffel bag filled with clothes and he had never felt less worthy. "You need to get ready. We're going out."

"Together? Whew," Henry said. "I thought maybe you were going somewhere without me."

"No, we're going out because of you. Live music. And think of one of your weird food places we can try."

"My food places are weird?"

"I'm going to find some shoes and a purse. You'd better be getting ready when I get done."

"Will I be punished if I'm not?" he asked.

"Yes. And not in a good way. That's for later. Get going."

He managed to steal one more kiss before she disappeared into her bedroom. He ached with longing, not just body, but mind and spirit too. He was startled by how badly he wanted to make this work.

～

FOR DINNER he took her to a busy place where they squeezed in at the counter and had big bowls of spicy ramen.

"Good choice," she said. "You have found my favorite food that I didn't know I was missing."

"That's what I was going for," he said. "You didn't say anything earlier. Did everything go okay with Grandpa?"

"It did. We're a happy family again. Everything is working out after all."

He hoped he was part of that. After dinner, she directed him to an unfamiliar area of town and told him to park. They walked along a street mixed with retail businesses, restaurants, and bars.

"So what's the live music?"

"I forget what they're called. Bash Monitor? Bashful Man Something?"

"And what do they play?"

"Ska? Ska fusion? Is ska already a fusion? Is ska the one—?" She twisted back and forth with her elbows bent at exaggerated angles.

"I guess so. You're taking me to see a band and you don't know what they're called or what they play?"

By this time they had arrived at the venue. The sign out front said: Meteor Manor. The bouncer checked their IDs at a gated archway. Once inside, Henry guessed the site must have been a church. There was a small landscaped courtyard with a few outdoor tables. Double doors led to a beautiful room with wood floors and small stage where the band was already playing. The music rang out over a loud sound system.

Rayanne swept her arm around in a *what do you think?* gesture.

He didn't hate the music but it wasn't his thing. She'd never mentioned being a fan of this or any particular style of music. But that was the fun of getting to know someone new. He leaned down to speak into her ear. "It's fun. I didn't know you were into this."

Rayanne smiled and flicked her eyes to the ceiling as if at the end of her patience. She held on to his arm and pulled him back down. "The room. What do you think of the room? For the Beat Braves?"

"Oh," Henry said, looking around with a new perspective. There were benches around the perimeter and a portable bar like you would bring in for a party in your back yard. She took his hand and pulled him to the back where they could hear each other better.

"They opened for shows a month ago so they are actively seeking bands. They don't have a liquor license but they serve nonalcoholic stuff and snacks. But that means you can do all ages."

Henry agreed. It was the right size for a band building a following. He was already calculating ways they could advertise and friends who could help them with the sound and the lights.

"This is great, thank you," Henry said. He wrapped his arms around her and gave her a grateful hug.

"Let's go," Rayanne said, nodding at the dance floor. "I want to do some sweaty dancing and then I want to go home and do some sweaty something else. I've got a little maneuver to show you. I call it the reverse Navajo."

"Reverse? That's new," Henry said, dizzy with a surge of lust. "Well, I have a few ideas of my own. I came up with something I'm going to call the Kiowa bomber."

"Ooh. And there's always the Sac and Fox, which is exactly what it sounds like," Rayanne said.

"Right," Henry said, following her to the dance floor.

3 6

$\mathcal{A}$fter a short discussion, Rayanne relented and they went into work together.

"No one is paying attention," Henry argued. "We work at the same desk. We're together all day. It's stupid to take two cars."

"*Hoo!* I spy bed hair," Ester said as soon as they got in. "What did you two get into this weekend?"

"Nothing," Rayanne said, involuntarily reaching up to her hair, which was smooth and in place.

"Teasing," Ester said. "But you should see the look on both your faces. At least someone around here is having a good time."

"Ester," Rayanne said, "someday you're going to meet a cute guy and start dating, and I'm going to do everything in my power to embarrass you within an inch of your life."

"Don't worry, I'm going to tell the guy how lucky he is," Henry said.

"Rayanne frightens me but, Henry, you're adorable," Ester said.

Rayanne threw her stuff on her chair. She was going to offer to get Henry a coffee but was self-conscious under Ester's watchful eyes. "Did you have something for us? For me?"

"For him," Ester said, using her elbow to point to Henry. "But you can listen, *together*. The programs are finished. The printer is delivering them this afternoon. I'm going to work on the website updates today. Can you make sure I have everything I need for that?"

"We will," Rayanne said.

"We will," Ester repeated in a singsong voice and wandered back to her office.

She sat down at her computer to check her email. Henry left and returned with her coffee. He set it down next to her and she absentmindedly patted his ass to thank him.

He cleared his throat.

"Oops," Rayanne said. "Won't happen again."

"It'd better," Henry said.

"You skipped out of this last time. Are you ready to do it now?" She pulled up the grant application on her screen. Henry moved to stand behind her chair.

"Nothing beats taking a class. We can find a decent streaming class to get you started," Rayanne said. "It's easy to learn but hard to be good at."

Henry dropped his hands and squeezed her shoulders, his fingers digging into all the right spots. Her eyes slid half-closed and she lost her train of thought.

"Knock it off. We have things to do," she said. The heat spread to her face and other places. She pushed his hands off and shook her head clear.

He moved his hands to the chair's backrest and leaned forward.

"You smell good."

"So do you. We used the exact same products this morning. At the same time."

"Yeah, I do remember that."

She grabbed his shirt and pulled him down close enough to give him a quick kiss on the side of the head. Then she tapped her finger to the computer screen. "This is the part you need to pay special attention to."

Henry looked where she pointed. "Remind me again what we're doing?"

"Seeking money so we can do things."

"Isn't that the story of life?" There was no humor in his tone.

There was an odd creaking rattle from the parking lot. Tommy's bus rolled into view.

"I can't believe they got it running," Henry said. They went out to the parking lot where the bus was idling. Inside, the bus had been scrubbed clean and smelled like pine soap.

"Looks great," Henry said.

"You're the hero, man," Tommy said. "Your friend Cody helped with parts and the whole thing."

"I was bound to get something right, eventually," Henry said.

Rayanne did a stealth ass-grab. "Good job, dude. We can plan outings and haul people all over town."

Linda's car pulled into the lot. Tommy tapped the horn. The blare was enough to make them jump but Linda headed straight for the doors without seeing them.

"What's up with her?" Tommy asked.

Linda wasn't known for Monday-morning pleasantries, but Rayanne detected something extra in her step. Some other weight had been dropped on her.

"Something happened." Rayanne jumped off the bus and hurried to catch up with her. "Linda? What is it? Is it Margie?"

Linda shook her head. "Gather everyone together and bring them into the meeting room."

"Did something happen?" Rayanne's mind sorted through the possibilities. "Is it the building?"

"I'll tell everyone together," Linda said, the defeat in her voice unmistakable.

"Oh no, what happened?"

Linda reached out to mock-strangle Rayanne and then stepped around her and went to the door. "I need everyone in here, now," she shouted.

The bus lurched forward and skidded to a stop. Tommy guided it to the side of the parking lot and shut off the engine. Henry and Ester jumped off the bus with Tommy not far behind.

Rayanne couldn't stop the cold panic rising inside her. What would happen now?

Linda came back inside and held up her hands. "We're all upset. We'll talk about it together."

Rayanne held back her questions but her stomach went tight. When Henry came in, she said, "It's something with the Chief. Did you hear anything?"

"You were with me all weekend," he said.

As soon as everyone was together, Linda burst out with the news. "No building." She held her hands up. There was nothing left to say.

"What happened?" Ester asked. She paced the back of the room.

"They told us there was a vote to terminate the sale."

"Can they do that?" Tommy asked.

"It's their building. They can do what they want," Linda said.

"Can Arnie do anything?" Henry asked.

"Arnie is having the attorneys investigate."

"Is it because we're Indians?" Tommy asked.

"I don't think so," Linda said. "Maybe they had a better offer? Maybe they learned that they need the land. I don't know. As of this minute, there is no deal to purchase a bigger building. Arnie said the board could use this as an excuse to pull support, which means our funding is in major crisis. Everything is uncertain." After a long pause, she said, "Wouldn't be a bad idea to polish your résumés, guys."

"Polish them with what?" Tommy asked.

Rayanne fought back an unwelcome urge to laugh. All this planning, strategizing, and consensus building, and they ended up nowhere. They had less now than when they started. How do you keep everyone pressing forward when there was so little in return?

"Is it too late to mention I got our bus running?" Tommy asked.

Linda managed a small smile. "Good work."

"What do we do about the festival?" Henry asked.

"I don't know what we can do," Linda said. "Maybe scale it down and have it here? That might be worse than not having it at all. Let's hold off making a decision on that for now. Arnie's hoping to convince everyone to keep us funded." Linda's voice broke and she wiped a tear from her eye. "We have enough to keep all of us paid for now. Enough time to wind down what we're doing and—"

"We can research money from other sources on our own, right?" Rayanne said.

"Yes, we can," Linda said. "But if it was so easy to get people to give us enough money, we'd have it, don't you think?"

"You're giving up?"

"Giving up sounds awfully dramatic. We're working on it but in the future, this organization may be different from what we've been envisioning."

"What about the elder services?"

"What about them?" Linda said. "Are you listening to what I'm talking about here?"

Everything about this was wrong. They should be celebrating right now. Rayanne head hurt, measuring everything they'd done right and wondering how it could be scrubbed away so easily.

"Doesn't it help the city when we help marginalized people?" Rayanne's voice came out as a whisper.

Linda came over to give her a hug. "We're all on the same team. Keep doing what you can do now. We'll make some decisions in the next few days. I need you to hold it together."

"I am together," Rayanne said. Tommy slouched back in his chair, staring at a point on the ceiling. Ester continued her pacing, like she might be getting closer to her destination. Henry's face was blank. He hadn't been around long enough to understand all they had lost.

37

*B*ad news or not, people were depending on a meal delivery and Henry wasn't going to let them down. Rayanne alternated between rage and despair, one moment pacing the room, listing off all the indignities the center had suffered, the next sinking back into the couch in defeat.

"We got hungry elders out there," Henry said. He stuck a finger in the barbecue sauce and tasted it. He added a couple more shakes of hot sauce and whisked it into the pan. "You wanted to see what I could come up with and this is it." He unpacked the various-sized containers and wrapping materials and spread them out on the counter.

She wandered over to watch him work. "How did you manage to make something that smells so good in my poorly stocked kitchen?" She used a spoon to taste it. "Wow. Tastes amazing."

"Secret family recipe," he said.

"Wasco Ind'n traditional?"

Henry laughed. "Got it from a friend. I can show you how to make it, if you want."

"Why would I? I've got you to make it."

Henry used a couple of forks to shred the meat from an elk roast that he'd slow-cooked.

"You want to help me assemble these?"

Rayanne unpacked the buns into the containers. Henry spread a small amount of sauce over the bottom half and then piled on the meat.

"I don't want the bread to get soggy during transportation so we're going to give them a slug of sauce on the side."

Rayanne portioned sauce into small plastic containers. Her movements had become more relaxed as they worked.

"Do you want to deal with the sides?" he asked.

Rayanne went to the refrigerator and brought out a giant bowl. "I hope people like sweet-potato salad. And by people I mean us too. We'll be eating this until the end of time."

"People who get meal deliveries aren't going to complain," Henry said. "But don't be stingy with the portions."

"I won't. We still need to make the other one." She rummaged through a kitchen drawer until she found a strainer. She opened a can of garbanzo beans and dumped them in and rinsed them under the sink. "They all complain about three bean salad. I don't know why."

"I like it," Henry said.

"Everyone likes it except these guys."

"You need to get past the grumpy." Henry gave her a companionable nudge and kissed her shoulder. He couldn't touch her with his hands all gunky with sauce.

"I am past grumpy. This isn't grumpy, this is grumpy that surrendered because there is no incentive to be grumpy." She sighed. "How am I going to tell my grandpa about this? He's going to be so disappointed."

"He's Indian. Isn't he used to disappointment?"

Rayanne made a sound between a sob and a laugh. She wiped the back of her hand across her face. "Yeah. But I don't want to be the one to disappoint him. I forgot to tell you, some of his drum circle friends are going to be there tonight. We're supposed to bring two more dinners."

Henry bit back a comment about maybe mentioning the extra meals earlier so he could be prepared. He reduced the sandwich meat on each sandwich. He could make it go around.

"We don't know for sure that it's doom yet." Henry pushed back the thought that if he lost the job, he wouldn't be able to get an apartment. No one would rent to an unemployed person. He couldn't make himself think about what would happen if he couldn't get an apartment. "There's a chance the board will keep the center going."

"I guess."

"But if we do prepare for the worst case, I haven't done a résumé since I got laid off. Could you help me?"

"Ugh, résumés. Yeah, I can help you. Especially if you want to promote your skills working with tribal organizations."

"Is that what you want me to do, or is that what résumé you're good at writing?"

This time Rayanne bumped into him. "The second one. Grandpa informed me that I can't go around trying to fix everyone. What kind of job do you want?"

"I don't know. But I want to prepare for the worst. Can we talk about something else?" Henry washed his hands, then grabbed a spoon to add the salads to the containers.

"What do you think of a food cart with delivery service to elders?" Rayanne closed up the containers and packed them into the padded bags.

"I like doing this," Henry said. "But I think I would hate it as a full-time job. Working long hours and being around food every day would get old fast."

"Yeah. Lots of jobs sound fun until you think about doing it day after day."

Rayanne brought out a plate of cookies and began counting out four and putting them into plastic bags. "New subject. How would you describe your cuddle style?"

The question startled him into laughter. "Do I have a cuddle style? I use my arms and squeeze."

"That's more like a hugging style," Rayanne said.

"Cuddling and hugging are two different things?"

"Sure. Cuddling is more like one extended hug, or a bunch of connected hugs."

"Is that definition in the dictionary?"

"Be serious," Rayanne said, pretending not to smile. "I'm asking to describe manner and method. Like my cuddle style is intense. I like cuddling in the morning, in front of the TV, after I've had a hard day. I like to cuddle even if sex isn't involved."

"So you want to cuddle tonight but you don't want sex?"

"No. I want sex. Stick with the program. The question concerns your cuddle style. With some guys the minute you touch them they're yanking your pants off. Or you finish fooling around and they put one arm around you while they check their phone. Which are you?"

Henry couldn't hide his amusement. "My cuddle style rates as less than intense. But at the same time it is conducted with serious skill and commitment. I enjoy cuddling before and after naked time, but also in front of the TV or a winter afternoon or when life is being wretched and you need someone to hang on to."

"Good answer," Rayanne said. "My high school boyfriend wasn't a big cuddler. He was, like, didn't we just hug yesterday? You're more fun to be with."

"Than your high school boyfriend? I should hope so." Henry finished rinsing the last of the dishes in the sink. He dried his hands on the back of Rayanne's pants and kissed her on the cheek. "The faster we get this done, the faster we get back."

THE RING of laughter carried all the way down the stairs. Rayanne smiled when she knocked on the door. Grandpa flung it open and welcomed them in. If an apartment was like a balloon, this one was close to bursting. Rayanne wished she'd brought extra chairs. The curtain to Grandpa's bedroom was closed and there was a single coffee cup next to the sink. He'd laid out silverware. As usual, a giant bottle of flat soda was out on the kitchen table. Maybe he let them go flat intentionally.

"I thought you'd never show up," Grandpa said. "We're starving."

"We saved the best for last," Rayanne said.

"Come say hello to my friends," Grandpa said. "You remember Big Stan," he said, referring to the taller man with two braids and chiseled cheek bones you would expect on a Plains Indian. "And this is Little Stan."

"Hello, Stan," Rayanne said and hugged the short man. He carried all his weight around the middle and had two skinny legs.

"We're brothers," Little Stan said.

Henry looked from one to the other, not sure what to think. "Your parents named you both Stan?"

That made everyone crack up.

"And this is the new guy, Knox." Knox had a weathered face and oversized glasses that didn't sit on his face quite right.

"I been wondering why Gus don't bring his family around more often," Knox said. He took her hand and held on to it.

"This is Rayanne's friend Henry," Grandpa said. "He's from out Warm Springs."

"Oh," the others said in unison. "Who's your family?"

"Jackson," Henry said. "Arnie's my uncle."

They nodded together but Grandpa said, "They don't know who he is. They like to ask questions."

"He's a councilman out there," Henry added. "It's nice to meet you all."

Rayanne got everyone situated and passed out the food. They were one container short. "Sorry," she mouthed at Henry. He waved the comment away. "We can split it," he mouthed back.

"So Knox. Is that, like, a life of hard knocks? Or like the fort?" Henry asked.

"Fort," he said. "But I don't know why. My brother was Buster. My sister is Flinsy."

"Flinsy?" Henry said.

"Yeah, she came out all right in spite of it. My people come from up Alaska. Tlingit. Haven't been up there in years. Miss it, but I don't like to travel so much anymore."

"One of our board members, Pauline, is Tlingit," Rayanne said.

"She pretty?"

"Her husband thinks so," Rayanne said.

Knox chuckled. "I guess I'd better leave her be, then."

"We wanted to ask your help," Gus said. "We need to break into Earl's house."

"This evening is going to be more fun than I thought," Henry said, rubbing his hands together. "Should we use my van?"

"Don't encourage them," Rayanne said.

"Bet you didn't know we were part-time criminals," Big Stan said, polishing off his sandwich. "This food is delicious."

"Glad you like it. But give Henry credit for this menu," Rayanne said. "Why do you need to go to Earl's?"

"We need the drum. We're going to sing at the rehab center," Gus said. Rayanne handed him another napkin.

"What does the rehab center have to say about that?" Rayanne asked.

"Nothing. What are they going to do? Arrest us?" Little Stan asked.

"No one is getting arrested," Rayanne said.

"If Earl wants his drum, I see no reason not to bring it to him," Henry said, his eyes bright.

"I can't stop you," Rayanne said. She imagined the creaky elders trying to sneak around carrying a big drum. There was a reason they waited for Henry.

The conversation moved on to their respective homelands. Big Stan grew up in Oklahoma. Little Stan grew up around Puget Sound. Knox had more stories about people with funny names. Rayanne loved the way everyone had a unique story about where they came from but they all had so much in common.

They ate every bite of food that Rayanne and Henry brought and asked to be included in future deliveries. By the end of the night, Rayanne's stomach hurt from laughing and her heart hurt because she was afraid the center might fail and what if they couldn't save it?

38

*R*ayanne typed a search string into her computer and scanned through the results. There was a multicultural center near downtown that had a ballroom and onsite parking. A hotel near the airport had a convention space that might work for them. She had a contact at the local community college. Perhaps there was an event center on campus that would work for them.

"What are you doing?" Henry sat down next to her.

"Looking for alternatives. We don't need a huge place, but bigger than here. Linda was addled in the head. We can barely work in this space much less host an event here. If we can find a place with a stage and enough room for a few booths, we could pull it off. Too bad Milk Creek Farm is so far out there, otherwise that place would be perfect. I'm wondering if—"

"I think Linda intends to cancel."

"She thinks it would be easier than changing to a different location. If we find the right place—"

"I thought you planned this to celebrate the opening of the Chief building."

He was right but she didn't want to say it out loud. Instead, she said, "I did. But it's become more than that. There's got to be a way. It's not ideal but we wouldn't have to disappoint anyone."

"We don't even know if we have a job going into the future."

"A couple weeks ago you didn't even want this job. Don't help. I don't care." She shouldn't be acting like this. But it was no longer disappointment, it was panic. Their time together with those elders was exactly the kind of family and community she wanted to bring together. Something would be lost if she couldn't keep things going. She hit a few keys on her keyboard and pointed to the screen.

"The old history museum has an event space." Even as she said the words she sensed how hopeless it was. They didn't have time, and even less money.

"I know how you feel about this," Henry said.

"I'm not ready to give up." She tapped the down arrow even though she could see how absurd it was, thinking they could move an event like that at the last minute. An event she'd designed to fit in the space they were not going to get.

"For so long I've been picturing this thing coming together. My grandpa and Margie and all these people we've been talking to. I want all the elders to be honored together."

Henry picked up her hands and kissed them. "Maybe you're asking the right questions but the festival is the wrong answer."

"I have no idea what that means," Rayanne said.

"I have an idea."

~

SHE DIDN'T KNOW what Henry's plan was, but she resisted.

"I'm not in the mood to go out," she said. She meant it too. "We were gone last night. Can't we stay home for one night?"

"You'll like this," he said.

"Whatever it is, I don't want to stay long," she said as he herded her out to the van.

"We won't."

He drove out to an industrial area with chain-link fence

surrounding heavy equipment and pallets of unidentifiable materials. They came to a series of single-story buildings constructed like a row of garages with identical blue doors. He pulled up to a gate and punched in a security code. The big metal door creaked open.

"You're taking me to a self-storage place?"

"Isn't it romantic?" Henry said.

"This is not what I was expecting. If I didn't know better, I would be worried."

Henry gave her his most glorious smile. "You shouldn't be worried."

The van traveled down a long alley. Light poured from an open door with a single car parked out front. She expected to see stacks of boxes or furniture. Instead, the Beat Braves had their gear set up. Their tribal flags hung across the walls. A carpet remnant covered half of the concrete floor.

"You made it," Jack said. "Welcome to our secret clubhouse."

"What are you doing here?" Rayanne asked.

"This is where we practice," Cody said. "White folks frown at loud Indians."

"Everybody frowns at loud everybody," Sam said. "You gotta give white people a pass on that one."

"Every day," Cody said. "We can make noise here at night and no one minds. There's a punk band the next row over but we get along." He offered a mysterious smile when he said it.

Sam said, "Did they tell you the good news?"

"That's why she's here," Jack said.

Henry smiled. "I booked the band at Meteor Manor."

"Already?" Rayanne said. "I thought you would futz around and put it off and then lose the contact information."

"I guess I deserve that," Henry said, "but you thought wrong. They loved what we're doing and they had an open night for us."

"Cody thinks there's something wrong with the place and it's a trap," Sam said.

"A trap for what? Do you have anything worth trapping?" Rayanne asked.

Sam pressed his hands to his chest. "I like to think that I do."

"Well, that's great. I can't wait to see you in a real club."

"If you like it, would you reconsider us for the festival?" Jack asked.

"We have to cancel the festival," she said.

"Why?" Sam said, more upset than she would have guessed. "We were all going to go and see what it was about."

"Long story," Rayanne said. "I think we'll try to have it again sometime."

"There's a reason I wanted all of us here," Henry said. "Rayanne's grandpa is in an intertribal drum circle and they need a place to play. I would like to invite them to play here sometime."

Rayanne smiled in surprise. She'd never thought of trying to find another place for them. "What a great idea."

"I thought of it last night. I don't think Earl's rehab center is going to be too welcoming."

"I always wanted to play with a drum group," Cody said. "I never had a chance before. Do they let young guys play?"

"I understand they're recruiting," Rayanne said. "Maybe we can do it later this week. Maybe we can break Earl out too."

39

*A*rnie suggested they go for a walk. He wanted to talk to Linda somewhere that wasn't the office or a meeting room. Someplace away from the phone.

They met at the greenway that ran along the river. Big stands of trees shaded a series of paths and trails. The park had plenty of picnic tables and a playground. There were too many people to pretend they were away from it all, but there was a hazy sky overhead and grass and trees all around.

Arnie put his phone in quiet mode and held it up. "Did you turn your phone off?"

Linda pretended to think for a moment, and then pulled it out of her pocket and fiddled with it before putting it away again.

"What if there's an emergency?" she said. "Oh, yeah, this entire thing is an emergency. What's the bad news?"

"Why do you think there's bad new?" Arnie said.

Linda laughed. "I figured you brought me out here so the staff won't hear my bitter cries of grief."

"It's not like they haven't heard that sound before," Arnie said, smiling at her sideways.

"True. But they haven't heard my 'all is lost' bellowing wails."

"And they won't. Yet. I came out here so we wouldn't get interrupted," Arnie said. A gentle breeze came up through the trees and blew her hair around her face. She pulled it around one shoulder and braided it and stuck the end into her blouse. He got a glimpse of collarbone and bra strap. He was surprised to find a twinge of something for this woman he'd been friends with for so long.

"What are we going to be doing?" she said, winking at him. "Plotting? Will we be fighting individuals or institutions?"

He'd never seen her this playful. She was always so serious. Arnie let out a breath he didn't realize he was holding. Business. They were there for business.

"I'm afraid I'm not confident—"

"We have got to stick together on this," Linda said.

"We are stuck together but we've got more than me," Arnie said. "You've got an entire executive board and no one is more surprised than I am about their reaction to this. They think it's time to quit."

A group of teenaged runners headed toward them, filling the path. Without thinking, Arnie put his hand on Linda's waist to guide her out of their way. He left it there until the group passed and the two of them continued on their way.

He continued. "Back when Margie was in charge, the center agreed to an ultimatum. And here we are. No building. Is there an arts festival without a building? You built something but it didn't grow."

Linda sighed. "They want us to shut down. That's final?"

"I don't know what choice you have. You're not going to have any funding."

Linda wandered off the trail. There was a bench that overlooked the river. Arnie joined her. The smooth gray-green water stretched out before them. Across the water there was a cluster of high-end homes with boat docks.

"Remember when they used to have a powwow at this park?" Linda asked.

Arnie shook his head.

"They had it when I first moved here after college. You could camp out here. There would be tents, and teepees, and Indian people from all over this area. I'm often uncomfortable in big groups of people, but when I was here I never felt nervous or out of place."

"How come they don't do it anymore?"

"The park turned to day-use only. I guess they couldn't find another site. Familiar theme, eh? When you're around town doing your thing, you forget how many of us are here. It was reassuring to have a place to see everyone."

"I get it," Arnie said. "Believe me, I understand what you want to see built. I think you're the one to do it, but I'm just one guy."

"If anyone can do it, you could change their minds. People who work in Indian Country know it's not easy. One more year. Can you get me enough for one more year?"

Arnie didn't want to make any promises. He'd come here to talk her into closing down. Here she was talking him into sticking with the fight. He'd had mixed success getting people with purse strings to change their minds.

"I thought that's what the last year was," he said, not unkindly.

"It was," Linda agreed. "I'll plan for the worst. Ester is so sharp, I think I can get her into one of the tribal health organizations in the region. Maybe we can hand over Tommy's program to one of the local schools." She sighed again. "Rayanne's capable of anything. I'm not worried about her."

"What about you?"

"I'm not worried about me, either," Linda said. "I heard that the city college is talking about a diversity program. I bet I could talk my way into that. That's not where my heart is but anything to raise the profile of red people."

"No thoughts of going back home?"

"Not enough for me there. I miss my family and I miss the mountains, but I like the opportunities here better."

Arnie wanted to think there was something behind the look she was giving him.

"What are we going to do with Henry?" she said. "I figure he's stuck around because he's got a thing for Rayanne, but I know your mission was to get him a job."

"Henry is the least of your problems. His mom has been wanting him to live on the rez. He got kicked out of his apartment so this is the perfect time. My brother back home has a room for him. I can get him a job out there."

"He's lucky to have family to fall back on," Linda said.

THEY TOOK their time walking back to the parking area. Linda had a lot to do but she was enjoying Arnie's company and hated to see him go. He wasn't in a suit today. Instead, he was wearing what most people referred to as business casual. She called it golf clothes. The polo shirt had the logo from his tribe's resort.

"It's been fun working together again," she said.

Arnie looked surprised. He held her eyes a half-second too long. Was he thinking about kissing her? Of course he wasn't. Arnie may have grown up on the rez but he'd spent every minute of college chasing after the opposite of Indian women. She remembered one time he showed up at a party with a slender blonde who was way out of his league. She'd overheard him fast-talking about rez life, over-selling it like you could to people who knew nothing about Indian people beyond what they'd seen on TV. He was still overbearing at times, but there was an appealing earnestness about him.

She put her hand in her pocket. "Permission to check my phone?"

Arnie laughed and shook his head. "As if you need my permission to do anything."

Linda nodded in agreement. She checked the time.

"I need to get back and mind what's left of my tiny empire." She gave it one last try. "Can you try for one more year? I don't think we're done yet."

Whatever moment had passed between them was gone. Arnie held his hands up in a gesture of surrender. "I hate not being able to come through."

"I know you do," Linda said. "I don't hold you personally responsible."

On the drive back to the office she thought about how to tell Margie. When they'd been working together, much as she loved Margie, there was always the sense that the elder was part of what was holding them back. Her thinking was old-school and simplistic. She didn't like risk. She never grasped what technology could do for them. She mistrusted some institutions that could be allies.

Linda didn't blame her. Margie had come up in a different time. When she had started out, Tribes had less opportunity for self-determination. It was a challenge to find a federal official who would listen. It was harder to assert tribal rights that still existed.

Margie was a great leader and wonderful role model but it had taken so long to get her to let go. Linda felt bad even articulating these thoughts. Margie would be heartbroken to see the organization she'd built from nothing disappear. She hoped she wouldn't have to give her that news.

Instead, she wanted to talk to her about the Chief deal. Margie had been there at the origins of the deal but how had it come about?

Linda changed direction and headed for Margie's.

"Hey, stranger," Margie said when she opened the door. "More bad news?"

"I hope not," Linda said. "Help me remember how we started the Chief building acquisition."

Margie moved to let her in. The TV was on but the screen flickered blank blue. There were three remotes on the table next to her chair.

"You need help with your TV?" Linda asked. She tried pressing buttons on each remote.

"Ester had it all set up for me but I did something wrong. I need her to come back."

"I'll let her know," Linda said. "So, the building. Who did you talk to first?"

Margie sat down. To Linda's relief, her voice was stronger and she moved more easily. Linda wished she had more time to spend with her.

"Paul Douglas. He was the facilities manager. He grew up in Tahlequah and knew something about Indian people. He said the city would like to work with us on the transfer."

"So we had their support and then we lost it. Someone withdrew support," Linda said.

"Can't get that pie back from the bear now," Margie said.

"I want to know what happened. I want to know why we got this close and then it all fell apart. It's not like we went to them with our hat in our hands."

Margie shook her head. "I don't know if it's worth trying to find out. Sounds like a lot of aggravation to me."

"Well, turns out I like aggravation," Linda said.

40

*H*enry almost picked up flowers but Mom would know he was sucking up. It was true but he didn't want to be obvious about it. He picked up a brownie mix instead.

Arnie was already there. They sat at the kitchen table together, drinking a beer. The house smelled like baked ham and Mom's best side dish, cheesy potatoes. It was funny to think of them as brother and sister sometimes because Arnie was so much younger. Mom liked to tell that when Arnie was a baby she often got stuck at home, taking care of him. She said that contributed to her getting knocked up so young. Her teenaged brain figured if she was going to be stuck taking care of a kid, she could be doing it with her own kid and live with her boyfriend. She was too young to know any better and being stuck at home with Henry and his loser dad ended up being worse than taking care of Arnie.

The story went a long way to explaining why it took the two of them so long to become friends.

"Hey, Mom," he said, kissing her cheek. He shook Arnie's hand. "I'm going to fix this real quick." He went into the kitchen and opened the mix. "I booked the Beat Braves a show. You guys should come." He found the big blue mixing bowl and threw everything in.

"What are you making?" Mom asked.

He showed her the box.

"What's the music like?" Arnie said.

"You'll like it," Henry said, pulling out the handheld mixer. "You can dance around. Make it rain."

"Careful," Mom said, "don't over-mix it."

"I can read the directions. It's right on the box. You should come too, Mom. See what I'm about."

"I know what you're about, and I don't like that kind of music."

"Someone once told me it's good for you to do something you don't want to do. You can come by for a half hour. You don't know this kind of music. They do their own thing. They're taking tradition and making it into something new."

Mom gave him a puzzled look. "Who are you, and what have you done with my son?"

"Very funny," Henry said. He scraped the batter into a pan. "Are you going to take your stuff out of the oven soon?"

Mom got up. "I'll get dinner on the table, and you can bake your thing."

"How's everything going at the center?" Arnie asked.

"You would know better than me, Mr. Executive Board. Linda said you want us to do the festival but Rayanne can't figure out how to pull it off. I am learning a lot."

"Who's Rayanne?" Mom asked.

"This woman I work with," Henry said, keeping his voice neutral. "I'm sure I mentioned her. If you come to the concert, you can meet her. She's the one who helped me find the venue."

"I thought you two were a thing," Arnie said.

Henry shot Arnie a look but it was too late.

"Is that the friend who has the couch you've been sleeping on?" Mom asked. "I should have known there was a reason you weren't back here, begging me for more time."

"She's native, Mom. You would like her." He wanted to add *she's a hard-ass like you*, but at the moment this would come off as an argument against him.

"Then why am I hearing about her now?"

"We're getting to know each other," Henry said.

"I bet," Mom said. "You're using condoms, aren't you?"

Arnie snorted with his mouth full of beer. He turned his head away to laugh.

"*Jeez*, Mom. Yes. She has tons of them," and realizing how that sounded, he added, "...that she won at a bachelor party. I mean bachelorette party."

"She sounds charming," Mom said.

"She is," Arnie said. "He's right. You'll like her. You can credit her for him sticking with the job as long as he did."

Henry stuck the pan in the oven and set the timer. He helped Mom carry food to the table and they sat down to eat.

"And I am doing the job," Henry said. "If the center keeps going, I have lots of my own ideas. I'm trying to learn which ones will work better than others. Rayanne is showing me how fundraising works so I'm learning all about that. We're going to have to figure out someplace to move. Arnie, maybe you have ideas how I could learn more about that."

Both Mom and Arnie were paying deep attention to their food.

"What is it?"

Arnie took his time before saying, "Unfortunately, your job at the center is going away."

"Did Linda say that?" Henry asked. A mixture of anger and insecurity stirred in his belly.

"No. Linda is fine with you but even if I can convince the board to keep the center going a little longer, it's not going to be enough to keep you on."

"I can take a salary cut," Henry said. "Or even find a part-time job until we can cover me."

"You don't have a place to live," Mom said.

"I'm working on it," Henry said.

"There's a job for you out on the rez," Arnie said. "Uncle Mike has a room for you. It would be good for you to try living out there. It wouldn't be forever."

"For years we've been talking about you living out there. When you were a kid and we went to visit, I could hardly get you to go home when it was time to leave," Mom said.

"I am an adult now," Henry said, keeping his voice calm. "You two don't get to make a plan and tell me what to do."

"It's a great opportunity," Arnie said.

"That's what you said about the job at the center," Henry said.

"Linda said you've been great. Think of what you can do in the Economic Development Office on the rez. It's a grunt job to start but you're smart. You can work your way up. Then you'll have more freedom to pick what you want."

"You forced that other job on me and I picked that," Henry said. "That's what I want to do."

"Henry, you don't have a choice," Mom said. "Please don't tell me you expect to live with that girl while you fiddle around at a part-time job."

"Her name is Rayanne and she's the one who gets to decide whether I'm a loser, not you. I want to be worthy of her, and I'm not going to sponge off her. If you can't say her name, don't talk about her." He turned to Arnie. "Is there a date I'm required to go out there, or were you thinking of abducting me or what?"

"It's not like that," Arnie said. "You can start in a week or so. Why not give it a chance? You can come back if it doesn't work out."

Henry scoffed. As tough as things were now, they would be harder if he left and tried to come back.

The timer for the brownies went off. Henry took his plate into the kitchen and dropped it in the sink. He pulled the pan out of the oven.

"Did you check it with a toothpick?" Mom said.

"No. I didn't. Why don't you do it for me?"

He stalked out the front door.

41

*R*ayanne heard the key in the lock and smiled when Henry came through the door. But instead of coming over to grope her like every other time he came into the house, he walked back and forth across the apartment, his eyes blazing.

"What's going on?" she asked.

He shook his head and waved the question away. His jaw clenched and his hands curled into fists. Every exhale was an audible snort. The tension radiated off him. She'd never seen him like this.

"Will you come sit with me?"

He stopped pacing and his look softened. He crawled onto the couch and put his head in her lap.

"Did you have dinner with your mom and Arnie?" she asked.

"Yeah," he said. "Arnie got me a job on the rez. Mom got me a room with Uncle Mike. I'm supposed to move out there next week."

"I thought they wanted you to have a job at the center. Did you tell them to take a hike?"

"It turns out I don't have a job at the center." Henry flopped onto his back and looked into her eyes.

"That's Linda's call, isn't it?"

"That's what I thought but it seems Arnie arranged to pay me through some temporary family-pity source, which is conveniently gone now. One of Arnie's schemes, I should have known. Even the job wasn't real."

"It was real. Did he say the center is closing?" Rayanne hated the idea but she hated the not knowing more.

"If he knows, he's not telling me. Whatever happens, there isn't a place for me. And as my mom never fails to point out, I am homeless. I can't find a place if I don't have a job."

Rayanne nudged him until he sat up and then she crawled up and straddled him so they were sitting face to face. "You're not homeless."

"I don't have my own place," he said.

She leaned into him and put her head on his shoulder.

"I wouldn't mind half as much if it weren't for you," Henry said. "Would you ever want to live on the rez? I bet Uncle Arnie could get you a kick-ass job."

Rayanne sighed. He was warm and his chest firm. She liked the way they fit together. "I wouldn't leave Grandpa. If I lived on a rez, I'd want to go home."

"I didn't expect that you would, but I had to ask." Henry smoothed her hair down her back.

"Have you decided to do this?" They'd just gotten together. She didn't want him to leave.

"I think the word to use is resigned. I am resigned to this."

Rayanne sat up and cupped his jaw in her hand. She brushed a line of kisses up and down his neck. He made a cute grunt and put his hands on her hips, shifting her body so they lined up better. Everywhere they met, they fit together. His hands slid down to grab her bottom and pulled it tightly against him. His eyes were closed, his smile lazy. "On the bright side, I get to have one epic going-away party with special guests, the Beat Braves."

"I wish you could live here," she said.

"Me too," Henry said. "But it's too soon. It needs to be because we're starting something together. Not because I'm a failure."

She pulled back and waited for him to open his eyes. "You're not a failure," she said. "The rez is, what, ninety miles? It's not forever, right? We can keep it together long distance."

"That's a great plan, what with our unreliable cars and upcoming winter weather." He snaked his hands under her shirt and stroked the bare skin on her back. "Plus this sort of fun stuff is going to be tough to manage from my room at Uncle Mike's house."

"You don't want to try to continue?" She hadn't even known she wanted a boyfriend, but now that he was here, she didn't want anyone but Henry.

"I want to try not to leave in the first place." Henry unsnapped her bra and her breasts floated loose under her shirt. "But if I have to go, of course I want to try. And I will work as hard as I can to move back here so we can be together."

"I have a bunch of ideas—"

Henry reached up and cupped a breast in each hand. His fingers circled around to squeeze the nipples, taking her breath away.

"I got my own ideas, thank you," he said. "Do you want go into the bedroom or should I do you right here?"

"Bedroom," she said. He took his time before removing his hands and helping her crawl off him. "Could I request a glow-in-the-dark condom?" she asked.

"Sure. But I'm in charge of the rest." His voice left no room for negotiation.

42

---

*R*ayanne couldn't put it off any longer. They had to cancel the festival. There was no place to have it, and she couldn't keep the participants hanging. And now, with Henry leaving, she had no heart left to try to save it.

"I'm dreading this," she told him. "An email blast strikes me as heartless."

"But easy," Henry said. "Why not go for easy?"

"Some of these people we had to sweet-talk into participating in the first place. They aren't going to be happy."

"Not a lot of joy on this end either," Henry said.

Ester came into the room with her video camera.

"I hear unhappy but I don't see it," she said. "Show me unhappy. Your motivation is disappointment. At this point in your life you have no incentive for hope because your dreams are crushed at every turn."

"What are you doing?" Rayanne asked.

Ester zoomed in closer. "I'm making a documentary. Instead of a documentary about our victory over the forces that endeavor to hold us back, it's a documentary about defeat. White man making promises and then taking them back."

"Who's going to watch that film?" Henry said.

Ester put the camera down. "People watch all kinds of depressing things. I think they like it. For the oppressed, it validates their hopelessness. For the oppressors, they can shift the blame rather than see how their own actions are part of the problem."

"Ester," Henry said, his face serious, "I think you are too smart to be here."

Ester shrugged. "I read that somewhere. I don't know what I'm talking about. Remember my true calling is healthcare-data-wonk. Linda has plans to pass me off to another tribal healthcare organization so I can make spreadsheets for them."

"Henry's moving to the rez," Rayanne said. The anger in her voice surprised her.

"Uh oh," Ester said. "What about your thing?" She flicked her gaze to Henry.

"It's going to turn into long-distance thing," Henry said.

"So you really like each other," Ester said. "That sucks. Not that you like each other but that you found each other and now you face even more obstacles. Shall I make a film about you two? Indians ripped apart as part of a postcolonial plan. They want you to shack up with non-Indians, dilute the blood until we vanish into the melting pot."

"No." Rayanne held up her hand to block the camera lens.

Linda came into the room. "Ester, I think you missed your true calling. You need to do something that involves theatrical narration."

"I will spiff up my résumé and change my job-search plans," Ester said. "Henry is moving."

"I heard. You're lucky to have your family," Linda said.

"That's funny. I don't feel lucky," Henry said.

"Arnie is proud of what you've accomplished here."

"I wasn't here long enough to accomplish anything."

Rayanne didn't feel lucky either, but she understood what Linda meant. She tapped the binder on the desk. "We need to get on this. Do we want to divide it up? Everyone can make a few calls. We're going to need to write some checks too."

Linda sighed. "It's too bad after all this work you did, we have nothing to show for it. That's what the board is beefing about. They wanted to see us do something besides respond somewhat effectively to a building flood. If we could pull off even a miniature festival, they could see the kind of thing we're trying to build."

She looked around the room. "Where's Tommy?"

"Job interview," Ester said. She shrugged at Linda. "It's not a secret, is it? You told us we were at the end."

"Not officially. Yet. What are we going to do with that bus?" Linda said.

"Load it up and drive off together into the sunset," Ester said. "Maybe to Warm Springs. Uncle Arnie can get us all jobs. Isn't there a good timber industry out there? I could learn about trees."

Henry pretended to laugh. "And we could all live in Uncle Mike's spare room. Here's a speck of good news: I'm having a blowout going-away party featuring the Beat Braves."

"Who are...?" Linda said.

"My friends' band. The one you didn't want at the festival. Rock with hip-hop and native pride, all rolled into one loud package," Henry said.

"It'll be fun," Rayanne said, forcing cheerfulness into her voice. "There's a place to sit outside, too, if the music and dancing get to be too much."

"Dancing?" Ester said. "I'm in. I'm a dancing machine." She rolled her hips in time with her arms and then spun into a full turn.

"You are full of surprises," Rayanne said.

"You have no idea," Ester said with a wink.

"And speaking of dancers... We have to call that youth group and let them know the event is off. They were so excited when we invited them to join the program." Rayanne sighed. "Disappointing the young and old alike."

"Maybe we can get them out for something else," Linda said. "Another school program or something."

"We thought it would be fun to see them perform with live music," Henry said. "They used a recording for their demonstration at the school."

"Those kids find lots of places to perform without our help," Rayanne said.

"Wait a minute." Henry stood up. He held up a finger like it was helping him think. "Live music. Dancing demonstration. A stage. A little courtyard outside."

He was giving her a knowing look but she had no idea what he was talking about.

"Meteor Manor?" Henry said, nodding his head.

"You want to do the arts festival at Meteor Manor?" Rayanne's brain cranked around the idea.

"You guys, you have to explain," Linda said.

"You just said even a small thing could work. We could do that. We already have a date. We could bring the kids out to dance with the Beat Braves." Henry looked at Rayanne. "We could have the Beat Braves, right?"

Rayanne was still trying to keep up with the idea.

"We could have a few vendors in the courtyard. A food truck, if they'll let us bring one in. It wouldn't be a festival as much as an inter-tribal event. Arnie could haul the board out there, and they could see us bringing people together."

"Do you think the Beat Braves would go for it?" Rayanne asked.

"Guys!"

"Meteor Manor is a new concert venue where the band is scheduled to play," Henry explained. "We could alter the show to include these other native performers. Beat Braves won't care. A week ago they didn't even have a gig."

"That area has a lot of nightlife too," Rayanne said. "Maybe we could attract people who might not normally check out a cultural event."

"You guys think you can pull it off?" Linda said. "I'll get Arnie to work on the board. Tommy can drive folks there."

"Social media, I'm on it," Ester said, racing for her computer.

"Wait, Ester! I need to talk to the band," Henry said. "I need to talk to the venue. I'm not sure we're even allowed to do all this."

Rayanne felt hopeful for the first time since they'd learned they'd lost the building. "Maybe we can get some city people to come too, and change their minds."

"Now you're dreaming, missy," Linda said. "But I will get on the phone and spread the word."

"It's a good idea," Rayanne said.

"I can't believe we didn't come up with this sooner," Henry said.

"You thought of it soon enough. Let's figure out what we need to do and get started."

43

The next few days were a frenzy of email, phone calls, and errands. Everyone on the staff had his or her own assigned duties. Henry created a Rayanne-style checklist of his own and made several trips to Meteor Manor to work out the details with the staff and get the technical specs for the Beat Braves. Ester was in charge of anything relating to promotion. Tommy mapped out a transportation scheme to get everyone who needed a ride to the venue. Rayanne was in charge of the artists and food. Linda and Arnie were tasked with getting the board to come.

His last few days at the center went by in a blur. The last nights with Rayanne didn't last long enough. He couldn't get enough of her. He tried not to think about the time when they would be apart.

The night of the event, Rayanne changed her outfit three times, downgrading from sexy to interesting to something that verged on schoolmarm.

"You should stick with the little blue dress that stops in the middle of your thighs." Henry hugged her from behind, pulling her softness close. She wore a pleasantly dull dress, like she might wear to a wedding or graduation.

"Don't distract me," she said, pushing his hands away. "I need to look professional."

"Professional compared to what?" He had his face buried in the crook of her neck. She twisted away from him.

"According to the community we hope will attend our event. I think you should wear that white shirt. The one where you roll up the sleeves and show a little bit of skin at the base of your throat. It's sexy."

"Much as I love to please you, woman, that shirt is dirty and balled up in some unknown location, seeing as how I'm living out of a duffel bag."

"That's a shame. What do you have that *is* clean?"

Henry backed away from her. "Really? We're going to have a policy meeting about my shirt? What does the committee recommend?"

"Forget it," she said, dismissing him with a wave. "Wear what you want. If you don't care, why should I?" She left the room.

Henry followed her. "Please, I don't want to fight with you tonight."

"We won't. We can save it for tomorrow. I'm ready when you are. Find an ugly shirt and let's go."

Henry brought out his duffel bag and dug through it, choosing and discarding several items. His ire grew, not only due to the dismal inadequacy of his wardrobe, but also with her, for putting the idea into his head that he needed to look decent for an event that had started out as nothing more than a concert with his friends' band.

"Rayanne," he said, exaggerating a contrite tone, "can you help me find a shirt?"

She glanced up from her phone, her eyebrows knitted together.

"Please?"

"You're cute when you're pitiful." She picked up his bag and put it on the couch and tore through it until she found the white shirt. She shook it out and inspected it carefully before holding it up to him.

"I'm going to iron this. The room isn't well lit so you can get away with it."

Henry grabbed the shirt away from her. "I can iron my own shirt. You stand there and enjoy the view."

That earned a half-smile from her.

By the time they got to the venue, Rayanne had relaxed a half-notch.

"This place looks great," she said. Strings of tiny white lights draped over the low branches of the trees in the courtyard. "Did you do this?"

Henry made a small bow.

Ester came out of the event space wearing a little black dress. She wore a messenger bag slung across her body.

"She wore a short skirt," Henry said.

"She did," Rayanne agreed, not hiding her surprise. "You look amazing. I didn't think you were the little-dress type."

"I'm not. This is an experiment. I feel like a greyhound wearing a tube sock." Ester patted the bag. "I've got the brochures and I made some fliers with a map that leads to our present location. You want to go walk the street with me?"

"I'm game, what about you?" Rayanne said, looking at Henry.

"I need to powwow with Jack and get those guys set up. I'll meet you by the stage at show time." Henry put his arm around Rayanne's waist and gave her a long kiss.

Ester made exaggerated motions of fanning her face. "Should I wait out front?"

Henry let Rayanne go but she hung on to his hand.

"Come on now," Ester said. "You can do it. Let's go."

A piece of his heart dropped as she disappeared through the gate. This separation was going to be hard to bear.

PART OF ESTER'S experiment included modest heels and so far it wasn't going well.

"I should have given it more thought," Ester said, a lopsided hitch to her gait.

"You want to go back?" Rayanne asked.

"No, I'm tough," Ester said.

They were having mixed results. Most of the bars were happy to take the information. The restaurants weren't quite so accommodating. One person, she wasn't sure if it was the hostess or the owner, shooed them out the door.

"What was up with that lady?" Ester said. "It was like we killed her puppy, made it into a sandwich, and then made her watch us eat it."

"What is up with you Plains Indians and the jokes about eating puppies?"

"I'm not a Plains Indian," Ester said, pretending to be annoyed. "Let's be honest. How many folks do we expect from this last-minute act of desperation?"

"You make it sound so grim," Rayanne said. "Let's sit for a minute." There was a bench outside one of the shops.

"Don't have to ask me twice," Ester said, sinking into the seat with a groan.

"Is Henry acting weird tonight?" Rayanne asked.

"I don't know him well enough to answer that question," Ester said. "What do you mean weird?"

"Like he was up to something."

"Maybe he's going to ask you to marry him," Ester said.

"Don't even joke about that. Even getting past the part where we barely know each other, he doesn't have a job. I'm not shacking up with a guy with no job."

"I'm glad to hear it. That's a good baseline standard." Ester adjusted the bag so the strap went over the opposite shoulder. "Still, it seems like you two are doing pretty well at, you know, being a couple."

"Absolutely. Success at grinding crotches together is a surefire way to predict future long-term success."

"You make it sound so dreamy," Ester said.

"It is dreamy," Rayanne said. "He's great. And now he's moving and everything is messed up."

"There are numerous layers of crap outcomes to the center's demise," Ester said. "At least we got this party. Maybe the board will see what we threw together and think, 'Half-assed is better than no ass. Let's give these kids another chance.'"

Rayanne couldn't help laughing. "Half-assed is better than no ass. Let's put that on a T-shirt. I want to try to hit a couple more businesses before we give up and go back."

~

HENRY WORKED on stage to help the guys arrange their gear. They needed to leave enough space for dancers to move around too. Cody and Sam went over the set list.

Jack checked and rechecked the cables and connections until Henry stopped him. "Are you nervous?"

Jack shrugged. "I didn't expect so many people to be here."

"That's what we wanted," Henry reminded him. The room filled up. He recognized many of the faces, but there were strangers there too. Rayanne and Ester's efforts were yielding results.

Tommy came and found him. "The bus is here, boss. Now what?"

"Can you bring it around the back? We can get them in through the load-in door. That way we can get them all seated now. It will be too confusing if we wait until the show starts." He checked his phone. They were close to start time. Jack had brought a couple guys who had experience with lights and sound and they were doing last-minute tests.

He texted Rayanne: *on your way back?*

She responded: *two minutes*

He spotted Arnie come through the door. Margie had her cane in one hand and held onto Arnie's arm with the other. Henry jumped down to say hello. He had to push through the crowd to get to where they were. By the time he got back there, Linda had come in. She helped Lou navigate the room. Pauline and Bernard weren't far behind.

"I got seats up here I saved for you," Henry said. He was surprised to see his mom come in after them too.

"What are you doing here?" he asked.

"You invited me, remember?" Mom said. She gave him the kind of hug proud mothers gave their sons. "Isn't this your going-away bash? I can't miss out on that."

"This event represents many things," Henry said. "You will be glad you came. Come and sit with the board." He'd arranged the chairs in a row along the side of the stage so they would be able to see.

Cody and Sam had finished with their set up and everyone was assembled. Everyone except for Rayanne and Ester.

He hoped they were on their way because it was time to get things rolling.

"I GUESS we walked farther than we thought," Rayanne said.

Ester hobbled along next to her. "Women wear shoes like this on purpose? How come there's never a pedicab when you want one?"

"Good question. It's only three blocks. Why don't you take your shoes off?"

"If my feet are dying in these godforsaken shoes, how are they going to do barefoot on these barbarian streets?"

"Maybe I can find a stick for you to bite down on," Rayanne said, trying to urge her along.

"And miss out on my amazing poetry?" Ester sped up her gait, a pained gasp spilling out every few steps. It was painful to walk next to her.

They were a half block away when Rayanne stopped. "Do you hear that?"

"I can't hear anything over the sound of my feet screaming," Ester said. She kept shuffling forward.

"I hear music. Do you think they would start without us?" Rayanne rushed ahead, momentarily abandoning Ester. She went back for her. "Jump on my back."

"You're joking," Ester said.

"It's not that far, I can do it." Rayanne turned around and bent her knees, one arm reaching back for Ester.

"I will snap you in two," Ester said.

"Get on my back or I'll throw you over my shoulder," Rayanne said, her voice firm and serious. She didn't know how she could make Ester do anything, but they didn't have time to argue.

"I would love to see you try to do that, but I'm wearing a short skirt," Ester said, climbing up and letting Rayanne grab her knees. "I hope I remembered to put on underwear."

"So do I," Rayanne said. She couldn't move fast but they made better time than they did when Ester was on her own.

"This the best you can do?" Ester asked.

"I can drop you and leave you on your own anytime," Rayanne said.

"I know, I tease you because I love you. You're one of my favorite people. Now, giddy-up!"

Rayanne loosened her grip on Ester's knees.

"We're almost there," Ester said. "And you're right, the eagle flew the nest without us."

They joined a group of people entering the gate. A heavy bass beat drifted out from the club.

"This is a good crowd," Ester said.

"You aren't kidding." Rayanne kept ahold of Ester as she crossed the courtyard. Light from the room spilled outside. When she got through the door, it was too crowded to hold Ester so she let her down. Ester held on to her arm as they worked their way up to the stage.

When she was close enough to see the stage, she was startled to see not only the Beat Braves, but Grandpa and his buddies sitting around a big drum. They'd managed to break out Earl because he was sitting there with them. She recognized him with his big head of gray-white hair and a beaded headband.

They pounded the drum, first singing together, and then Earl singing solo, the voices rising and falling together. This style of singing wasn't part of her tradition but the music moved through her, familiar and thrilling. Jack was up there, working on his computer and the band joined in, the modern sounds building off the traditional drum group.

Grandpa grinned like he'd won the lottery. He and the others were bent over the drum. The drumsticks rose up and down together and struck in unison.

"This is amazing," Ester said in her ear.

Rayanne nodded. Henry stood at the side of the stage. The executive board was lined up in chairs, their eyes on the performance. Henry must not have spotted her come in because he kept scanning the room. He left for the back door and returned a minute later and pointed to the front of the stage. The youth dancers came out single file, spinning and dancing, their regalia clacking and jangling as they moved. Their faces were as joyful as the elders. Everybody had a part.

By this time the audience was bouncing around too. Rayanne could see that many people were from the native community, but there were others too. From where she stood, it was hard to see the board members' faces. This was better than half-assed. Whatever her original vision, this one turned out better. Rayanne was ready to burst with happiness. If this was the last thing she did for the center, at least it was something good.

Everyone performed together for several songs before winding down. The elders sat at attention by the drum as if ready to go another few rounds.

Linda and Arnie went to the front of the stage to the main microphone.

Arnie took it first, like he was going to say something, but he handed it to Linda.

"Thank you, everyone, for sharing our celebration of the Crooked Rock Urban Indian Center." She went on to tell a little bit about the center, skipping over the part about how their future was in jeopardy.

Someone squeezed Rayanne's shoulder. It was Henry. She put her arms around his waist.

"You did this?"

"You did this," he said. "I embellished."

"We did it together." Standing there in the crowded room, filled with the people that meant so much to her, and with Henry's warm body at her side, the feelings of happiness and pride were bursting inside of her.

Henry tilted her face up to his. "You okay?"

"Yeah," she said, losing herself in his gaze. "I just…uh…I have very strong feelings for you."

Henry smiled. "Very strong feelings? Sounds serious. Do these feelings have a name?"

"They might," she said smiling back.

He kissed her. "I have very strong feelings for you, too."

"Good," she said, squeezing him tight.

"I look forward to talking more about this," Henry said, "but you need to get your adorable hiney up there to do your elder-honoring."

"Tonight?"

"Why not?" Henry took her to the stage where Linda was introducing the board. Then she introduced Rayanne.

The room looked cozier from the stage. The faces in the audience were friendly and curious. Now that she had an opportunity to speak, she wished she'd had more time to plan. She took a deep breath and concentrated on the most important message she wanted to get across.

"In our culture we honor our elders because they are our teachers. I've had so many wonderful people who helped me so I could do the things I do now. But I'm still learning. It hurts my heart when I see elders who are neglected or lonely. They don't know we need them unless we let them be needed. I've always wanted to do an elder-honoring like tonight."

One by one she introduced Grandpa and his drum circle. Then Margie and Lou were honored. There were some elders among the audience and she brought them up and honored them too. Too quickly, it was finished, and Linda was thanking her and thanking everyone who had come.

"We're going to end the program and let the band play so you can dance," Linda said.

Jack took the microphone back and thanked everyone while they got the stage cleared and the kids took off. Rayanne helped pack the elders up and said goodbye to Grandpa.

The tone in the room shifted as the band kicked into gear. Rayanne danced with Ester until Henry reappeared.

"I took Margie home," he told her.

He grabbed her arm and spun her around with a lustful gleam in his eye. And when it was their time to go home, he loved every inch of her body until she was thoroughly sated and dropped off to sleep, her limbs tangled with his.

44

They said goodbye when Rayanne left for work. They'd already gone through so many emotions, it was hard to know how to feel when he finally left. A quiet sob escaped when he handed her the key.

"That was a guest key," he reminded her. "When we're ready for real, you can give it back to me. Or we'll find a place together."

"Okay," she said, her voice scratchy with tears.

Back at the office, she could barely hold it together. She was supposed to be researching places to move to but she didn't see the point until they knew what the future held.

"Remember when Arnie put him on the job, you thought he was a turd," Ester said.

"Are you asking me or telling me?" Rayanne said, unable to shake the bleak cloud that floated over her head. Henry had said she might see him sooner than she thought but at best she'd have to wait for the weekend. She already mourned sleeping alone and she hadn't even had to do it yet. She was going to have to do meal delivery by herself too.

Ester and Tommy stood by her desk, their own moving chores on hold while they waited to see what the board was going to decide.

Linda had been in there with them for over an hour. At one point there were raised voices but at the moment it was suspiciously quiet.

"Should I listen at the door?" Tommy asked. "I mean, as a courtesy, to make sure they haven't murdered each other. What if they're heaped together in a pool of blood?"

"Remember what it took to get the carpet right after the flood? And that was just water," Ester said.

"Can you imagine what they would do to us if they caught us listening at the door?" Rayanne said.

"I should learn how to plant bugs," Ester said. "Isn't there a spy store on the Internet? I wonder how much spy stuff costs."

"They aren't going to work through lunch, are they?" Tommy asked.

Linda opened the door and they all hopped to their feet. She shook her head. "Can you order sandwiches and chips, please?"

She shut the door before they could find out what kind.

"What's the weirdest kind of sandwich we could get?" Rayanne said. "And if either of you says anything about puppy, I will kill you with my bare hands."

"*Ew*," Tommy said. "What is wrong with you? I heard there's a food truck that sells macaroni-and-cheese sandwiches."

"Not bad," Ester said. "I would eat one of those."

Linda opened the door again and waved Rayanne over. She handed her a piece of paper and whisked the door shut again.

"One salami, one roast beef and four roast turkey. Double U must mean wheat. No M. No mustard, or no mayo? C. Cheddar?" Rayanne took her best guess and entered the order into the website. She found petty cash and sent Ester and Tommy to pick up the food.

While they were gone, she scrolled through job announcements. No harm in seeing what was out there. The festival night was such a success she was sure they would give them another year, but then why was it taking so long for them to decide? She could imagine the lengths Linda must be going through to convince them. But they should have decided by now.

She heard the front door open and figured it was Tommy and Ester, but when she didn't hear their voices she looked up.

"Henry!" She bounded across the room in three steps and threw herself into his arms, relief and happiness washing over her.

"You know, you saw me a little over four hours ago," Henry said.

"Yeah, but I didn't know when I would see you again so I've been missing you."

"I brought you lunch. Tortas." He handed her something wrapped in wax paper.

"You came back to bring me lunch?" She unwrapped a huge sandwich with chunks of meat falling out. She leaned down to take a sniff. "This smells incredible."

"I haven't left yet," Henry said. He pulled a chair over to sit next to her and unwrapped his sandwich too.

"I thought they were expecting you on the rez?" Rayanne said, her elation fading. This only extended the agony. If he wasn't gone now, he would be soon. Her appetite faded.

"I'm not going," he said.

"What are you going to do?"

"I'm becoming a personal support worker. It was in one of the brochures in your elder research. I'm going to move into Margie's basement and get paid to help her out. I can take her to appointments and move furniture."

"That's what you want to do?"

"That's what I want to do right now. Margie is going to help me find some classes like the grant-writing thing we talked about. I can learn new stuff while I look for a career job. And I will have a home close to you, and a little bit of money."

Warmth flooded into her heart. "Whose idea was this?"

"Mine," he said. "But it took only three seconds to convince Margie. It gives her more time in her house, and she has someone to boss around. Everybody wins."

Rayanne jumped up and squeezed Henry tight.

"I'm going to make this thing work with you," he said.

"Me too," Rayanne said.

"You again." Ester's voice came through the front door. "Can't stay away. Hey, what are those sandwiches?"

Tommy took the bags from the sandwich shop and disappeared into the meeting room. He hurried back out.

"Can you tell us what's going on?" Rayanne asked.

"Everyone's tense," Tommy said.

"That's not good."

"Hunger does things to people. Things could turn around after they eat," Tommy said.

Ester brought a knife from the break room and cut Rayanne's sandwich in half. "You can't eat this whole thing."

"I'll be lucky if I eat three bites," Rayanne said. "Too much going on."

They shared Henry's news and the four ate at the front desk, keeping a careful eye on the meeting-room door.

"Does Uncle Arnie know about this?" Ester asked.

"Not yet," Henry said. "Neither does Mom. She will not be pleased that I foiled her plan."

Linda burst out of the meeting with her face shiny-bright and two thumbs pointing to the sky. Rayanne ran over to hug her with Ester and Tommy joining.

"They're giving us another year, and that's it," Linda said. "It's not going to be easy but if we stick together and have a good plan, we can do it."

Rayanne nodded in agreement. "We can do it, but we still need to find a place to move."

"After lunch," Linda said.

Arnie came out and spotted Henry. "Shouldn't you be back home by now?"

Henry put his arm around Rayanne. "I am home."

Rayanne squeezed him back.

Ester came out with her camera. "The Indians, giddy with victory, plot their next move."

AFTERWORD

This isn't the end of the Crooked Rock Urban Indian Center.

Book 2 will feature Ester and her love interest, Theo, who will be introduced in the next book. The story of finding a home for Crooked Rock, and Arnie and Linda will continue too.

Estimated release date: Early 2017.

Visit my website at www.pamelasanderson.com to join my mailing list and get updates when new releases are coming out.

There so much misinformation and misunderstanding about native people in the mainstream. I don't have all the answers, either.

Trying to define the typical Indian or tribe would be like trying to define the typical American or state. And just like the Indian Tribes across America, there is no typical organization that serves urban Indians.

Indian communities, individuals and organizations are different depending on their history, culture, traditions, geography and leaders —this is true of individual tribes, and is true of urban Indian communities.

I've created Crooked Rock as a place to serve my stories. My intentions are always respectful and based on my experience and observations as an Indian, and in the course of my work in Indian Country.

You might be wondering about the cover. Are those native people?

Unfortunately, no. The cover is made from standard stock photos. The selection of stock photos of indigenous people is skimpy, and sadly, my numerous attempts to set up a photo session of my own failed. If you can provide pro-quality stock photos of cute Indian couples, please get in touch at pam@pamelasanderson.com. I would love to work with you.

ACKNOWLEDGMENTS

Once again, thanks to all the terrific friends, relatives, and readers who support what I'm doing. I appreciate you until the end of time.

Special thanks go to Kira Walsh, Marguerite Croft, Michelle Osbourne and Sinead Talley. I am also eternally grateful to superstar editor Lorelei Logsdon (www.loreleilogsdon.com) and the multi-talented cover artist Holly Heisey (www.hollyheiseydesign.com).

Huge thanks to my sweetheart, Bob Hughes who did all the laundry and dinners when I was drafting. Another shout out to Mom for making sure everyone has a copy.

Last but not least, thank you Reader. If you made it this far, I hope you enjoyed the book. Book reviews will help other readers find this book. Please consider writing a review—I appreciate them all.

ABOUT THE AUTHOR

Pamela Sanderson is a citizen of the Karuk Tribe and lives in the Pacific Northwest. She is employed as a legal assistant working on behalf of Indian tribes and tribal organizations. When she isn't working or writing, she enjoys baking, gardening and following Major League Soccer.

CPSIA information can be obtained
at www.ICGtesting.com
Printed in the USA
BVHW031954300122
627573BV00016B/256